KATE WELSH
HIS CALIFORNIAN COUNTESS

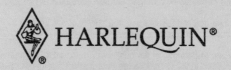

HARLEQUIN®

TORONTO • NEW YORK • LONDON
AMSTERDAM • PARIS • SYDNEY • HAMBURG
STOCKHOLM • ATHENS • TOKYO • MILAN • MADRID
PRAGUE • WARSAW • BUDAPEST • AUCKLAND

Recycling programs
for this product may
not exist in your area.

ISBN-13: 978-0-373-29588-3

HIS CALIFORNIAN COUNTESS

www.eHarlequin.com

Printed in U.S.A.

The wind freshened and the sun reflected off the rippling water like dancing diamonds.

"This is all such...such an adventure." Amber's smile was even broader now, showing more of her even, white teeth. Her eyes had gone wide with wonder, too.

Jamie looked away from her, feeling things he shouldn't for an unescorted female. His gaze fell on the water, and through her battery of questions he experienced again the excitement of his first journey.

"So, does your adventure end with the voyage?" he asked. He looked back at her. The attraction he felt for this woman showed him how little he'd known of true desire before.

"End of the adventure?" his lovely rail partner asked, calling him back from his mental wanderings. That endearing frown reappeared. It made her eyebrows arch downward in the middle.

"I hope the adventure continues for a long time."

* * *

His Californian Countess
Harlequin® Historical #988—April 2010

HIS CALIFORNIAN COUNTESS

Chapter One

1876—New York, New York

Jamie took a sip of tea and winced at how scratchy his throat felt. Leaning back, he looked around the sitting room of the town house he'd bought and decorated with the best in French furnishings. It was what he'd needed it to be—a fitting setting for the Earl of Adair, a wealthy British lord. When he'd first arrived in New York City he'd needed the businessmen of New York to trust his finances and ignore the rumors his uncle had spread that he was penniless.

They had.

And Jamie had done what he'd come to America to do. He'd invested his late wife's inheritance in the growing country, filling the Adair family's coffers to overflowing. His title—Earl of Adair—had opened the doors to success, but he'd unexpectedly found the United States offered more. It offered freedom, something he'd craved his whole life. He much preferred the name he'd lost when he became earl, Jamie Reynolds.

Lord, he was exhausted. He dropped his head back and stared up at one of the crystal chandeliers gracing the ornate ceiling. His eyes wouldn't focus and the effect blurred the beauty of the teardrop pendants.

He blinked. He hadn't caught scarlet fever from his daughter Meara. Of course, he hadn't. The doctor said it was nearly impossible for an adult to contract it. He was only tired. He wouldn't be ill. He didn't have time. Now that Meara was on the mend he had to redirect his attention to finding Helena.

Jamie glanced at the breakfast Mimm had laid out as he reached for the newspaper on the silver tray next to him. He couldn't bring himself to eat, but to sit with his tea and actually read a newspaper felt wonderful—such a normal activity after days of dealing with one crisis after another with Meara.

Then his relief over his daughter's recovery bloomed into a new worry in an instant. He sat dumbfounded and stared in horror at the masthead. "May sixteenth?" he gasped as he crumpled the edges of the newspaper in his fists. "This can't be right. How could it be six days since she fell ill?"

But of course, the *New York Times* didn't misprint its date. Last he remembered it was ten days into May. He'd still had nearly a week—one last-ditch effort to find Helena before the *Young America* sailed.

She'd eluded him for months since his search began back in Pennsylvania when the mine owner there told him Helena had run off to New York to catch a clipper to California. He'd hoped to find her before she boarded the ship. But he'd failed. Thank God he'd booked passage just in case he didn't locate her before the sailing. *Today's sailing.* At this point, he'd be lucky to make the ship himself.

So what was he doing just sitting there? He'd not a moment to spare. Jamie jumped to his feet and shouted, "Mimm! I have to leave."

His rotund housekeeper rushed in. "What on earth is wrong, lamb?"

"Her ship sails in a little more than two hours. I must get to the *Young America*. Find her. Stop her."

Mimm arched one of her eyebrows, giving him one of her shrewd looks. "Yer lady love, my lord? 'Pears to me she's not sharin' yer feelings."

"Helena was never my 'lady love' as you keep calling her. You know how I feel about that. I promised her father I'd see to it she was safe. I only offered for her to keep her off her damned guardian's auction block. Now because I failed to explain why I was offering marriage she's traveling as an unprotected miss. Her feelings for *me* are immaterial to my search." Too agitated to stand still, Jamie paced across the fine Oriental rug, closing the distance between them. He'd given his word to a dying man. A man he very much feared had died in his place.

"You need sleep, not to go hying off after someone who don't want nothin' to do with you," Mimm said. "Besides which, Meara's out of danger, but not able to face such a journey. And frankly neither am I."

"And I am not proposing either of you come along. I'll meet you in California," he said, then rushed off to see his trunk was packed.

Miriam Trimble had never learned there were things best left unsaid. But she'd been more than a mother to him. He owed Mimm for his very life so he guessed that gave her the right to say whatever she wished.

* * *

She eyed him when he met her in the hall outside Meara's room several minutes later. "I still say this isn't a good idea. You're lookin' a bit peaked to me, me lamb."

He took her shoulders in his hands. "I'm sorry I snapped before, Mimm. I'm okay, as Americans say. It's a childhood disease Meara had. You heard the doctor. All I could get is a lesser form. Besides, I don't have time to be sick and that's all there is to it."

"Sickness isn't all that cooperative, darlin'. I'm worried for you."

He nodded and shrugged on his coat. "You needn't be. I'll be fine. Is Meara sleeping?"

"Aye."

Meara needed sleep more than a farewell hug from her da. "I hate leaving her after being gone nearly all winter, especially without saying goodbye. Give her my love and tell her she'll have a great adventure seeing this vast country from the rail car when you all travel to join me in San Francisco. I think perhaps the doctor is right about the air at Cape May. I asked Palmer to see that the house there is opened when he was here…was it yesterday?"

Mimm sighed. "Last evening after the little one's fever broke."

Jamie raked a hand through his hair. He really was exhausted. "I'll make sure there's a pony waiting in New Jersey for her birthday. That ought to help get her strength back and make up for my missing her special day. Tell her I'll see her by mid-September."

"We'll miss you, lamb. Take care," Mimm ordered.

When he looked back down the hall, she had tears in her eyes.

"I'll be fine," he promised, then turned away and hurried from the town house. He couldn't let the clipper sail without him. He stopped on his way to the docks to see his man of business. There, he and Palmer put in place the plans for Meara and her entourage, as well as the purchase of the pony. Then he hastened down Dover Street to Pier 28 where the *Young America*, black hull gleaming in the late morning light, stood ready for departure.

He arrived just as several longshoremen prepared to hoist the gangplank off the clipper's gunwale, making him the last to board. Mindful of his driver carting his trunk behind him, Jamie strode up the gangplank, his knees growing weaker by the minute. He knew he didn't present the aristocratic image his uncle would expect, but he'd finally gotten to a place where that didn't matter. America had not only allowed him to amass a sizeable fortune and given him a buoyant sense of freedom; it had helped him put most of the ghosts of his past to rest.

Except for the reason he needed to watch over Helena. Because if he was right that Harry Conwell had given his life for him, Jamie's past was still a threat to his present and future.

Many of the passengers were on deck, but Jamie didn't see Helena. He found the steward and asked if she'd boarded. The man returned to him rather quickly with the news that she had and so Jamie began his search again.

Then he saw her. Sunlight gleaming in her blond hair, she stood at the rail, looking down at the murky water. He walked over and tapped her on the shoulder.

She whirled to face him. Though there was a strong resemblance, this young woman wasn't Helena. She had
the same heart shape to her face and the same perfectly
turned-up nose, but rather than blue, she had the biggest,
darkest brown eyes he'd ever seen. A poet would say a
man could fall into their depths and not care if he were
ever seen again.

He felt a primeval punch to his gut. He'd never felt
this before. It was attraction that went past that to desire,
but was untainted by lust. He was quite unprepared.

She tilted her head and frowned a bit. "May I help
you, sir?"

It was only then he realized he'd been staring. He
blinked and the deck shifted under his feet. "Sorry. At
first I thought you were someone else. But you aren't
her a'tal." He nearly cringed at the sound of the Irish
lilt in his voice before he remembered. He was free. He
could talk as he wished. His uncle had drilled repress-
ing that accent into him all his life, but he was his own
man now. Jamie Reynolds answered to no one.

"Should I be sorry I'm not her?" the young woman
asked.

"Definitely not." He didn't know what surprised him
most, her sweet, warm smile, her answer, or his. Nor did
he know why she'd unnerved him so completely. "Is this
your first trip at sea?" he asked, needing, for some
reason, to keep the conversation going. He knew he
should probably continue his search for Helena, but now
that the ship was under way, all urgency deserted him.
He pushed thoughts of Helena away, suddenly wanting
to know more about this lovely, innocent-eyed woman.

"I was born in California, but my family died of
fever. I was sent to live with my aunt and uncle but I

traveled overland. I remember little of the journey and only a bit more of the state. This is my first trip anywhere since except to Poughkeepsie, New York. I went to a college there."

He raised his eyebrows. "College?"

She nodded. "Vassar."

"Beautiful *and* intelligent. Not qualities I've seen in combination all that often."

Her little pointed chin notched up a bit. "Are you saying it is mostly homely girls who have good minds?"

She had backbone. He liked that. "I was speaking of London and the young women of its marriage-mart Season. Beauty and pretty manners are prized. Intelligence isn't." He hoped she hadn't noticed the bitterness in his tone.

She blushed prettily and he relaxed. "That was a compliment, then?" she asked, her head tilted a bit.

"Of course. Colleges for women are rare, aren't they? England has Girton College, but they don't offer a degree."

"Vassar does and there will be more colleges that do, I assure you. You find London's women distasteful for some reason."

And she was perceptive. "Many of them are only interested in learning how to trap a man into marriage, then to run his house and his life afterward. They aren't beating down Girton's doors, I assure you."

She smiled. "And you had to come all the way to America to escape them?"

"I had other purposes in coming here. It's a happy coincidence that they're there and I'm not."

She seemed to ponder his answer with an adorable little frown wrinkling her smooth forehead. "It wasn't very smart of them to let you escape."

He laughed. "So if they'd been smarter, I wouldn't be here? Intelligent women can be dangerous then. I must remember that."

It was her turn to laugh. And it was such a low and sensual sound it reminded him he'd been too long without a woman's warm body beneath his.

She flashed a look at him from head to toe, then gave him a teasing grin when her eyes met his. "You look quite capable of defending yourself against danger of any sort," she said. Then she did the strangest thing. She looked out over the water and her expression changed from temptress to pixie in an instant. "Oh, look! We're moving. It's so beautiful," she cried, so animated she fairly vibrated with glee.

"We've been moving since we began talking."

"I hadn't thought there'd be so much water! Which is rather silly of me, isn't it? It's only that this is all such…such an adventure." Her smile was even broader now, showing more of her even white teeth. Her eyes had gone wide with wonder, too. Innocent eyes.

He looked away from her, feeling things he shouldn't for an unescorted female. An innocent one at that. His gaze fell on the water and through her battery of questions, he experienced again the excitement of his first voyage.

Growing a bit tired, but not wanting this interlude to end, he leaned on the rail and pointed out Brooklyn with its verdant-green rolling landscape, Manhattan and the few landmarks within it that he'd learned to spot on earlier trips.

The wind freshened and the sun reflected off the rippling water like dancing diamonds. The ship vibrated and the deck shifted under his feet. Crewmen seemed to fly up the ratlines. A whooshing sound from the bow cutting through the water filled the air, disturbed only by a drone of conversation from the passengers still on deck or the occasional shout of a crewman going about his business.

"So, does your adventure end with the voyage?" he asked now that they entered the harbor. He looked back at her. It was a lowering thing to admit, but the attraction he felt for this woman showed him how little he'd known of true desire before. He certainly hadn't felt anything like this for Helena for whom he'd embarked on this voyage. For her he felt only duty and obligation. Perhaps he should be looking for her now, but he had the whole voyage to relay her father's worry for her safety and to offer whatever assistance she needed.

"End of the adventure?" his lovely rail-partner asked, calling him back from his mental wonderings. That endearing frown reappeared. It made her eyebrows arch downward in the middle.

I must get her name.

"I hope the adventure continues for a long time."

"Where did it begin, if I may ask?"

"Begin? I grew up in the mountains in Pennsylvania. I'd been to Poughkeepsie, New York, for college, but that city is small, especially compared to New York City. I'd been through there on the way to the school, but I never left the rail station. The cities have been very exciting."

"Cities, not city?"

She laid her hand over his on the rail and smiled at clearly happy memories. "I stopped off in Philadelphia. For the Centennial Exposition and—oops." She lifted her hand from his and covered her mouth with it. His gaze flew to her eyes and found them widened. He didn't know what could have alarmed her when all he felt was the loss of her innocent touch. "I shouldn't have mentioned our Centennial, should I?"

He smiled. "I took my daughter to see it. I assure you most people in Britain have got over the revolt. It has been a hundred years, after all. Though there are those who still insist on referring to America as the colonies." His smile widened. "I suppose it follows that a country bold enough to revolt against an ancient power would spawn colleges for women and female adventurers," he teased.

"Adventurer?" She took a deep breath, which made her breasts swell inside the pretty blouse she wore. "My, but I like the sound of that! I'm an *adventurer!*"

He dragged his gaze off the sight of her lovely bust line, but it fell on her mouth. Then what she'd said sank into his muddled mind. Jamie laughed as the ship fell out a bit from under them, and by some fortuitous hand of fate, she fell right into him. Glad he was anchored against the rail, he caught her in his arms and enjoyed the feel of her petite form from the instant their bodies came into contact. Then he steeled himself and regretfully helped her get on her own feet.

Flushed, she ducked her head and apologized for her clumsiness. "Not to worry," he told her, while keeping his enjoyment to himself. "You'll get your sea legs under you quick enough."

She hugged herself and shivered. "Well, unless I want to take a chill, I must get to my cabin and unpack. I may come up again after finding my shawl. It's been nice talking with you. I suppose I'll run into you again. Large as the *Young America* is, it is small in the general scheme of life. Thank you for helping occupy my mind. I was a bit nervous about leaving the docks."

"I didn't get your name," he said as she turned to walk away.

She pivoted and shot him that enchanting frown for a split second before her lovely smile blossomed. "No, you didn't," she replied, then hurried away.

His bark of laugher turned several heads, but he didn't care if they thought him odd or gauche. She was really quite refreshing and he was sorry to see her go. But she was correct. During more or less the next one-hundred-and-thirty days if the ship had fair winds, they would see each other constantly. He couldn't help but be glad of it. He'd get her name when next they met.

Jamie turned back toward the river and leaned his forearms against the gleaming gunwales. After several minutes, his eyes began to burn and the reflected sunlight became annoying rather than appealing. Perhaps his pixie had taken the magic of the sailing with her and perhaps she'd had a good idea about settling in.

But for the life of him, he couldn't remember what cabin he'd secured for himself. He started off and realized his legs were less steady than they'd been all day. He made a grab for the rail. The movement of the ship made walking difficult so he stayed put for a few minutes longer. Finally, a boy dressed in what appeared to be a uniform, passed near him. "My name is Reynolds," Jamie said, his voice sounded rough and strained. "I wonder if you could direct me to my cabin and help me locate another passenger, Miss Helena Conwell."

The crewmember, a boy of perhaps fifteen or sixteen, stared in obvious surprise for a moment, then his confusion seemed to clear. "Ah. Lord Reynolds, is it? We'd begun to despair, thinking you'd missed the ship." The lad had it wrong—he was Lord Adair, not Lord Reynolds—but British titles were confusing and mostly unimportant to Americans. That was why he dropped its use whenever possible. But arranging for a specific cabin near a woman who was not in his party had needed a certain amount of diplomacy and prestige, as well as extra funds.

"Sir, are you quite all right?" the crewman asked.

Jamie straightened and shook his head, trying to rid his mind of the swirling thoughts muddling his brain. His mind bounced next to Mimm and all her fussing that he might be ill. It was ridiculous that he could have gotten what his daughter had. Meara's doctor had all but promised it was only a disease of childhood. But even if Jamie was sick in some more minor way, he still couldn't let on. They'd surely put him off the ship. Helena was on the *Young America* and he had to make sure she was safe and that she understood all that had happened.

"I'm perfectly fine," he answered finally, then stiffened his back and notched his chin up.

The crewman nodded, but looked a bit dubious. "Your cabin is actually across the saloon from Miss Conwell's. Close as possible, as you requested. This way, sir."

Jamie's exhaustion increased as he moved below, following the crewman through the saloon in the raised poop deck until he stopped before a cabin door.

"Stateroom six is yours, sir. The lady's is just over there. Stateroom three," the crewman explained and indicated Helena's door or hatch or whatever the hell it was called aboard a sailing ship. The lad tried unsuccessfully to cover a smirk. "I'll be steward for both staterooms during the graveyard shift. Just hang that little sign on the door if you're needing privacy with her."

Jamie felt his temper instantly rise. "Miss Conwell is a *lady*, sir, and I'll thank you to keep that in mind when you speak of her or to her. Her late father was a great friend of mine. I am merely here to pay a debt to him by seeing she reaches her chosen destination unmolested. She is alone in the world or she'd never be traveling unchaperoned."

The young man had the grace to blush. "I'm sorry, my lord. I apologize for repeating what the doc said…" He cleared his throat, then continued, "I'll do what I can to put an end to the gossip."

"See that you do," Jamie ordered. "The doctor is a drunk from what I saw when I was aboard to arrange passage. I cannot imagine why Captain Baker keeps him on." Then for some reason he thought of the pixie-woman he'd been talking with. She also seemed to be alone and he couldn't help be worried for her, too.

"Is there anything more I can do for you, my lord?" the lad asked, looking as if he'd rather be anywhere else.

Jamie was so annoyed he waved him away when he could very well have used his help unpacking. He'd left Hadley, his valet, at the town house. The man was more liability on the sea than an asset and Jamie had no wish to make the poor fellow miserable for the four months it would take them to arrive in San Francisco.

He looked at Helena's door, tempted to knock, but he didn't want to give anyone the idea there was even a hint of scandal brewing about her. He had wanted to see her immediately, damn it. It had been weeks since they'd danced at her birthday ball. He'd been disappointed when he'd realized her friendliness that evening had been a ruse. He'd wanted to establish at least a degree of peace between them and he'd failed. That night she'd run from her guardian and it would seem from him, as well.

He felt unsettled and unsure. It was as if a curtain had risen on his life, as if he were part of a comedy. Worst of all, he was as powerless as a marionette controlled by some sadistic specter. Nothing made sense and he could not reason it all out.

Except the vow he'd made at his wife's graveside. That was written firmly on his heart. He would never again deviate from his chosen course as he almost had with his offer of marriage to Helena. He would only marry again for love. But as he didn't understand what love meant or trust the nebulous emotion when declared, marriage was for him not a possibility.

It seemed to him that thus far those who declared love expected the object of that rather unstable emotion to declare it in return. Yet those who'd so far declared it to him had deserted or betrayed him. Consequently, the very idea of surrendering his heart to anyone caused a visceral fear to course through him. No, he'd had enough of that painful emotion to last him the rest of his life. His heart was locked up and he'd tossed away the key.

He stood in the doorway, staring at her door. He'd finally caught up to her.

After a while, his thoughts swirling, he wondered why he was still there in his doorway when he felt so very awful. So heavy. His throat so sore. He turned into the room behind him and was hit by a wave of dizziness. He looked around, his mind spinning like a child's top. Why was the room tipping? Swaying? Why was the room so dark? His town house was always bright.

He looked around again, confusion swamping his mind even more. Where was he? This was not home. He should find out where he was. The room spun out of control as he turned back to the door. He grabbed for it, but missed and it swung away from him. Then the floor rushed up at him as blackness descended. And two thoughts revolved in his head. He needed to confess to Helena his part in her father's death. And he didn't know the pixie's name.

Amber turned and took a survey of her pretty cabin. Yes, it looked perfect. This was the cabin of an *adventurer. The handsome man* she'd flirted with on deck had called her an adventurer and that had given her the idea to make the cabin reflect her new path in life.

On the wall near her porthole she'd tacked the image of Memorial Hall in Philadelphia painted on rose-colored silk. It looked lovely against the cherry wainscoting. It had come from her unscheduled stay in the City of Brotherly Love. As she'd told *the handsome man*—that was how she thought of him—she hadn't wanted to pass up seeing the Great Philadelphia Centennial Exposition and World's Fair.

Above the bed she'd tacked the postcards from all her adventures. There was one of the Women's Pavilion and Memorial Hall and some postcards from the Philadelphia Zoo where she'd seen too many exotic animals to count. And all the colorful tickets from everything she'd seen. It was a week she'd never forget.

Taking in the fair and zoo hadn't been the first adventurous thing she'd done, though. The first had been applying for a post of governess to two small girls of a wealthy California family curious about the state where she'd been born. Then, rather than travel the whole way by train as she'd originally planned, Amber had decided to play decoy to help a friend. She'd left town wearing the clothes of a young woman named Helena Conwell, who was in love with a mineworker Amber had known since childhood. But Helena's guardian was bent on keeping the lovers apart even though he no longer had any legal control over her. The happy couple had escaped west while Amber, still playing decoy, would travel by clipper to San Francisco while using Helena's name.

Amber sympathized with Helena's wish to marry the man she loved. Amber herself would never marry, though. She'd never have the children she'd always wanted, either. Those dreams had vanished the day Joseph died.

He'd been gone a year now. But the memory of his final moments when they'd carried him from the mine, clinging to life, would always haunt her. He'd loved her so deeply, so perfectly, that he'd fought pain and death itself just to see her one last time. The memory brought with it a pain so sharp that each time it rose in her mind she still needed to press upon her broken heart to get past the moment. She would never risk that kind of pain again.

So now she would build other memories.

Alone.

She had no choice in that. She'd given her heart and Joseph had taken at least half of it with him. The rest would remain hers and hers alone.

Now she would help raise two precious little girls. The little darlings had even written her from their home in San Francisco with the help of their mother so they could tell her how excited they were to meet her.

Excitement was what all this was about. Excitement kept the pain at bay. That was why she'd flirted with *the handsome man.*

Amber used to spend holidays and summers with her friends from Vassar at their families' summer homes on the banks of the Hudson River near the college. She'd always watched those carefree young women act the coquette and now she'd finally done it herself. But she was a bit embarrassed that she had. He must think she was terribly bold. Or a bluestocking, which she supposed wasn't as bad. Of course he may have thought she was both. The absurdity of that made Amber giggle. No one at home would believe it of her.

But this voyage was about a change as well as excitement. A different life from the one she led as a teacher in the town where the mine had taken Joseph seemed the only way to forget her pain. With any luck someday she would remember the happiness she'd felt in the arms of her own sweet Joseph without the accompanying hurt.

Enough of this! She'd said goodbye to that old life. A life better left behind if she could not share it with Joseph. It was time to greet a new day. One on the high seas!

Suddenly tired from all the turmoil of getting to the pier and the sailing and, yes, of flirting, then remembering all that had brought her to this place, Amber decided not to go back up on deck. She tossed her shawl over the chair in her stateroom and lay on the charming bed. She stared up at the elaborate canopy and realized she dreaded seeing the man from deck again anyway. She'd run out of flippant things to say and she'd been terribly affected in physical ways that she'd never been with Joseph.

After a while she fell asleep, only to have *the handsome man* invade her dreams, and she felt things she'd never felt before, either. Oh, goodness, she wished she hadn't had that conversation about "marriage duties" with her soon-to-be mother-in-law. Joseph's mother had laughed, saying she found nothing of a duty about the experience and if her husband had done his job with Joseph he would make sure Amber didn't see it as a duty, either. She had told Amber much of what she should expect and feel. And in her sleep, she finally felt most of these emotions. She didn't wake again until morning's light beamed through her small porthole. Though her room was cool, her skin felt flushed and somehow needy.

Damn that *handsome man.*

Chapter Two

⁂

Amber straightened the velvet bow around the collar of her pink blouse. It matched her navy-blue wool skirt perfectly. Then she took one last look at her hair in the little mirror over the dresser. Time to go for breakfast, she told herself, but her gaze remained locked with her eyes in the mirror as thoughts spun through her mind.

Would she see him? Amber bit her bottom lip, unsure if she wished for a "yes" or "no" answer. She supposed she would see him. It was inevitable after all. So when she did, what should she say after the reckless way she'd flirted?

The real question was how she could even face him. And if they did speak to each other, it stood to reason he'd ask her name again. She would be forced to give Helena Conwell's name. That was the trouble about lies. They seemed to multiply. She sat down on the bed, tempted to skip the meal altogether.

But no. That would only put off the inevitable anyway and it would be cowardly. She'd flirted on purpose. This was her *adventure,* though she had not named it as such until then. She had promised to travel as Helena. It had even been her own idea and she'd given her word. That thought helped her get a grip on herself. Honor demanded she continue as planned.

She stood, marched to the door and pulled it open. As she turned the key in the door to lock it, she heard a deep groan come from behind her. She whirled and another low moan drifted out of the cabin across from hers. Amber noticed the door stood ever so slightly ajar. Hesitant to offer aid to what sounded like a man, she looked around the deserted saloon. Perhaps she should go for help, but he sounded to be in dire need and Amber had never been one to stand by and do nothing.

She advanced on the door and carefully pushed it open a bit, but after little more than a foot she met with resistance. "Hello," she called out. "Sir, do you need assistance?"

Another groan was the only answer. Concerned for her fellow traveler, she thanked God she'd worn her own plain blue twill that was unencumbered by a bustle. She took a deep breath, squeezed around the door and nearly stepped on the gentleman's outstretched hand. He lay on the floor with his face turned away from her.

"Sir," she called, her voice trembling as she stepped around him. Then she could only stare. It was *the handsome man.* He was clearly sick or injured.

She sank down and laid her hand on his forehead. He was burning up. She looked around and hurried across the stateroom to the washstand. After pouring water into the washbowl, she rushed back with a cool cloth to bathe his face.

His eyes opened and he stared up at her with glazed

violet eyes. She didn't know what startled her more—
their pure violet irises, or his words.

"Helena?" he asked, his voice weak with fever. "Is
it you?" He reached up and traced her cheek with his
burning fingers.

She told herself it was the fever that made that slight
touch radiate heat through her. It had to be, for she
didn't want to feel anything for one of the men trying
to stop Helena from living her life as she saw fit. "How
dare you seek to interfere with—" she began.

He grabbed her wrist and seemed not to hear her.
"I'm so sorry. I didn't know Franklin was inventing
evidence against Kane. Please, believe I didn't know."
There was such vehemence in his gaze that she found
herself transfixed. "Harry was so worried for you as he
died in my arms. I must keep my promise. I must protect
you, Helena. You must be wary of Gowery. More wary
even than you were. He is not what he seems."

Amber decided not to argue names or intentions at
that point. "Yes. Certainly," she told him in her gentlest
tone. "Put all that from your mind. Right now you must
get to your bed. Let me help you." She might well have
saved her breath for he seemed to lapse into sleep. She
tried to tug him upward, but he was dead weight. Kindness had failed… "Listen to me, you large galoot. Sit.
Up."

"Yes, Mimm," he answered and rolled up onto his
knees. "I'm hot, Mimm. I'm so hot." He dragged himself
to his feet with help from her. Once standing, he looked
in her eyes. "Goodness, Mimm, you've shrunk. But
you're very pretty, suddenly." He frowned. "You're not
lookin' a bit like yourself." Once again she heard the
touch of an Irish accent in his speech and fought a smile.

"Come… You're not far from the bed. One foot in front of the other," she ordered as they wove across the floor. And then his weight got the better of her and he toppled, pushing her on to the bed. Stunned, she lost her breath as he landed half on top of her. Amber tried to shift out from under his body, but no matter how she squirmed and tugged, she couldn't get her dress free. Desperate, she pushed on his shoulder so she could take a breath. He opened his eyes and stared into hers. "You aren't Helena."

"No, I'm Amber."

"You're my pixie. Did you just appear there?"

"No. You fell upon me," Amber explained. She'd been so busy trying to help him, she'd forgotten all about the fact that *the handsome man* knew Helena. But her anger had cooled. He seemed to only want to help the woman she'd promised to impersonate. He'd talked as if he were an old friend of her family's, but not a friend to Helena's guardian.

A knock sounded in the cabin. "Is there a problem, ma'am? I heard a shout."

"Oh, yes," she called back. "I came to this man's aid and he's collapsed on top of me."

"Has the gentleman perished?" he asked, sounding suspicious.

Her patient tried to push himself off her. "Are you my angel instead?" he asked. "Am I dead after all?" He stared at her with heartbreak in his violet eyes. "What will happen to Meara?"

His eyelids drooped closed then and his weight pressed more heavily on her. "He's not dead, but he is very ill," she called the man at the door. "I just need help to get up, then we can summon the ship's surgeon."

"You'll have to extricate yourself," the man at the door shouted. "I am a minister—Reverend Willis. I will pray for the man, but I fall ill very easily. I shall go find the doctor, though."

"Then find him quickly, for God's sake!" she shouted back, though she had to admit it came out like more of a croak, what with a man's weight all but crushing her.

In the next moment, she managed to twist herself free, but her skirts were still trapped under him. So there she sat, showing more ankle than she had since she was in short skirts, but at least she was no longer trapped.

The doctor bustled in, wearing a rumpled light-colored suit of clothes and dingy waistcoat, his face bearded, a pair of glasses perched on his florid nose. And enough alcohol on his breath to knock out a room full of sailors. "What is this about a woman of ill repute trapped under a sick man? And why didn't I know you were available?"

"How dare you!" Amber gasped and stared at him in speechless horror. Then she took a deep breath, trying to get hold of her anger. From the other girls at Vassar she'd learned that disdain got a woman further than anger. Amber notched her chin higher and tried to look down her nose at the man who stood half a head taller than her. "I am nothing of the sort!" She shook with rage inside, but explained in a cold haughty voice how events had transpired.

The doctor nodded and walked around behind her. His only response to all she'd said was a short phrase. "Do *not* leave this cabin."

And with that ominous statement, she felt a tug as he yanked her skirts free. Sparing her no more than a glance when she hopped down off the high canopied bed, he went about examining his patient, unbuttoning the man's brocade waistcoat and fine cotton shirt. Then the doctor began muttering and swearing.

Averting her gaze, she backed toward the door. "Well, thank you very much for your help. I'll just return to my own cabin."

"You will remain here, my dear."

She froze. "Why?"

He turned to face her. "You may wish you hadn't meddled. You have been exposed to whatever disease this man has. You must be quarantined with him for the duration."

"The duration?"

"Of his illness and yours should you fall ill."

"I most certainly will not! I won't get whatever he has. I'm extremely healthy. Besides which, I am an unmarried lady. I cannot stay in here. I have a stateroom just across the saloon that is paid for. If necessary, I shall go there until you're convinced I will not take sick with whatever has stricken him. What, by the way, is wrong with him?"

"He is a victim of scarlet fever."

Normally she wouldn't question a physician, but this man had clearly been drinking. "Isn't that a child's illness?"

"I have seen it in the odd adult. And he is quite seriously ill with it."

He sounded so positive. "Oh, the poor man."

The doctor narrowed his eyes, pegging her with his penetrating gaze. "And you will stay and lend yourself to nursing him. If not, he'll die."

Her ears had surely failed her. "Lend myself toward

nursing him? I spoke with him only briefly on deck! And, as I told you, I am unmarried."

The doctor locked his gaze on her. "Do not take me for a fool. Or simply a drunk. I am quite sober today. Lord Adair asked for a stateroom near yours. I was there when he booked passage. And I found you trapped on the bed with him." He shook his finger at her. "You apparently know the man quite a bit better than I. If you refuse, you would be signing this man's death warrant. He may not survive anyway. But I cannot help that."

"Not help it? You are supposed to be the ship's doctor."

He backed toward the door. "There are many others aboard who may need my care on this voyage. For their sakes, I cannot help him at the risk of my own health. If you refuse, the captain might well order him cast overboard rather than wait until he perishes."

Her heart wrenched. Could he do that? "You will not!" Her gaze shot to the man on the bed. To think of the kind, funny and, yes, handsome man, who'd teased her being thrown away like refuse broke her heart. If she declined, he would at best be left to his own devices and would most certainly die. Women back home often nursed injured miners. If they could do it, she could do it, too.

She looked back at the doctor and bit her lip. "I know less about nursing than I do about him," she admitted. "You called him Lord Adair. What is his Christian name?"

"I believe I remember him saying he preferred to be called James…no…it was Jamie. Not at all what one would expect from Britain's ruling class. Am I to assume you are willing to care for him?"

She took a deep breath. "You give me little choice if

he is to have any chance, Dr.…uh…what *is* your name? I think I should know the name of the man coercing me to do something so far beyond my experience and propriety."

"I am Dr. Bertram Bennet, late of New York, and ports east, west, north and south."

"Fine, Dr. Bennet, what do I do?"

"Bathe him with cool water to lessen the fever. I will see nourishing broth is delivered to keep up his strength and—" he whipped off his worn black neckcloth "—put this on the door if he perishes." His eyes softened a bit. "We will have to consign him to the deep if he does. It is the way of the sea."

"Have you no powders or remedies?" she demanded as the doctor made for the door.

He stopped and sighed. "I will send something for the fever, but it rarely works for a pernicious disease such as scarlet fever. Mostly I believe such illnesses must run their course."

"Doctor…what…what about his…um…his clothing?" she managed to ask, her cheeks burning like fire. She was sure he would need to be undressed. How else would she bathe him? How had she gotten herself into this? Oh, yes. She'd forgotten adventures often lead to difficulty.

The doctor considered her, raising one of his eyebrows. Her cheeks heated further. "Perhaps you don't know the gentleman as well as we all believed. Just cut his clothing off. He can afford the loss. The earl is as rich as Croesus. I will have your trunk pushed in here. I am sorry your life has been thrust on this new path. Do you know why he insisted upon a cabin near yours?"

"From his ramblings, I have deciphered that he was a friend of…my father." She hesitated. Lying was difficult for her.

"That is what he told the steward, but no one believed it," Dr. Bennet said.

"He was apparently with my…uh…father at his death. It has left him feeling some duty to see to my safety."

The doctor nodded. "I hope for Adair's sake he has the chance to fulfill his mission." Then he turned away sharply and left, closing the door with such a resounding thud that Amber jumped. It felt as if the door had closed on every plan she'd made for the rest of her life. As if nothing would be the same again.

She turned back to the bed and took a deep breath. The earl didn't look very lordly at the moment. He looked rumpled and sick. And he needed her help. She wanted him to get well, but if he did, she wouldn't look forward to his learning of the ruse that had put both of them aboard this ship.

If he was to get well, she first had to deal with his clothing. After the dreams she'd had all night long, she didn't know how she would care for him so personally and not think of them. But she had no choice.

He murmured and tossed on the bed as she rummaged in his trunk. She found only a straight razor and a rather nasty-looking double-edged knife. The latter didn't look as if it should be part of the accoutrements of an English earl and that gave her pause. What kind of man was he really? She especially had to wonder after not finding any sort of nightshirt. That, too, was outrageously scandalizing—at least to her.

She walked back to the washstand and wet a cloth to place it on his burning forehead, then, using the razor, split his seams, unable to just destroy such fine clothing. She had just finished when a cabin boy quickly shoved her trunk into the room. She rolled her eyes. There was a perfectly acceptable pair of scissors that would have made the job ever so much easier.

Next arrived the powders the doctor had promised. By the time she got the powder mixed with water and into him, her blouse was soaked. Since it had gone nearly transparent with the water, she decided to change. While she rummaged through her badly packed things, the earl called out for the woman named Mimm and someone named Meara.

Amber quickly changed her blouse and put on an apron. She thanked God she'd added her serviceable clothes to the spectacular wardrobe Helena Conwell had given her. Then she pulled out her grandmother's carefully written book of remedies and medicines. Her aunt, the wonderful woman who'd raised her from an early age, had added some of her own. She quickly looked through it for any reference to scarlet fever. What she found worried her. He was in for some hard days ahead.

And so was she.

She dropped the book in her lap and sighed. The healing book hadn't contradicted the doctor, but it did add some suggestions. She quickly went to the door and asked the cabin boy stationed there to request several herbs she was supposed to make into a tea.

"Oh, my head," Amber heard the earl mutter as she turned away from the door. He stabbed his hand into his hair as he tried to sit. "What in God's name did I drink last night?"

She rushed to the bed and pushed him back down. "You are quite ill with scarlet fever."

"Pixie. What are you doing here?" he asked, his voice very hoarse and a little slurred; she saw that it pained him to speak.

"I heard you earlier. You'd collapsed. I foolishly entered your cabin and sent for the doctor. He quarantined me in here with you. I've been named your nurse, your lordship," she said, leaving out the embarrassing, yet pertinent, facts.

This time he managed to sit up. "Oh, please, do lay off the your lordship business. I've become rather fond of American lack of deference." He looked down at himself, then back up at her. "It seems as though we should be on a first-name basis." He glanced again at his lap. She had left him in only his underdrawers. The sheet slid to his waist, leaving his torso quite bare, and she couldn't look away from the sight of his muscular chest.

Then he sank back to his pillows. "Devil take it! I cannot be ill. My daughter was, but I thought myself above it."

"Do calm down," she begged, noting his overly bright eyes and the very scarlet look of the rash covering his body. "You'll get well. See if you don't."

"I won't *see* anything at all if I don't," he grumbled crossly.

Her grandmother's book had warned of nervous irritability and this was certainly a change from what she'd seen of him on deck. "I don't know much about caring for the sick, but I promise to follow all the doctor's instructions. And I have my grandmother's healing book for guidance, as well."

"Are you speaking of that drunken sot I met the day I booked passage?"

"He was quite sober today, I think."

"Oh, lovely!" he groused and tried to sit up again. "My life is in the hands of a drunken doctor and the observations of a backwoods grandmother and her granddaughter who is barely out of the schoolroom."

"Well!"

His over-bright eyes widened and he grimaced, then put a shaking hand to his forehead. "I am so sorry. I'm not usually so easily annoyed. Where have my manners gone?"

"You're sick. But perhaps you're hungry. I have some broth for you."

He shook his head. "No, I'm not in the least hungry. What I am is worried for my daughter."

So he was married. That should make caring for him easier. She set to bathing his face and neck to lessen the fever. "What is your daughter's name?" she asked, needing to learn as much as possible about him in case a letter had to be written to his kin.

"Meara," he said quietly. "She's only seven years old. I've raised her here with the help of my old nurse."

"Do mothers in England not help raise their children?"

"She died a few months after Meara's birth."

"I am so sorry. I understand your worry for your child. But have you no family to care for her? Not that I think you will not survive," she added quickly.

"I became the earl at a tender age. My uncle was my guardian and he made my life miserable. If I die, Meara would have him as her guardian and he will succeed me. What if I die of this?" He grasped her arm in a steely grip and gazed up at her with fever-bright eyes. "I can't die!"

Before Amber could respond, he started to breathe oddly. Almost panting. After a minute or so between breaths he said, "Oh. God. Chamber pot. Hurry."

She got the pot to him before he was violently sick, losing all the medicine she'd fought to get into him. She stood there, feeling inadequate and embarrassed for him.

When he was finished, he nearly pitched out of the narrow bed from weakness. Amber made a grab for both his shoulder and the pot. She pushed him to the pillow, then took the foul-smelling pot to the porthole and dumped it. The sea air smelled so refreshing she left it open.

When she looked back at him he was no longer awake, lying so still it frightened her till she saw his chest rise with a breath. Her worry over treating him as a patient, after the sensual dreams she'd had, vanished. She hesitantly laid her hand over his heart. And wished she hadn't, for his heart didn't beat at the same rate as hers. It fluttered in so quick a rhythm she could scarcely count the beats.

His skin beneath her hand was dry and burning to the touch. His neck, shoulders and most of his torso were bright red with the rash. And her only weapons in the battle were a cool cloth, the powders Dr. Bennet had given her and the herbal teas she'd concocted.

She worked at it hour upon hour. Sometimes she wiped him down and, occasionally, when her arms and legs grew too tired to work, she covered his torso, limbs and forehead with wet cloths. That respite gave her the strength to begin all over again.

Twice more through the night she spooned the powders mixed with water into his mouth. She constantly tried to get him to drink the tea. He was often like a little bird, taking what was offered, but with his eyes shut. Other times he shook his head, refusing anything nourishing.

He developed a rattling cough about the noon hour the next day. She looked in her book, but neither there nor in the doctor's instructions was a cough mentioned. Exhausted, with little sleep since the first night aboard, Amber sat next to his bed, put her head back and slept.

In her dreams Lord Adair visited. Manly, healthy and hungry—for her. Now that she knew his name she moaned it aloud as he kissed her. "Jamie."

Chapter Three

Jamie woke, his skin on fire. His bed pitched and tilted, making his head swim. "Stop!" he yelled and was immediately sorry. He took a gasping breath past a throat that must have been sliced to ribbons by some fiend with a knife. Then someone raked fire across his chest. But the fire was cold. He shivered. Cold should feel good, but it made his skin burn all the more.

"I'm so sorry," a sweet voice crooned. "I'm trying to keep your fever down. Maybe if I just laid the cloth on your chest. Would that feel better? I'm sorry I didn't know this hurt you so."

The voice. He knew that voice. He forced his eyes open. "Pixie? Is it you?"

"My name is Amber. I do believe thinking of me as Helena is less annoying than this fixation you have with pixies. Why do you persist in this?"

What a foolish question, he thought. "You look… like a pixie," he gasped. "Tiny."

"I'm quite capable." His pixie grew somehow, then seemed to float over him, frowning down at him. Her frown wasn't the least threatening, though. It was quite the most adorable frown he'd ever seen. He smiled at that. Although he felt like death, she lightened his spirits. "Ever met…a pixie?" he challenged. "Wily… creatures. Eire's full of…the little people."

"But we're in America. Well, not exactly there just now, as we're on the high seas, but this is an American ship. It's even called the *Young America*."

He struggled to grasp that. "On a ship? Why am I…on a ship?"

"You were searching for Helena Conwell and mistook me for her," his pixie explained.

He was looking for Helena? Oh, yes. He had to make sure she was safe. And he'd left Meara in New York recuperating. He swallowed. Oh, God. He was sick. He wasn't supposed to get sick. Not like this. What if he died and left Meara to the mercy of Uncle Oswald? She wasn't safe.

Tears blinded him and he closed his eyes to hide the depth of his emotions. "Meara," he said, wanting to explain why his lovely nursemaid had to make sure he lived, but the name came out sounding as if he were crying. He kept his eyes closed, feeling the tears he couldn't stop run into his hair. Embarrassed and desperate, he decided to hide in the sleep that called to him. He'd hidden the real him for years and done a good job of it. He could do it again.

The next time he woke it was night and a lantern lit the room. He lay, watching the lantern swing to the same rhythm as the rocking of the room. Why would a room move? he asked himself. Earthquake? He'd felt minor tremors in California, but those never made the room rock this way. He closed his eyes, dizziness swamping him, and groaned.

"Jamie?"

It was the pixie calling softly to him. She laid a cool cloth over his forehead. He opened his eyes again. Bathed in the light from overhead, he saw her. "You've returned," he said, then winced at how painful his throat was.

"I didn't leave. You fell asleep. You must try to stay with me this time. Could you eat some fresh broth?"

He shook his head. He hated to disappoint her, but he couldn't imagine eating anything with the room swaying as it was.

"We could talk," she said hopefully.

He winced. "Hurts."

"Then I'll talk."

And talk she did. She told him about her adventures. About her visit to the Centennial Exposition in Philadelphia and to Atlantic City, New Jersey, where she'd worn her Easter finery on their famous boardwalk by the sea. She told amusing stories about the students she'd taught, and about going to college and the wealthy girls who'd been kind and shared their clothes and family holidays with her.

He fell asleep again to the sound of her sweet voice and she followed him into his dreams. But worry followed him, too. He was suddenly young again and Pixie was his teacher. Uncle Oswald was there and Jamie was under his uncle's control again.

Then Meara was in the house.

And it changed. It was wrong. Now the object of his uncle's ire was Meara. And as a young boy Jamie tried to protect her, but had no power to do so. He screamed her name as the blows fell on her and he cursed his uncle to hell.

His eyes flew open to find his magical pixie staring down at him with concerned eyes. "You shouted. Are you all right? Can I help?" she asked and took the hot cloth off his head.

"I'm worse," he whispered and grabbed her wrist after she set the cooled cloth back on his forehead. "You know I am."

She covered his hand with her free one. "You're warmer. I'm trying everything I know."

He let go of her. "I know you are…Pixie."

"My name is Amber. I'm not magic," she said, and there were tears in her eyes and voice. "If I were, you'd be on the mend."

"How long?"

"Don't talk like that. You have to get better for your Meara."

"Not till…I die. How long…have I…been sick?"

She wiped her pert nose on a dainty handkerchief. "It's been a week."

"And you're…so tired…else you wouldn't…be crying…over me." Her image wavered and he tried to see her more clearly, but to no avail. "Don't even like me," he muttered. "Never have."

Amber frowned and pushed an annoying stray hair off her forehead. What was going through that fevered mind of his? "It isn't true that I don't like you. I hardly knew you before needing to care for you. If I didn't like you, I'd have told the doctor to go hang."

He narrowed his eyes as if trying to puzzle something out. "Would you marry me, Helena?"

Disappointment pressed in on Amber. He'd seemed to know her. And now he didn't. He'd closed his eyes again. Amber called softly to him, but she knew it was futile. She'd lost him again.

As long as she didn't lose him altogether. He was so worried about his poor motherless daughter. It was poignant, but confusing. Why was he not with her? Would he neglect the child he loved because this obsession of his with Helena was so all consuming? Sadly it seemed to be. He'd just asked the woman to marry him, hadn't he?

It made her a bit cross with him. He had a child who relied on him. What she wouldn't give for the chance to be a parent. Nothing would be more important to her than her child. She knew what it was like to be orphaned. The loneliness and grief had nearly torn her apart on that long train ride east. But she'd been lucky enough to have her aunt and uncle meet her and envelope her in loving arms. Even though Aunty had been sick for so long before she was gone, too, Amber had been secure in the love of the adults in her life even when it was only her and Uncle Charles.

It wasn't long after Aunty died that he began talking of her going to a two-year boarding school where she'd be further educated with the idea that she would advance from there to Vassar. It wasn't merely the education he'd wanted for her, though. He'd wanted her away from the coal patch. And away from men like Joseph. Men who were miners. Men who could go to work one day and never return. He'd wanted more for her than pain and loss. So he'd sent her away where someone else could see she met the right people.

But as soon as the ink was dry on her prestigious

diploma, she'd moved back to the coal patch, to a town where the mine owner wanted to educate the children of his miners. And there she'd met and fallen in love with Joseph—a miner. Then, just after the banns were read the third time, Joseph died.

She'd continued to teach, but the heart had gone out of her. In the state she was in, she'd nearly let Joseph's mother push her on her other son. She'd woken up one day, looked around at the soot and death and seen Uncle Charles's wisdom. And that had put her right where she was now.

Coming to care too much for a man she was beginning to fear was about to die.

Amber shook her head and went back to bathing him, careful of the rash he'd said hurt when she ran the wet cloths over it. She'd checked her grandmother's book and sure enough, it mentioned that the rash was painful and burned.

"No, Uncle Oswald. Please don't! No! Damn you to hell for hurting her!" Jamie called out, tossing on the narrow bed.

Amber grabbed his shoulders while trying to hold on to him. The stool she stood on rocked under her feet. "Jamie! Calm down," she ordered in her school-room voice.

He stilled instantly and opened his eyes. His voice rawer for his shouting, he rasped out, "You can't…let it happen. She's sweet and innocent. He…he's a monster."

"All I can do is keep taking care of you."

"Marry me. Be Meara's mother. She needs you. You don't know what he'd do. He'd break her. Nearly broke me, but I had Mimm and Alex. She'd love you, Pixie."

He knew her again. He knew who he was asking— begging to marry him before it was too late to help his child. Could she do it? Could she marry him and care for the child he spoke of with such love? She'd wanted children for as long as she could remember. But she'd buried that dream with Joseph.

"Don't think it…to death." He chuckled, but it was a heartbreaking sound.

Amber wanted to remember the man on deck, handsome and smiling and kind. Not this hollow-eyed near-corpse. She forced her thoughts to his strange proposal. "I'm all alone, Jamie. How could I care for a child?"

"How can you not? I'm dying. You know it. I know it. There's money. You wouldn't have to worry about means. That old pile in Ireland would go to Oswald and he can have it along with the title he's wanted my whole life. But please don't let him have Meara. You have to promise to protect her."

"He's powerful. He'd take all the money, Jamie. I couldn't fight him. I'm going to be a governess in California. What kind of life would that be for a little girl who should have been wealthy?"

He frowned, looking thoughtful. "I'll write a codicil," he said at last.

"You could barely hold a pen."

"Then you write it. I'll sign it. Make Captain Baker witness it. Figure it out. Save her, damn it. Please. At least let me rest in peace."

"Stop it! I'm not letting you die! Then you'd be stuck with me when all this turns out okay. I'm not countess material no matter where I spent the years I was at college."

Again that thoughtful look entered his eyes. "Then, if I live, when the voyage ends, we'll annul it."

Amber bit her lip. A child. A little girl who'd be all alone but for a man her father clearly loathed. He said there'd be money so Meara would never want for anything. There was little she could do but agree and that made it just a bit vexing. Everyone else's problems kept forcing her into doing outrageous things.

"All right," she said, annoyed. "I'll call out to the young man assigned to us. He can see if the captain will do what you want about the codicil and if the minister I met will marry us. He's very afraid of becoming ill, so he may refuse. He most likely should."

"So fierce, Pixie." He reached up and traced her jawline.

She shivered at his touch.

"And fierce is what I need just now. Protect my princess."

"You most likely won't remember all this when you wake up again, but I'll ask."

Amber knocked on the door and asked the cabin boy to fetch Captain Baker and the reverend. Then she went back to the bed with her notebook. "Are you still with me?"

"Aye. Write this. To the firm of Bootey and Fowler, New York, New York. This is a codicil to my last will and testament. I hereby appoint my wife…" He waved his hand weakly toward her notebook and swallowed. After a breath and a long pause he said, "Put your whole name there, Pixie, and…uh…add the date…my wife as guardian…to my Meara…Reynolds, my daughter."

He stopped talking, closed his eyes, then, just when she thought that was all he wanted to say, he blinked his eyes open and added, "She is to administer the trust set up at the Brooklyn Trust Company. The rest of my financial estate shall pass into her ownership. Under no circumstances should any other individual lay claim to any part of my estate or to the guardianship of the child, Meara Reynolds.

"That ought to do it," he said. "Where the hell is Baker? And that minister."

A knock sounded on the door and Amber hurried to it. "Captain E. C. Baker, ma'am. What can be done to assist you?"

"The earl wishes to—to—" The words stuck in her throat. "He wishes to marry me for the sake of his daughter. He fears he will perish and leave her orphaned."

Reverend Willis had apparently accompanied Captain Baker and he shouted through the door, "You wish me to perform a marriage ceremony?"

This bellowing through the door was just stupid. It had been a week and a day and she had not sickened. She flung the door open and was surprised to see a well turned-out officer standing next to a tall, thin man in unrelieved black. Captain Baker had tightly curling salt-and-pepper hair and a full closely trimmed beard to match. After her meeting with Dr. Bennet and his smelly liquor breath, she'd not known what to expect of another ship's officer. "No, *he* does," she said. "I think this an *absurd* idea, but there is his motherless child to consider, though I have assured him he will live through this sickness."

"I am sorry Dr. Bennet has caused you so much trouble. He should have quarantined you in your cabin and cared for the man himself. Unfortunately, the best doctors do not accept positions on sailing ships."

"We are well past that point now, sir."

"The will," Jamie rasped from the bed.

"What was that?" Captain Baker demanded, frowning.

Of course, he had not heard. It had been said much too softly to have been heard even the seven or eight feet to the door. "The earl has dictated a change to his will. He wants you to witness it."

"My dear young woman, this is unconscionable. You are clearly taking advantage. I do not think this is wise, milord," E. C. Baker called into the room.

"My…idea," Jamie rasped back louder than before, then took a gasping breath.

"I've disputed this," Amber told the captain. "He is resolute. And this arguing is sapping his strength."

The captain pursed his lips and stroked his beard as he thought over the problem. "Very well. Has he signed this codicil to his will?"

"I thought it would be better if you sign before he touches the page. I have a health book that says objects the sick person touches can carry infection."

Baker raised an eyebrow and stared as if considering her. Then he nodded. "Fine. We will do the ceremony first," Baker said to Reverend Willis.

Willis nodded back. "I'll need the names."

"The man taken ill is Lord Jamie Reynolds, Earl of Adair, and this is Miss Helena Conwell."

"Excuse me," Amber interrupted. "My name is Amber Dodd. I am merely traveling in Helena's stead. We traded places in our accommodations."

"So you truly didn't know the earl?" Captain Baker asked.

"I didn't. It was a bit of a mistaken identity," she said. "Helena failed to inform the earl of the change in her travel plans." She glanced at the bed. "Jamie, are you still with us?"

"What's holding…this back?"

She looked toward the men in the doorway. "Captain? Reverend?"

Reverend Willis cleared his throat and motioned Amber back to the bed. "I don't know how to address a man of English peerage so we'll just go with both his names. Make sure this is all legal and binding. Jamie Reynolds, Earl of Adair," he said in a loud voice, "do you take this woman, Amber Dodd, for your lawfully wedded wife?"

"I do, Pixie," Jamie rasped and smiled sadly.

The minister went on, unaware of the poignant moment. "And do you, Amber Dodd, take Jamie Reynolds, Earl of Adair, for your lawfully wedded husband?"

"I do," she said.

Amber was grateful he had dispensed with all the promises they'd likely never be called on to test. And he certainly needn't mention that death would part them. It was standing in the room, a dark witness, ready to claim him.

Captain Baker then read aloud the codicil and signed it at Jamie's nod. Then Jamie scrawled his signature upon it. She returned to the door. "I will pray for his life, ma'am," the captain said.

"And I will continue to do the same," Reverend Willis added. "I will also write up the marriage papers and give them into the captain's keeping."

She nodded her thanks, then closed the door.

"It is done then?" Jamie asked.

"It is, but the entire affair was unnecessary. You're going to get well. I've promised, haven't I? I never break a promise."

His energy spent, he nodded slightly, smiled sadly, then took a ring off his little finger and slid it on hers.

It fit. She wondered if that was prophetic. And if it was a prophecy, what did it mean? Was she destined to wear it as his widow or, queer thought that it was, did it mean they were destined for each other? Whichever it was, while she stared at her left hand, he fell back to sleep.

Amber stored the codicil in her trunk and resumed bathing him, fighting the fever ravaging his body. She wanted him to live, but the longer he hung on, hovering between life and death, the more she cared about him. She prayed that if he were to die God would take him before she cared even more for him. But then she quickly revised her thought because the truth was…she already cared for him too much.

And now she was married to him.

This adventure had become her worst nightmare come true.

Chapter Four

Jamie opened his eyes and found her standing over him. He'd never have thought such selflessness would be part of her character. And the plainness of her dress and even plainer hairstyle surprised him, too. He hadn't thought Helena, an upper-class princess, would own a garment so worn and simple. "Oh, you're back again," she said in that sweet voice. It lured him from sleep time and again even though pain awaited.

"And you're still here," he quipped, scarcely recognizing the hoarse sound of his own voice.

"I promised you I'd be here. Will you try to take some broth and tea? I think my grandmother's recipe is keeping your fever down a bit."

Just then sunlight flooded through the skylight and illuminated her lovely face. It wasn't Helena. It was Pixie. He struggled to gather a name from his fevered brain. She was Amber. He'd thought she must be part of a dream, but she was real. So he *had* met her on deck.

Jamie nodded to her question about the broth and tea. He didn't feel up to eating or drinking, but he didn't want to disappoint her. She was taking care of him. The least he could do was cooperate and help himself.

Her lovely smile made the agony of swallowing worth the pain. He didn't feel the same way when he tasted the bitter liquid he'd watched her mix with water and the contents of an envelope. "That last...quite disgusting," he complained.

She laughed and laid a cool cloth on his forehead. "Your opinion of the doctor notwithstanding, we need to do everything we can to get you well. Meara is counting on us."

Us? Jamie frowned as a fog rose between them and he felt his mind begin to descend into chaos. He fought to hold on to clarity, but could feel it slipping away. "Meara? You know my wee one?"

The pixie frowned. "No, you told me of her nearly a week ago. It's easy to see how much you love her."

Meara. His sweet trusting little angel. He shouldn't have left. "Been...away...too much," he tried to explain. He wanted to hide in his mind. He forced his eyes open and beheld captivating Helena. She floated next to his bed. Seeing her there made no sense. She hated him. But she needed protection. He had to make her see reason. "I gave...my word." Speaking had grown agonizing, but she had to understand. "His blood...on my hands. Promised... Least...I can do. Died to save me."

Amber sighed. So she was Helena again. Why did that bother her so much? She stared down at Jamie's tortured expression and forgot her own upset. She knew the story of Harry Conwell's murder and it clearly haunted Jamie.

He stared up at her, now engulfed in delirium. She

decided to play along. What difference did it make if a delirious man thought she was someone else?

"It wasn't your fault," she told him. "It was someone angry over his mining interests."

"Not sure," Jamie whispered. "Gowery said…but…I wonder—" His eyelids slid closed.

He was gone again, but he had been lucid for a longer time than he'd been in nearly a week. Since the day he'd pushed her to marry him.

Amber plunked down on the stool next to the bed. Lord above! She'd married him. She'd come to care for him. And he could still die. His fever kept spiking toward sundown. She wanted to believe he'd live so badly, but even his recovery posed a huge problem for her—for her heart. While he'd been lost in delusions and delirium, she'd seen the honorable man his unguarded mind revealed him to be. And more and more she became ensnared and enthralled by a pair of fevered violet eyes.

Several hours later Jamie's fever spiked again. It raged for hours as if in response to her refusal to give up hope. Then he began sweating and she prayed the fever would break for good.

Exhaustion pressed in on her as she blotted his forehead to keep the sweat from running into his eyes. He tossed and turned and once again muttered names and the occasional coherent phrases about his terrible upbringing and his need to protect his child from the same man English law would have made her guardian.

It surprised her that he was such a good man considering his life under his uncle's cruel tutelage. No matter what happened between them in the future, she was at peace with her decision to marry him for Meara.

His skin had begun to peel quite severely a few days earlier and, according to the healing book, the disease had about run its course.

The sweating continued into the long, hot afternoon. She changed his soaking sheet several times. The crew had refused to get close to the diseased bed linens, but they did bring her fresh buckets of water so she could wash them. After she changed the bed, she dropped the sheets into a bucket of vinegar and water. After they'd soaked for a while, she rinsed them in a second tub of clean water, then gave them a soak in baking soda. That was how the book, which had almost become as precious to her as her Bible, said to clean everything that came in contact with him.

Their quick wedding seemed forever ago. In her weariness she'd lost count of exactly how many days that was. That she'd become Lady Adair that day seemed impossible. She looked down at herself and chuckled. She'd certainly set the entire aristocracy on its ear if right then they could see the woman the Earl of Adair had married.

Jamie finally quieted and the profuse sweating lessened. He was cooler to the touch than he'd been since the day she'd entered the cabin. By sunset her back ached and exhaustion licked at her heels. Though he'd not awakened since morning, he finally slept comfortably. She was no longer in the least squeamish about the personal nature of the tasks the doctor had pushed her to perform. She bathed him thoroughly, and found it difficult not to admire the beauty of him.

At last she had a few minutes for herself. Behind a blanket she'd hung in the corner, she washed in cool water and changed into one of Helena's silk shifts. After pushing the buckets of dirty water out to the cabin boy for disposal, she sank onto a pallet she'd made on the floor. Praying they'd both sleep all night and that Jamie was on the mend at last, Amber fell into exhausted sleep.

Soft breathing came from somewhere next to Jamie. From below and next to him. He glanced down and found his golden sprite curled up on the floor amid twisted sheets and blankets. It was the pixie from his dreams.

He must still be dreaming. Only in a dream would someone so lovely and innocent be there, ready to fulfill his most deep-seated wishes. If only she were real.

But whatever she was, wherever he was, he was drawn like a moth to a flame. Wondering which of them would be singed, he slipped from the bed to the floor and reached out to touch her golden hair. As he tangled his fingers in her wavy tresses, he waited, anxious for the burn.

But the fire was only in his blood.

She sighed and turned her face into his hand. He hardened and melted at once. It seemed the most natural action in the world to sink down next to her and pull her close. He captured her chin as he settled his lips over hers. The moan that escaped her called to him. Captured him.

Made him want.

Her.

Made him need.

Only her.

He parted her lips with his tongue and she granted him entrance with another sigh. He tasted sweetness and hunger and prayed it was hunger for him. Sliding his palms lower, he found her fine-boned, delicate shoulders and ever so gently kneaded them. Then he stroked downward over her back, her gently rounded buttocks. Her warmth heated his blood, especially when he realized that only a thin silken shift separated them. That knowledge tempted him as nothing before ever had. Finally his fingers found the hem of her shift.

His palms came in contact with her thighs and he was amazed that her skin was silkier than her shift. He was obsessed with her. "So silky. So soft," he whispered. He had to have her.

He skimmed his fingertips upward over her thighs and feathered them over her hipbones. She shivered and made strangled little sounds, tempting sounds that provoked a desperate need in him. He wanted to hold those perfect hips and mount her, but he fought the urge. There was all that enticing territory above to explore and he had all day and night. That was the beauty of a dream. He had as long as he wanted or needed. He trailed his fingers over her flat belly. It was even softer than the rest of her.

When he cupped her smooth, tempting breasts, she moaned again and a whispered word burst from her lips. "Please." And then again, "Please."

"I know," he murmured, hoping to soothe her. He didn't know how he knew what she wanted—what she needed. But this was his dream so, of course, what he wanted she wanted. And he wanted to pleasure her. A dream lover like his pixie deserved his best efforts.

He sought and found her warm, hot center and stroked her moist core, first one finger, then two. With his thumb he circled the one spot he knew would drive her wild.

It did. She cried out and tipped her hips as if seeking more, rocking against his hand. "Please," she sobbed.

"I…I need—I need…." She tossed her head and held her arms out to him.

She might not understand all he'd made her feel, but he did. "Oh, yes, sprite, I do, too," he assured her. They needed to lose themselves in each other. He gave in to all his secret desires. He shifted over her and covered one of her sweet nipples with his mouth and suckled her till she cried out again. Her scent—a combination of flowers and musk—seemed to surround him, then desire overwhelmed him.

He pulled her hips toward his and entered her tight core.

She made a small distressed sound and he tensed. Even a dream lover deserved care and consideration. "It's all right. Don't worry. I'll make it good for you."

Something was different about this coupling from those he'd had with his wife. Try though he might, his mind was too clouded with passion and need to identify what he'd missed or to consider anything beyond the desire this dream woman had stirred in him. He was no longer sure of even who she was—the sprite or Helena, he could no longer tell.

Knowing he had to coax her back to him, he covered her mouth with his and caressed her lips with his own. When she opened them on a gasp, he twined his tongue with hers. She was soon with him again and he re-warded her trust by carefully pressing forward, then pulling back. He rocked on her till he was buried to the hilt in her sweet depths. "Better? My God, tell me it's better!"

She nodded, sucking in a breath. "Better than better. Perfect," she breathed. Her tightness caressed him and rapture called, but he struggled to hold himself in check.

He supported his weight on his forearms as best as he could, but soon, shaking with need, he lost himself. All thought fled his mind when she circled his waist with her long, slender limbs.

Somehow he managed to fight back from the precipice of satisfaction, desperate to ensure pleasure for the magical woman in his arms. Sweet breath puffed from her lungs in the rhythm of his thrusts. Then when he could no longer hold off reaching for the ultimate rapture, her muscles began to pulse around him and he gave himself over to the wonder of the dream. Her cries of ecstasy tore through the little room and he gladly followed her. As he emptied his seed into her keeping, he cried out her name.

Helena.

Feeling as if she'd drained every ounce of strength from him, he rolled to his side to keep from collapsing on her. Chilled, he flipped the blanket over them both, and then pulled her along his side, settling her head against his shoulder. Exhaustion closed in on him, but he managed one more coherent thought. Who would have thought Helena would be so passionate a lover? This dream was better than any he'd had before he'd given up the idea of marriage between them.

As the fog in his mind closed in on him, Jamie felt a tear drop on to his shoulder, then another. But he couldn't manage to ask why she'd cry.

Amber tried to hold on to her emotions, but one tear fell then another and another. How could a heart break and allow the owner to live with such pain? She would rather die than have him know the destruction one word—one name—had wrought within her.

It had all seemed like a dream at first. Indeed, she had

had similar dreams for days. With every fiber of her being Amber had believed this was a dream, as well. He'd been so sick and she'd been so afraid to believe he was on the mend that awaking in his arms had truly felt like a secret wish come true.

A fantasy.

A dream.

Then, when things she'd never imagined or heard of began to happen between them, she'd fully awakened and thought the real Jamie had come to her, wanting to make their desperate unromantic marriage a real one. And God help her, after all her protestations that she wanted no man in her life, in her exhausted sleep-deprived mind she'd wanted him. She'd believed the beautiful act they'd performed together came from feelings in each of them that matched perfectly.

Those traitorous emotions had grown against her will while she'd nursed him. Now she'd have to use all her willpower to obliterate them. Because he'd turned the dream she'd awakened to from beautiful reality to a nightmare with the shouted name of the woman he believed her to be.

Not Amber. Not even Pixie.

Helena.

Beautiful, wealthy and proper Helena.

So now Amber lay, silently weeping, unable to move away without risking his awakening and seeing how deeply he'd wounded her. The abyss of troubled sleep claimed her before she could stem the flow of her tears. While she slept in his arms, her dreams were full of confrontations that featured Jamie and Helena with Amber in the role of their child's governess or some other lowly servant.

* * *

Jamie stirred and Amber woke with a start. Morning light flooded through the porthole, illuminating the cabin and sending reality crashing in on her like a mighty wave, assaulting her heart and soul. Everything between them last night had been a fraud.

She recoiled and tried to scramble away when Jamie's gaze fell upon her face and anger marched across his features. He tightened his grip on her shoulder and pushed himself up on one bent arm, staring down at her with narrowed, furious eyes.

It was then that she remembered she was ignominiously nearly naked in the arms of her counterfeit husband. He'd taken her body when he thought she was his high-society love. Or maybe it was she who was the counterfeit in this marriage. After all, it was she who was not the woman he thought he'd wed. She was not his precious Helena.

Amber wished he'd say something.

Anything.

"What is this about? Was our meeting on deck an accident, Pixie?" His beautiful mouth twisted in a sneer and "pixie" ceased to be a sweet pet name. "I thought you were a disadvantaged innocent, forced to travel alone."

"I had my reasons for being alone."

"I must wonder if your reason was to lure me into this trap so you could then demand marriage. It worked for my late wife, but I won't be trapped that way again. I care not about my reputation here in America."

Amber felt her temper rise. Now she scrambled away, dragging the blanket with her as she stood. What did she care if it left him naked and exposed? She'd bathed him and cared for his needs for days on end. She could look at his naked form all day and feel nothing but contempt.

But then he stood in all his naked glory—bold as you please—and captured her gaze with his own narrowed, hard-as-amethyst eyes. It was she who broke away from their locked gazes. When her lowered eyes fell on to his manhood, her face heated in a betraying blush. She looked away quickly, but the damage was done. And that set fire to a temper few had ever seen.

"Luring you into marriage?" she shouted. "You must still be suffering from delirium. Your uncle has apparently already done his worst by freezing your heart. I did not need to trap you into marriage. We're already married. It was you who begged me to marry you to protect Meara. You promised an annulment if you survived the fever and I wished for one."

He opened his mouth to speak, but she rushed on, not caring what he planned to say. She had heard all she wished. "It was you who crawled on to my pallet last night and made annulment impossible. This is my thanks for caring for you all these long days? I should have let the captain toss you overboard. You endangered everyone on board just to follow your obsession with Helena!"

She stormed out into the saloon, her shoulders and back stiff as the deck she'd been sleeping on. Still wrapped in the blanket, the neckline of her pretty silk shift peeking out, she was mortified to bump into the ever-present cabin boy. But she raised her chin and stomped by him, refusing to show her embarrassment.

"Have my trunk sent to me," she told the boy over her shoulder as she stalked across the wide, elegantly appointed companionway and saloon. "I'll stay in my cabin under quarantine for the rest of the voyage, if I must, but I will not spend one more day in there. With *him*."

"Yes, ma'am," the boy answered, staring at her as if she were mad.

Perhaps she was.

Because she was afraid she'd fallen in love with that…that obnoxious person whose miserable life she'd probably saved.

Then her tears welled up again as she remembered all he'd revealed during his illness. He was a good man, worthy of her love even though he didn't want it. It had been the scars of his youth speaking just now. She knew that, but she hardened her heart. She'd never wanted to care. To love.

And she wouldn't.

She just wouldn't!

Chapter Five

Jamie's hand trembled as he ran it through his hair. He sank to the bed. His mind was less foggy; still, he was not completely sure of a good part of what had happened, in particular why he'd been standing naked, arguing with Amber. He winced when the door slammed behind her.

He sighed. Pixie was Amber. That much he was sure of. Their meeting on deck was engraved in his mind clearly, in sharp contrast to the murky uncertainty of the present.

He closed his eyes, trying to sort the jumble of images swimming to the surface. And now, God, now even snatches of the past days started to come into focus.

Too late.

He groaned. He remembered the burning fever. The pain of being touched. He would have died without her selfless care. Amber had agreed to marry him for Meara's sake when he'd been so sure he would die. She'd tried to give him hope, but she'd finally agreed to the marriage. Only after warning him she'd be un-suitable as his countess, however.

That meant she'd been willing to protect his child. As far as he was concerned, that proved she would make a wonderful countess because she'd make Meara a wonderful mother.

And he wasn't being in any way selfless, resigning himself to marriage to her because he suddenly recalled another of his lost memories—their lovemaking last the night. Memories of her skin, her hair, her scent.

As he went over those moments on her pallet, he knew he'd made an even more egregious error than he'd feared. Rising in his mind like a condemning specter was the look on her face—in her eyes—as he'd made her his. Her uncertainty of the unknown had all been written there. Then her expression changed to the one she'd worn as she scrambled to her feet and faced him this morning.

What had he done? What had he destroyed?

Jamie pinched the bridge of his nose and sighed again. The answer to that was as simple and as compli-cated as human nature. He'd allowed his past to color the present. He'd painted Amber with the motives of his late wife, Iris, a social-climbing whore, and of his cruel, manipulative guardian.

A knock at the door drew him back to the present and his eyes flew open. Hope that Amber had decided to return surged through him. Refusing to greet her naked as the day he was born, he made his way to his trunk and hurriedly located his dressing gown. After shrug-ging into it and knotting the tie at his waist, he hurried to the door on wobbly limbs. "I'm relieved you've reconsid—" he said as he pulled the heavy door open.

And his heart fell.

The drunken doctor he'd met the day he booked passage was not the person he wished to see. The older man wore an imperious look on his face as he said, "I'm told your nurse has deserted you."

"I no longer have need of nursing care, and where my wife is cannot be of great interest to you."

"It is of great interest to me until I've become certain she's not about to take ill. I must pronounce you healthy, as well."

Jamie spread his arms in mock surrender. "By all means."

The doctor took no time at all in making the pronouncement that Jamie had indeed come out at the other side of an illness that should by all rights have killed him. Jamie did not waste his time telling the doctor that he'd been doing that all his life, thanks to good women like Mimm and the pixie. Amber, he corrected silently.

Her name was Amber.

He rested a few minutes and began to dress so he could go talk to that young lady. His wife. His countess. He'd only managed to don his small clothes and trousers when another knock sounded hollowly in the room. He was less hopeful this time about who might be there. Yet he was still disappointed when a young boy in uniform stood there.

"I'm to fetch her trunk, sir," he said without preamble.

"Trunk?"

The cabin boy looked behind him at the door across the saloon. "The lady, sir. She said I was to fetch her trunk."

"Her cabin is that one? I was told that cabin was assigned to Miss Helena Conwell."

"Oh, no, sir. That confusion was put to rest days ago along with all the rumors about her…uh…her character. She and the one you was expecting switched travel accommodation, ya' see."

"No, I don't see. Is Miss Conwell elsewhere on the ship?"

"Oh, no, sir. She never boarded."

"But when I came on board you said she had."

"'Cause she give her name as Miss Conwell."

Jamie felt his head would split open at any moment. Perhaps too much information was flooding into his brain box. "So how was the confusion cleared up?" he demanded, frowning, not even sure he wanted to know. Had he been duped into this voyage? If that had been the intent, he'd fallen into the trap. He could be with Meara right then or looking for Helena. Perhaps *that* had been the plan.

Plan?

He was nearly sure neither Helena nor Amber would have *targeted* him as the butt of a prank or worse. Amber would have been trying to do what he, Jamie, had been trying to do. Protect Helena from Franklin Gowery. *He* was the man Helena had been fleeing. Not Jamie. And if Jamie had handled things with Helena better, she'd have run *to* him. Not away.

"We got her real name when she was to marry you," the boy said, calling Jamie back to the problem at hand. His wife and who she was. "She gave it so the reverend could fill out marriage papers, and for the ceremony." He sounded as if he were explaining the thing to a dolt. And that was how Jamie felt. "I was in the hall," the boy went on. "The second witness, sir," he went on. "I was round a lot, giving the lady water to wash yer sheets and…um…such. Always smiled even though she was all done in most of the time."

Jamie heard everything the lad said, but one fact stood out, reminding him of the overarching truth of the situation. Not only had she been trying to protect Helena, but she had saved his life. His anger at her deception, while perhaps justified in some way, was immaterial when weighed against the truth of it. Amber had saved his life, and at the risk of her own. She was his wife now and though he knew things about her—that she was sweet and bold, caring and brave—he had no idea of her full name. "Amber what?" he demanded, not feeling the least in control of his own destiny at the moment.

"Her name?" the cabin boy asked. At Jamie's nod he said, "Her name was Dodd, sir. Miss Amber Dodd."

Jamie nodded. Was. Yes. Of course. Now he supposed it would be Amber Reynolds. Countess Adair. Lady Adair. Oh, God! He was married.

"May I get the trunk for her?"

Once again, remembering how he continued to appear, Jamie stepped back and waved the boy in. "How did it get in here, anyway?"

"I was permitted to bring it as far as the door. And… uh…just now she…um…she seems in great need of her clothing."

Jamie cringed for the second time in less than an hour. She'd looked a bit like Venus Rising earlier, but now he realized she'd stormed off like that. It would be talked of endlessly aboard the ship, for lack of anything more interesting.

"I would appreciate it if you would keep that part of all this under wraps," he told the boy. "I wouldn't like to see the countess embarrassed because I became a difficult patient."

"About how she wasn't dressed after the fight you two had, you mean? Oh, no, sir. I didn't even tell the doctor. His lips get to flappin' when he's in his cups. Just said she was wantin' her privacy now that you were on the mend. That's what brought the doctor. I had to tell him, as I was ordered to, if either of you left the cabin. But I wasn't ordered to say what she was wearing—or wasn't—when she left. She was quite upset, sir."

Jamie couldn't fight a wry smile when he remembered her wonderful Irish temper exploding all over him. That thought lightened his mood a bit. "Yes, I believe she was ready to attempt to do murder when she stormed off. I did not remember our marriage and was confused as to why she was in my cabin in her state of undress."

The cabin boy's eyes widened. "That would do it, sir."

Jamie was tempted to loiter about in the saloon as the boy dragged the trunk across to the pixie's door, but he didn't want to risk another explosion in front of the lad. He did not even know why he'd stood there trading confidences with a stranger barely out of short pants. A cabin boy was certainly far below his station, but that was one of the things he liked about America. Birth was of no consequence.

When the door had closed behind the boy, Jamie knew why he'd stood there chatting. He was lonely.

He didn't know how to win her back, but he knew he wanted to. Needed to. She could even now be carrying his child. He would think of something while gaining his strength. He'd leave her alone, then he would find a way to tempt her back to him. Like it or not, they were wed. This voyage would last at least another three months, and he had this time to woo his wife. They might as well make the best of the situation.

Amber, having donned a wrapper she'd left hanging on a hook behind the door, forced herself to smile at the young cabin boy, hoping he didn't notice evidence of the tears she'd dashed away when he'd knocked. He set down her trunk and turned toward where she stood in the doorway.

"Is that all, my lady?"

Amber blinked. The title weighed on her. And now she was stuck with it. "I'll have a coin for you once I unearth my funds from somewhere amongst my things. Thank you for all your help while the earl was ill. Have a lovely day."

She nearly sobbed as she hastily closed the door behind him. She should not have mentioned *his lordship*. Anger toward him had quickly given way to heartbreak and she didn't want to chance creating more gossip about their relationship. Though she knew it was probably impossible on this voyage, she didn't want her name linked further with his.

She wanted no link to him at all.

Liar, whispered her secret heart.

Amber sank to the boudoir chair in the corner of her stateroom, trying to hold back her tears. She was afraid if she gave in to the need to cry out her pain and disappointment she'd never be able to stop.

It was hard for her to believe that not long ago she'd looked around this room and been so excited about all the possibilities and adventures ahead of her. That marriage was the last thing she'd wanted for herself.

Now she just wanted to hide in there and forget the rest of the world even existed. Especially a certain English lord across the saloon who thought he was so utterly desirable that she would stoop to trapping him.

Humph! More like the other way around. She opened her trunk and looked for something to wear. Something to make her feel confident. "Of all the nerve," she muttered and pulled out a no-nonsense traveling skirt and blouse. "He begged!"

Begged her to wed him.

The last thing she'd wanted was marriage to a dying man. A man to grieve for. "The very last thing."

Then, after fighting for his life for days on end, after learning what a good man he was, after finding love in her heart for a man once again, she'd awakened to his fiery kisses and bold caresses. She'd thought he felt as she did. That he must. That they were fated for each other.

Then he'd called her Helena.

She slammed the trunk shut and plunked herself down into the chair. The whole mess was so ironic. It was Amber who'd come up with the idea for this travel charade. She'd felt sorry for Helena Conwell and had felt a kinship for her, as well. They'd both lost their parents and had both been passed into the care of another. Rather than finding a person like Amber's sweet and caring Uncle Charles, Helena had been saddled with Franklin Gowery, one of the most feared and hated men in the entire Pennsylvania coal patch.

It angered her beyond bearing that this was her fault. She felt stupid and foolish for trusting Jamie Reynolds, Earl of Adair. Father of Meara. Meara, the stepchild she'd thought she would raise alone.

It made no sense. He couldn't believe such things of

her. She'd seen his honorable character at his most vulnerable moments while he lay delirious. He'd worried about his child, not himself. Not his fortune except that it be used to provide a good life for Meara. How could that morally upstanding man have said those awful things to her? Thought those things *of* her? How could the laughing, lighthearted man she'd met on deck have turned into a bitter cad who'd all but called her a whore?

And after all she'd done to save him!

A knock at the door startled Amber. She couldn't imagine who it could be. The doctor had already been there and gone, having pronounced her healthy. Though she didn't know why she'd cared to be granted the freedom of the ship. After this morning she didn't want to leave her cabin until they arrived in San Francisco.

Of course, nearly three months in her cabin might be a bit too much time for introspection. Perhaps she'd go up on deck in the middle of the night. That would probably be a time when she could take in some air and not meet anyone other than the crew.

She took a shuddering sigh. It was a plan, admittedly not a very good one, but a plan nonetheless.

She looked toward the door, thinking of all those days ago when she'd left her stateroom on her way to the dining hall, only to hear Jamie moan and find him on the floor.

And change her life forever.

She nearly jumped out of her skin when another more determined knock on the door resounded in the cabin. She would not answer it. She'd lost her appetite, so if it was someone inquiring as to her appearance at breakfast or which sitting she wished at the dinner hour, they could wait all day. She had no reason to speak to anyone.

"Amber. Amber, I know you're in there. I had Jerome watching your door while I dressed. Please. We need to talk."

She pressed her lips together. She wouldn't give him the satisfaction of even responding. But who in blue blazes was Jerome? Curiosity was not going to get the better of her, much as she wondered. She wouldn't open her door to him.

"Amber, please. Won't you open up, Pixie?"

She heard the murmur of conversation in the saloon. More curious than ever, she tiptoed cautiously to the door, trying to hear. A moment later Jamie spoke to someone. "No. Truly. We're fine. She's a bit upset."

"Bridal jitters, I'm sure," a woman responded.

Then a man who was clearly the woman's husband said, "You need to be a bit easier on her. Isn't that right, Mother? The wife, here, hid in her room for nearly a fortnight after our wedding night."

"It was scarcely a day or two, Stewart!"

"Well, I'm sure it just seemed that long to me, dearest. Your little bride will come around just as mine did."

Amber pressed her ear to the door, but still couldn't understand what the woman was going on about until her voice rose. "Let me know if she needs a woman's support. I noticed she had no older woman along to advise her and she looks quite young."

Good God! She'd never leave her stateroom again.

"Let. Me. In," came Jamie's tight demand moments later.

She couldn't fight the smile that bloomed unbidden. So she wasn't the only one mortified by this situation. Good! But oh, Lord, her face felt as if it was on fire. She doubted she would even leave the cabin in the very middle of the night after this. The passengers must all be talking about their argument. Argument was so civilized a word for that donnybrook! They'd screamed at each other. No, actually, she'd screamed. At the top of her lungs. He'd just stood there naked and sure of himself.

She backed away from the door, her eyes still trained on it.

"I can stand here all day," he threatened now.

And wasn't that a lovely thought. She turned her back to the door. Him out there, drawing attention to them. "Go away. I'm never coming out and you're not up to standing there all day anyway."

"See." His voice dropped. "You still care even though I acted like an ass."

She balled her hands into fists. She pulled the skirt over her head, then donned, buttoned and tucked the blouse inside the dark serge before buttoning the smart front placket. It was nearly too much for Amber—that mocking tone in his voice even if he'd mocked himself. And he *had* acted like an ass.

Oh, how she wished she had the nerve to say something like that out loud. Instead she finally said the only thing that came into her head. "I don't need your limp and lifeless body lying across my doorway. I prefer to make my way to meals unimpeded."

"Excellent. We're getting somewhere. You admit you have to come out some time. We can go to the dining hall together. I can't wait to see your lovely face. Take your time dressing, though. I'll wait. And so you won't worry, I'll just sit on this comfortable sofa outside our cabin."

Our cabin? Amber felt it happen again. Her long, well-controlled temper erupted for the second time in one single morning. She didn't know why he had the ability to anger her so severely, but having him call that cabin theirs just ran her patience right out to the end. She whirled around, stalked to the door and yanked it open before she could stop herself.

And there he was, still as tall as she remembered, his broad shoulders filling the doorway, long, lean legs crossed. He was leaning against the doorjamb, a little smile tipping his lips up at the corners. "Pixie," he said, "your ensemble is lovely."

"Don't you dare try to jolly me!" she said breathlessly, rage constricting her muscles. "You are a cad! I had my whole life planned. And you...you stand there smiling while that life becomes more and more out of my reach."

He held his hands up as if in surrender. "I'm sorry. I'm so sorry. I wasn't myself earlier. At least not the kind person I try to be."

"You try to be kind? You failed. Spectacularly!" She pushed on the door to slam it in his face, but his foot stopped her.

After a momentary tussle, he pressed his hand against it and asked, "How can I prove I'm sorry for the things I said? Please allow me to come in so we can be private. Or maybe we could find a quiet place on deck."

"Very well," she said, stepping back to allow him entry. The last thing she wanted was to have a conversation with him on deck with the other passengers listening. Unfortunately, his presence seemed to shrink the comfortable cabin to the size of a teacup. She backed away, gestured to the chair she'd occupied just minutes earlier. Her stomach flipped around like a landed carp. With nowhere else to sit, she sank to the edge of the bed.

"How can I make it up to you?" he asked as soon as she was seated.

She clasped her hands together, trying to maintain control. "Make it up to me?" she demanded through her teeth. "Give me back my reputation. The life I had planned. My virginity so I can get the annulment you promised. I gave you back your life by taking care of you. As thanks, you stole mine."

A look very much like pain crossed his face. "That wasn't what I intended. And I *am* sorry. For that and for what I said this morning when I woke. I wasn't thinking clearly yet, you see. Just reacting. I woke in the night, but I thought it was still a dream. I suppose because so much of my time spent in there was spent in delirium I had trouble telling the real from the imagined. There you were, sleeping so near—so lovely. My pixie. And when I touched you, it was all so perfect—*you* were so perfect. Then when I woke and…"

He raked a hand through his already tousled hair. "It was something in my past that made me react so poorly. But that is no excuse. I did not take the time to think it through. I lashed out. I was wrong. And I *am* sorry."

She nodded, not knowing what to say. He seemed sincere. But her heart broke just a bit for herself. And for him. He was stuck with her. And his next words confirmed it.

"As you say, an annulment is not possible now, but a quiet divorce here in your country will set you free to pursue the life you seem to be mourning."

Was he this dense? Did he think Americans so lax in morals that divorce was not frowned upon? "Do you think this story won't leave the ship with its passengers? That the family who hired me as governess to their little girls will want me even near them once they hear about it? And about a divorce?"

"I don't know. I am trying to make it up to you."

"As I have just explained, you cannot."

He shook his head. "I remember snatches of the days of my illness. I care for you, as well. How could I not? You've done so much for me. Is there no chance of you coming to care for me? But perhaps not." He smiled. "We agreed, did we not, that the annulment was only to occur if at the end of the voyage, we felt we did not suit?"

That *had* been the plan. She nodded.

"Though annulment is no longer possible," he went on, "why not follow that original plan? Get to know each other during the voyage? Decide upon our futures together? Will you trust me that far?"

She looked down at her hands. "I do not know. This was not the way I thought to return to California."

"As before, if we do not suit, we will separate. I am sorry about your plans, but I would settle a good sum on you. You would not have to work at all."

She could retire to a town home in San Francisco and live out her days alone with a "past" to be lived down. Pride forced her to say, "I don't need your charity," though she didn't know what she would do without it now.

"But it appears I need yours. A divorce in my country is a difficult thing. A very public embarrassment. Only if I proved you an adulterer, would I be permitted to divorce. I couldn't do that to you. Regardless of our marital status, you need not work and raise the children of others. You could remain with me—with us—and raise Meara. Mimm is only her nanny. She isn't educated enough to be Meara's governess. You could fill that role in my home and be my countess at the same time."

Amber dropped her gaze to her hands where they lay folded in her lap. Countess—the one position she wasn't sure she could fill. Nor did she think she would be able to live under Jamie's roof and not love him. It would open her up to heartache eventually. But wouldn't losing him now with so few good memories be worse than losing him later with many? She honestly didn't know.

"I had a position," she said. "The one thing I didn't want for my life was to live on someone's charity."

She could see he was running out of patience. "A wife doesn't live on her husband's charity. Think about what I've said. I don't give up easily," he said, his gaze piercing. "I warn you I will spend this entire voyage trying to woo you. I intend to give you the courtship our hasty marriage cheated you of. Right now, though, I'm famished." He stood. "Would you accompany me to the dining hall and breakfast with me, my lady? Together we'll put an end to any rumors and gossip."

Amber shook her head. She needed time. She'd given up on marriage and it was very difficult to change direction so suddenly. It was true she had few options but she had to carefully examine them. The most important was that she wasn't Helena. Hadn't he called her name in the throes of passion? Because of that she knew he loved the other woman even though Helena was beyond his reach.

And Helena would have made him a fine countess.

"Very well," he said on a sigh and looked disappointed. "I'll have a meal sent to you. But be warned. Mimm says I am the most stubborn person she has ever come across and no one knows me better. We could have a good life based on respect, common goals. And attraction. I *will* win you over."

Oh, she was so very afraid he already had. And she was just as afraid, if not more, that Helena Conwell would always have his heart. He hadn't offered love, after all. She was just his inconvenient wife.

Chapter Six

~~~~~~~~~~∽∽∽∽∽~~~~~~~~~~

Jamie leaned his forearms on the teak rail and stared down at the water below. It was clear as glass, a curious mix of blue and green. He saw no answers in its depths nor heard one in the gentle hiss of the bow cutting through the sea. Amber had proven herself to be as stubborn an adversary as he'd come across.

How could they reach an understanding when she kept her door closed and sent him away? Every morning. Every afternoon. Every evening.

A hand clapped on his shoulder and Jamie glanced to his left. Captain E. C. Baker stood there, a look of concern in his eyes. "Your bride still being stubborn?"

"She may have coined the word. For the life of me I don't know how to tempt her out of that cabin. I cannot imagine spending a week in there. I'd think it the worst of punishments." He chuckled bitterly. "Did, in fact, as a boy. And it was a room ten times larger and I had my nanny."

Captain Baker grinned, his gray eyes alive with mirth. "She's not in there at all times. She comes on deck at about midnight just after eight bells sound to the start of the graveyard shift. She remains topside till eight bells sound again."

Jamie frowned. "Is that safe?"

"I have my second in command watch out for her after I've smoked the last of my cigar and retired."

With a curious mixture of annoyance and admiration bubbling in his veins for the woman he'd taken in marriage, Jamie gave in to a smile. "The little scoundrel. She sleeps all day and enjoys the stars from midnight till dawn." Jamie straightened. "Thank you. I'll use the information wisely."

Baker raised a bushy eyebrow. "See that you use it as quietly as possible. It wouldn't do to awaken everyone when the ship is mostly bedded down."

Jamie nodded, regretting that he'd caused a stir before with his ill treatment of Amber. "I promise to retire the field before hostilities occur."

"It isn't you I worry about, son," the captain quipped, a grin splitting his weathered face. Jamie returned to his cabin then, needing to get to sleep so he'd be awake and alert at midnight.

A cabin door in the companionway opened, then ever so quietly snapped shut again. Jamie sat up. He'd heard eight bells ring just moments before. *Amber.*

The sound of the sails heightened for a moment, then another door shut, dimming the sound. She was on deck now. He'd not seen her face in over a week and waiting till the count of one hundred was agony. But he wanted to make sure she was under the careful eyes of the on-duty crew members. Hopefully her wish to avoid a scene would keep her from fleeing his company.

Two minutes later, Jamie quietly followed her topside. The brisk wind alleviated the ever-present heat so close to the African continent, where the captain had steered the vessel in the hope of avoiding the currents of the Gulf Stream. Having rested all day in his cabin, Jamie had come to understand what a hardship that was. The cabins were far warmer than he'd realized when the captain told him of Amber's nighttime activities.

She stood a bit beyond amidships where the whoosh of the bow cutting through the water was more pronounced. The sail, full of wind, flew above like giant wings, accompanied by the creaks and groans of the lines holding them fast to the masts and braces.

Jamie moved toward her. She stood, her face raised to meet the wind, her blond tresses flowed over her shoulders like a river of gold, shimmering in the light from the moon and lanterns. Her beautiful sherry-colored eyes were closed. She had a tight grip on the teak gunwale and stood breathing in the blessed coolness of the night.

"Amber," he said quietly as he settled a hand at her back, afraid she'd lose her footing if he startled her. But his bride was not faint of heart.

She turned her head and looked at him steadily for a long, silent moment. "I'm surprised it took so long for gossip about my nightly movements to reach your ears. Whom should I *thank* for your presence?" she asked, sarcasm rife in her voice.

"The captain took pity on me as I loitered about this afternoon devastated by your continued absence."

Her lips tipped up into a mysterious half-smile. "I'm sure you were no such thing."

"You're wrong, my dear. We agreed we would

attempt to get to know each other. That cannot happen if you insist upon keeping a door between us. We move closer and closer to the equator each day. It will grow more uncomfortable and unhealthy each day for you to hide in your cabin."

"I am not hiding."

Jamie smiled at that. "We both know you are. I'm just not sure if it's me you're hiding from or the other passengers. I assure you there aren't that many."

"I heard the conversation you had with that couple outside my door. I have no desire to further any gossip."

"You've greatly misjudged the situation, Pixie." He was gratified when she didn't protest the pet name. He still had trouble thinking of her as Amber, especially when she looked so wild and free.

"How?" she demanded, drawing her straight eyebrows into a near V.

"The other passengers know I was ill when the voyage began and they know we wed after you cared for me. Baker did not let it out how ill I was or that we are virtual strangers to each other. He thought our nuptials would seem much less remarkable that way and much less likely to be remarked upon later. I agree with him."

"Oh. I must appear to be a complete ninny." She'd said it so quietly he'd had to lean forward to hear her. She put her hand on his chest, but he didn't know why. His heart began to pound. Did she crave touching him as much as he craved touching her?

In a blinding flash Jamie understood. She loved him and he'd rejected her before he'd understood the gift she'd given him. A woman like this didn't give her body without her love. Her honor was too bred in the bone. Her moral code too deeply felt. What was he to do now?

He was loath to release her from their marriage, knowing that to set her free would be to all but brand her a fallen woman. He might be unable to love her. Love for him meant only pain and loss. But he could show her she was respected and valued. That the gift of her heart was valued. It wasn't all she deserved, but it was the best he could give.

Iris's voice, sharp and vindictive, still rang in his ears. And resounded in his heart. Try though he might, he couldn't silence her voice or the things she'd said after Meara's birth. "Love you? Are you a fool? I loved the idea of your title. Who has ever loved you? Your mother? She never knew you! Your father? Was it love that allowed him to take his own life and leave you behind? Your uncle could barely abide being in the same room with you. Your beloved cousin will probably shoot you on sight when next you meet. That nanny you've already hired to take care of that worthless whelp I was forced to give birth to? You pay her to love Meara. And you. When did she ever love you when a salary wasn't forthcoming?"

The last had been a lie. Mimm had moved halfway across Britain and secured employment at his boarding school and later at Edinburgh to be near him. So why could he not ignore the rest as the ravings of a bitter, spoiled woman?

Because he feared the rest was true. It sounded true.

Taking a chance on a future with Amber, Jamie gathered her hand in his. "Don't be sorry. Just promise to change the situation. Walk with me in the day. Eat meals with me. Share your time with me. That is all that should be required. That, and accept a sincere apology."

"I have accepted it," she said quickly and pulled her hand free of his.

"I cannot believe that or you would agree to be in my company. I hurt you. Words alone would never take away the sting of all the terrible things that tumbled from my mouth that morning. Had I not hurt you deeply, you would agree to learn who I am and allow me to know who you are."

"I have said it, have I not?" she answered and went to turn away. Before she could, he took her shoulders in his hands. For a long moment he tried to equate the delicate bones beneath his palms with the Valkyrie's heart beating within her and the spine of iron hidden in so delicate a body. He couldn't have chosen a better mother for Meara had he searched the world.

Because she didn't protest the truth in his words, he went on, "Our lovemaking formed a bond between us. We didn't mean it to happen, but the bond is there, is it not? Don't we owe it to ourselves to explore this curious state of affairs?"

Amber couldn't seem to look away from his glittering eyes, her heart pounding with fear over the hidden danger in his question. Of course there was a bond. Those beautiful moments in his cabin had somehow imprinted him upon her very soul. She'd known he was on deck well before he'd spoken. Everything about him stayed in her mind and body like a living thing, possessed of a will its own.

She would wake in the night, thinking the curls at the nape of his neck lay beneath her hands, only to find her pillow twisted in her fingers. In her dreams those haunting violet eyes drew her to him, then cruelly rejected her as it became a nightmare. Her breasts would ache after sensual dreams of him being in her bed. It was as if his hard chest with its crisp hair had gently abraded her nipples, making them sensitive for all time. She couldn't even wish those accursed dreams away. She ached for him.

She needed what she'd never missed before. What she'd made herself believe she didn't want. A man. This man.

With Joseph there had been that nebulous joining in the near future that had worried her and made her curious at the same time. Now she knew the act held nothing—and everything—to worry about.

Lovemaking had created sensations in her that had blasted her mind into millions of pieces, but still allowed her to think. It held a consequence—a bond, as he called it—that she didn't want, but that she felt the need of in the depths of her soul.

There was a look of longing in his eyes and she didn't think it came only from physical need. She couldn't forget the man she'd come to know when he'd been at his most vulnerable. A good man when delirious was the same fully aware.

She still didn't know what to do about it all. Doing nothing had seemed the best course. She'd clearly been wrong. "I don't know what to do."

"Do you want to go on punishing us both for a situation not entirely of our own creation?"

Was she doing that? She honestly wasn't sure, but wouldn't admit that. "I am not trying to punish you or myself. That would be foolish. May we just take it a day at a time?"

He tilted his head as if considering her request, then

he smiled, and her heart skipped several beats. "As long as tomorrow is one of those days," he said, the moon and wind in his hair making it shine almost as much as the light from within that she always saw sparkling in his striking violet eyes.

She nodded.

"Then may I walk you to your cabin, my lady?"

Again she nodded and he took her hand, placing it tenderly on his forearm and covering it with his own hand. "I worry about you topside all alone," he said, bending his head to hers. "Please don't come up here this way. Tap on my door any time you feel the need to take air. I'll be available."

They'd reached her door and her heart began to hammer again. Would he try to kiss her? More important—did she wish him to?

Amber looked up and could see it was what he wanted, but after a protracted moment, he let her hand go. "I'll see you in the morning then. Sweet dreams, Pixie." Then he turned away, but not before she saw the longing in his gaze. She went in and leaned against the door, a bit sorry he'd shown such restraint.

Amber walked hesitantly to the door to answer the knock she'd awaited with equal parts dread and antici-pation. *Stop it! He's just a man.* The admonition did no good. She'd been telling herself the same thing for days—and nights.

Because he wasn't just a man. He was *her* man.

Or at least he could be.

All she had to do was let go of the hurt. Let go of her fear. Fear of losing him. Pushing him away had seemed safer.

She'd agreed to spend time with him, though she wasn't yet sure if she dare open her heart to the possibilities time with him opened to her.

The knock came again. It sounded a bit more impatient this time. She smiled, hopeful. Restrained restlessness was so very Jamie, whereas the starchy manners and slightly imperious requests were all lord of the realm. Now to discover which man stood at her door.

She opened it and caught him just about to knock again. "Goodness, you must be starving," she said, raising her eyebrows. "Do they often run out of food even this early?"

"It isn't missing the breakfast I'm worried about, but the company I feared missing out on. And that I have missed."

What drivel. "I don't see how you could miss me when you only met me on this misbegotten voyage."

"Haven't you ever missed what you've never had? I greatly missed having a mother, though I don't remember mine. I had a nanny who was like a mother, but she didn't have the power of a real mother."

"And that nanny was Mimm?" she asked, remembering the name from the time of his illness.

He nodded. "And in that same manner it's all the possibilities of you I'm impatient for."

It was definitely Jamie awaiting her company. Relieved, she smiled. "Suppose we just begin with the meal? The rest is overwhelming to me at this hour."

"Then let us retire to the dining saloon and see what the cook has prepared." He reached out a hand.

She took it and they walked in silence toward the dining saloon along the outside deck. The closer she got the more apprehensive she grew. The scent of frying bacon wafting into the small hallway didn't help. "Actually, the meal itself is a bit much this early," she told him, not at all ready to face eating, especially with witnesses to their first meal together.

She peered into the lovely room. The walls were done in rich mahogany with raised zebrawood panels with creamy white scrollwork stenciled in gold leaf above. The coffered ceiling was partially mahogany as well, with carved inset panels that had also been gilded. There were two round tables that appeared to seat eight. They were elegantly set with crisp linens, blue-and-white china edged in gold and gleaming silverware.

Jamie must have felt her hesitate on the threshold. His hand on the small of her back reassured her even as she suppressed a shiver of delicious awareness at his nearness and his sheer masculine size. "We are the first here, Pixie," he said, his breath stirring the fine hairs at her nape as he steered her into the room.

"The other is for the ship's officers," he explained and steered her toward the first table and around to the back so they would face the door. As he pulled her chair out, he added, "This is why I wished to arrive so early. Now the others must join us. I have placed you in a position of power."

"Queen of all I survey, eh? Did your Mimm teach you that?"

He shook his head and smiled grimly. "My uncle saw to it I was raised to be an earl. Mimm would not know how to go on in society. She is not a governess, you will remember."

"That is the position you offered me."

"No. If we found we didn't suit, that is the pursuit I

offered you within the boundaries of my household. You said you didn't want to feel you were taking my charity. I would prefer you be my wife and a mother to Meara."

"How can you know that? We are still strangers," she countered and stared at him. Her stomach flipped as if they'd suddenly found themselves in a squall. But the ship was not to blame. It was the heat in his eyes. The violet had deepened so much they resembled bluebonnets, the Texas wildflower she'd seen on display at the Centennial Exhibition in Philadelphia.

He caressed her cheek with the back of his fingers, sending her heart tripping over itself and her stomach dropping into yet another trough. "But there is that bond I cannot forget," he said quietly. "And I don't believe you can, either."

If only he weren't right.

Chapter Seven

During the meal Amber shared her education and love of teaching with the passengers. She dodged any questions into their personal lives so the meal progressed with general conversation.

They returned to the saloon outside their staterooms. Like the dining room, it was ornately decorated, with exotic wood wainscoting and padded silk panels above. A beautiful stained-glass skylight cast a rosy glow over the lovely room. A glow reflected in mirrors set in a wall of gilded arches.

"Would you sit a while with me?" Jamie asked. "The sofa looks quite comfortable. Perhaps we'll have a few private moments to ask the most pressing questions we have for each other.

"I may invest in the bank of that Jones fellow I was talking with. It is an interstate concern. It would be convenient for me to have a branch of the same bank in New York and San Francisco since I have residences in both cities now."

"What businesses are you involved in?"

"I began by investing funds in American railroads, then in a few mining operations in Pennsylvania." He frowned slightly and stared at nothing in particular.

Amber's stomach tightened, remembering all that looking for Helena implied. "Did you have anything to do with the Pinkertons and what they did there last summer?"

He grimaced. "Yes and no. I worked undercover with them until I learned exactly what Franklin Gowery had planned. He lied to me from the first or I'd never have become involved. It all had very little to do with learning who was sabotaging mining operations around the coal patch and more about a way to expand his power over the miners."

"What do you intend to do with that information?" she asked, hoping he was the person she'd come to believe he was.

"I've divested my stake in American mines and refused to have anything to do with the trials of those arrested. Not that I condone the sabotage and murders some of them committed. The entire affair left me with a bad taste and I want nothing to do with most men who run American coal mines."

His narrowed gaze studied her. "Why did you switch your accommodations with Helena Conwell?" She could see he was angry and trying to hide it. Perhaps fight it.

Amber couldn't look away, though she was terribly uncomfortable. She wished she didn't care what he'd think of what she'd done. She was the author of his heartbreak after all. But no matter the consequence, she had to tell the truth. Otherwise it would hang over her head like the sword of Damocles.

She took a fortifying breath. "Because when I visited my uncle in Wheatonburg, I saw her and realized how much we look like each other. I was a decoy the night she left town. I traveled in one direction wearing her clothes while she went in another. It was supposed to confuse her guardian and the men he was sure to have looking for her. She wanted him and anyone connected with him out of her life."

Jamie's eyes narrowed further. "So you are why she isn't aboard. Where did she go?"

"She never intended to be aboard. California wasn't her destination. Before you ask, I don't know where she went. That way I couldn't be forced to reveal anything of her plans."

That he was in love with Helena was apparent by the annoyance in his tone. Amber's heart fell. She and Helena might look alike, but no one who knew them would confuse them. Especially if that someone was in love with Helena. Even wearing her clothes, Amber would never measure up.

Jamie's lips thinned. "Did she leave alone?"

She had to keep silent. It was the least she could do for the man Helena had fallen in love with, Brendan, Amber's childhood friend. After all, Brendan could still be in danger from Franklin Gowery and his Pinkerton agents.

"She'd reached her majority. She was free of her guardian. Helena didn't trust him. He was bent on forcing her to marry a man of his choice."

"Do you think I don't know that!" he snapped. He stared at her for a long moment, then looked away.

"I am sorry, Jamie. You were caught up in our web of deception and I fear in Helena's mind you were tarred with the same brush as Franklin Gowery."

He didn't rail at her. Instead, he sighed and raked a

hand though his hair. "Helena misread my intentions. She thought I was after her money, which is ironic, when one contemplates it. I hope her ruse worked and she's rid of him. The man is dangerous. It sickens me that I was taken in by him for so long."

She lay her hand over his. "It sounds as if you've done all you can to lessen the impact of your actions. I imagine you would have done more to repair any damage you caused if you hadn't followed me on to the ship. I am truly sorry. You could have died."

"I'd have been as ill on land and with nowhere near as pretty a nurse. Perhaps, as Mimm is always telling me, everything happens for the best."

Before either of them could say more, the other passengers arrived in the saloon and Amber excused herself to rest. She had to find a way to keep Jamie from burrowing further into her heart. Because she didn't believe Mimm's axiom. Her parents, brothers, aunt and Joseph were all dead. There was no way all those losses could be for the best.

Jamie sat on the sofa in the saloon outside their staterooms. It had been a week since he'd learned exactly why Amber had been traveling under Helena's name. He hadn't spent all that much private time with her since. The ship didn't lend itself to alone time outside their staterooms and that Amber wouldn't consider. Anger had simmered in his heart at her, but only for a few hours. He hadn't been able to hold on to it. Not against her sunny smiles and the very real truth that it had been his mishandling of Helena that had caused any number of problems, all of which she held against him.

Full of nervous energy, he checked his appearance

in the saloon's arched mirrors. He tugged on his black waistcoat, brushed a bit of lint off the sleeve of his gray frock coat, frowning at his reflection. He tried to see himself from Amber's viewpoint, hoping he didn't look too somber. His black satin cravat wasn't tied with the skill Hadley showed, but since his valet would have spent the voyage sick and miserable he was traveling with Mimm and Meara.

He sighed and turned away in disgust. Why worry about his appearance? What did it matter? He'd already made the worst impression possible on his new wife and he hadn't been wearing a stitch at the time. Still, though she continued to keep him at arm's length, he was getting to know her better. Amber was intelligent, kind-hearted and quick-witted.

He was trying not to rush her, but he wanted her more every day. He was not, however, a callow youth who couldn't rein in his needs. And he had.

So far.

He was sure Amber had no idea he dreamed of her every night and often woke painfully aroused. He paced back across the saloon, checked his watch, then slid it back into his pocket. Tonight they were invited to eat with the captain in his quarters. He'd promised to find them some time alone.

If Captain Baker said it, Jamie knew it would come to pass. The older man had become a trusted male adviser to Jamie. That was something he hadn't had since his father selfishly took his own life and left Jamie at the mercy of Oswald Reynolds.

The captain had suggested he not pressure Amber, but the lack of progress with her worried Jamie. He'd find her staring at him with a troubled look in her eyes he couldn't decipher. And there was a sadness in her now that hadn't been there when they sailed. A sadness he knew was his fault. The guilt was killing him. Tonight he planned to use whatever alone time Baker bought him to discover a way to fix some of the damage he'd caused to her heart.

Behind him a door opened and Jamie pivoted. Amber wore a dress that shone golden in the light beaming in through the skylight above her head. The gown had an underdress of gleaming white satin that was covered with yards and yards of ruffled golden lace. She was a vision of loveliness, but it was the neckline that held him transfixed. To be more exact, it was the extensive display of her creamy bosom and shoulders that held his gaze prisoner.

"You're staring." Amber grasped her shawl together in front. "What was I thinking?" she cried. "I cannot wear this. Whatever was Miss Conwell thinking to commission it?" she rushed on. A blush spread from her cheeks to her neck before she turned back toward her doorway. "I will make us late. You should go on without me."

Jamie reached over her head and barred the door with his arm. "I'll do no such thing. And neither will you. I'm the worst clod in creation if I made you feel anything but gloriously lovely. I'm sorry."

She tipped her head up and stared at him. "You think I look lovely?"

Encouraged by the hopeful wonder in her words, he nodded and kissed her ripe pink lips. He thought to make it a quick salute, but his mouth seemed to have developed a mind and hunger all its own, until her sweet moan called him back to sanity. He took charge of his errant body and straightened. Her eyes flew open and she covered her mouth with her fingertips. He thought it best not to mention the moisture gathering in her eyes or that she'd dropped the shawl.

"Have you no mirror in there?" he asked and took her by the shoulders, trying to ignore the soft skin beneath his hands. He brought her unresisting into the saloon and turned her to face her reflection.

It was a moment of clarity for him, as well. The mirror framed him standing behind her. They looked so perfectly right together. He ached with need, but forced his thoughts to her. "Look at yourself," he demanded. "How can you not know? I am the luckiest devil alive to have you on my arm."

"I don't know what to say." She stared at his refection. "If you're sure…"

"I've never been more sure of anything in my life," he lied. Oh, he was sure he wanted her. Leaving her at her door later that night would be a nearly impossible task. He pulled the door shut and held out his hand, gesturing with the other toward the narrow companionway leading to the captain's quarters. "We shouldn't keep Captain Baker waiting."

Chapter Eight

Amber heard Jamie curse under his breath, but then he smiled. There was something so mischievous about his look she had to question it. "What are you smiling about?" she demanded.

His gaze flicked to his reflection in one of the saloon mirrors as they passed it. He looked over at her, then looked away, clearly searching for a response.

If he thought the dress was inappropriate, why didn't he just say so? She wished she'd tried it on before having it ironed for dinner. Amber stepped in front of him. "You're blushing, my lord. Perhaps I do need to change."

"Why? You look like an angel." He groaned. "It was your gloves, if you must know. I was mentally cursing them. I would like to at least be permitted to hold your hand in mine without a glove between us." Now it was her turn to blush. "I'm such an utter clod. Now I've scandalized you. I should have warned you that I've managed to avoid most social occasions here and back in Britain. I didn't go about in society all that much before my first marriage, you see. And even less since I've been a widower."

Was he trying to convince her he was unsophisticated? It wouldn't work. He was too astute and canny. Too handsome for his own good, as well. "I'm not fooled. You've been married so—"

"I attended exactly three balls during London's Season that year before I married a woman my uncle chose…"

"The woman who somehow caused you to be caught in a compromising position with her thus forcing you into marriage."

He grimaced. "I wish I could go back and redo that morning I shouted at you."

"That is the problem with mistakes, my lord. They cannot be so easily undone. But I've always thought that was their purpose. Consequence is the great teacher, is it not?"

She'd certainly learned a lesson from this whole fiasco. She'd never let herself be talked into anything that she thought was a bad idea again. She should have been more afraid for her heart and less for his daughter.

The only problem was that she wasn't sure that was a lesson she wanted to learn. Children were her weakness, but a weakness she refused to regret.

"You're very wise for one so young."

"Young? I was twenty-four at my last birthday. I was taking Helena under *my* wing when I came up with this idea to masquerade as her."

"There, you see. You have me at a great disadvantage. You seem to be privy to a good deal of personal and often humiliating information about me, while I scarcely know anything about you."

She raised one of her delicate eyebrows. "And yet

you claim to wish our marriage to continue. I have to conclude that is because you feel you have no choice and are bound by duty."

He paused steps from the captain's door. "That isn't true. I wish the marriage to continue because I know enough about you to be nearly sure we'll suit. You are good. Kind. And moral. In Britain, and indeed in the upper echelon of your society here in America, pretense is often all that is shared before marriage."

She shrugged. That was true. Patience, her friend from college, had married one of the wealthiest men in New York and was miserable. He was not what he had seemed to be when they'd courted. She lived as a virtual prisoner and was only permitted to leave their house in his company.

So perhaps Jamie was right. He needed to understand that Amber knew how to fit into drawing rooms, but that she didn't want to live with such rigid constraints, either. Hoping to shock some sense into him, Amber put her fingertip in her mouth and bit down on the tip of the glove, then pulled, stripping off the offending gloves one finger after another. One glove after the other. A silent statement that she was of another class than Helena Conwell and the late countess.

But Jamie was a contrary man. Instead of being shocked to his toes, he threw his head back and laughed. "I don't imagine you learned that efficient method of glove removal at Vassar. Are you sure you want to do away with them? I don't wish to push you."

She wasn't sure, but she'd always hated to back down from a challenge. It always felt like failure. "They're hot anyway," she quipped, then she handed them to him. "Perhaps you have somewhere to stash these."

He grinned. "I suppose overboard wouldn't be acceptable?"

She wanted to kiss that smile off his face, but didn't. She wasn't brave enough to initiate a kiss. "We'll eventually come to colder weather."

He folded them and put them in his inside breast pocket. "I'll return them eventually, then." When he took her left hand in his, he stared at it for a long moment as a delicious shiver raced through her. Then he stroked a fingertip across the gold-and-onyx ring he'd placed on her finger the day they'd married for the sake of his daughter's safety. "I will have to take care of this. You need a real wedding band."

Why did he continue to pretend everything between them was normal? She wasn't the woman he wanted and he wasn't— No, she wouldn't lie to herself. She was afraid of being hurt, but want him she did.

He led her to the door of the captain's large aft cabin and knocked. The door opened as if the busy man had actually been awaiting them. "Lord Adair. Your ladyship. Thank you for allowing me to entertain you this evening." He gestured them inside. "Come in. Come in. Welcome to my quarters. Dinner should arrive momentarily."

On Jamie's arm, Amber stepped inside the handsome room. Baker's cabin reminded her of a library in a grand home. The walls were lined with cherrywood panels, his big desk sat before a wall that was the stern of the ship. Set in it were three square windows that were open, admitting the whisper of a breeze that teased her nostrils with salt air. They afforded a lovely view of the wide blue ocean.

A light lyrical air played on a music box sitting front

and center on Baker's large desk. "Oh, how lovely," Amber said, staring at the rosewood music box that had filled the room with its delightful tune. "May I?"

Captain Baker smiled gently and walked to the box. She and Jamie followed. "It is so lovely," she told the captain. Delighted, she lifted the inlaid rosewood lid. Inside were the whirling golden works.

"I thought perhaps you'd find it as fascinating as I do."

A knock at the door drew their attention. "Ah, that will be our meal," the captain said and left them standing by the music box while he went to admit the steward.

They sat down a few minutes later to a meal Baker called New England fare. It was tasty and informal, both of which she was grateful for. She had just sunk her teeth into the tender corned beef when another knock came on the door. Baker frowned and called out, "Come."

A cabin boy came in carrying a folded piece of paper. Baker took it, read it then sighed as he put his napkin on the table. "It seems I am needed to solve a dilemma of sorts. Please continue with your meal. I'll return as soon as possible."

"Perhaps we should join the other passengers," Amber said, suddenly nervous at being alone with Jamie in so private a setting. Heart pounding, she twisted her napkin in her lap, noting that both Captain Baker and Jamie frowned at her. She felt like a complete ninny.

"Oh, I'm sorry, my dear," the captain said into the strained silence as he stood. "They wouldn't be ready to serve you in the dining hall. It's perfectly fine for you to continue on here as before. Enjoy your meal and the company of your husband."

Her pounding heart settled a bit until the door closed behind Captain Baker. "I am quite tired and not very hungry." She got to her feet. "Perhaps I should…"

"Am I such an ogre that my wife is terrified to be alone with me?"

Oh, she hadn't meant him to insult him. It was she who was the wrong woman. "Of course you're not an ogre."

"Then stay and talk with me while we eat. We can't continue to avoid private moments or we'll arrive in San Francisco still near strangers. Ask me questions. And I will answer and ask you some, as well."

She sank her teeth into her bottom lip. She did want to know more about his marriage. "How long did it take you to realize you didn't love Meara's mother?" she asked and took a bit of potato off her fork.

Jamie finished chewing and set his fork down. "I might not be the most quick-witted of men about the ways of women, but you have steered me into dangerous territory. Are you looking for some mysterious woman's way of linking my first marriage with the circumstances of ours?"

"I'm curious."

Jamie nodded and gave her a small wry smile. "It was not a realization, Pixie. I never loved Iris. My uncle promoted the match. She was a beauty. The daughter of a businessman who wanted a title for his only child. My uncle knew her dowry would rescue the Adair estates."

Amber frowned, confused. "I thought the aristocracy didn't like to associate with people in trade. My friend traveled to London for the Season. Patience said she was pecked at zealously by most of the débutantes and cut constantly by the others. Except, of course, by the fortune hunters who pursued her relentlessly."

No sooner were the words out than she realized how insulting she must have sounded. "Oh, my. I'm so sorry. I'm sure that isn't why you married your wife."

Jamie stiffened almost imperceptibly. "*You* are my wife. And money and titles were at the root of my first marriage, but not on my part. I didn't want the match. My cousin was in love with her, but he is a mere Mister. At my uncle's insistence, I went to London for the Season to look for a bride. He sent my cousin Alexander off to Scotland on some pretext to get him out of the way."

"He would do that to his own son?" she asked, then took a sip of her tea.

"Never doubt it. My uncle knew I wasn't about to betray Alex by marrying the woman my cousin loved. But at the time, I didn't see how determined Oswald was that I marry Iris. Then, at a ball, she lured me into the gardens, saying she had a dilemma she needed to speak with me about. I assumed it was about Alex, their feelings for each other and her father's plans for her. But that wasn't it at all.

"She told me she had no feelings for Alexander. That he'd made a pest of himself. She said she was actually quite taken with me. Then she went on to compliment everything from my eyes to my shoulders and even my thighs, for God's sake! It was quite embarrassing. Before I realized what she was about, she was climbing into my lap. Her gown became disarranged showing more flesh than proper. That is when my uncle and her father discovered us."

"Discovered or sprung their trap?"

Jamie smiled sadly. "Very astute of you, Pixie. I was too gullible to prevent the disaster in the making, however."

"You can hardly blame yourself."

"I betrayed Alex. I caved in to my uncle. I was young, stupid and, most appalling of all, I was weak. I was so conditioned to giving in to his demands that I agreed even though soon he'd no longer have any power over me. I fooled myself into thinking I was at least getting a passionate woman as my life's mate. Alex returned to find I'd married the woman he loved. Our relationship hasn't been the same since. After getting to know Iris, and seeing how much she wanted to be my countess—anyone's countess—I came to believe she'd led him on to gather information on how to entice me." Jamie stopped, looking more than sad. Haunted, perhaps. "Why else pretend feelings for him, then marry me? Except, of course, for Mimm's theory that he fed her information on how to entrap me. He did tell her things about me, but I believed he was just making conversation."

Amber wasn't about to try to draw a conclusion. She knew none of those involved, save Jamie. "All this was arranged by the uncle you don't trust?"

Jamie smiled bitterly. "My one and only. Thank God he's only one man."

His uncle's actions made no sense to her. "Why wouldn't he want his son to acquire her dowry?"

"Alexander hates his father as much as I do and Oswald knew he'd never see a jot of her dowry."

"Did you give him some, then?"

"As earl, I am more or less obligated to take care of the entire family. But he'd miscalculated just how cowed

I was. Alex was the most important person in my life save Mimm. I reached my majority a month after the wedding and that was when Alexander returned, not wanting to miss that event in my life. I witnessed my cousin's heartbreak at the news of our marriage. I found my spine that day, you might say. Though I hadn't a clue how to run the estates or how bad the situation actually was, I tossed my uncle out on his ear. Months later, Iris's father died and his entire estate fell into my lap, as well."

"Then your uncle's plan failed."

"I have since come to understand there was more to his plan. The marriage was supposed to rescue the family finances. Once that was done, I think I was to meet my doom. Oswald would then inherit the title, lands and everything that went with it."

Amber felt a familiar knot in her stomach at the thought of his dying. "What happened? You obviously didn't meet with an early end. Has your cousin forgiven you?"

A strange look shadowed Jamie's expression. After pressing his lips together for a moment, he nodded, but followed it with a shrug. "Meara's birth made him come around, but we had another falling out when Iris was killed. He blamed me for her death. More so because I refused to mourn her. She was vain, selfish and unfaithful, not to mention a horror of a mother."

He shook his head sadly. "Alexander never saw a fault in Iris and he took exception to my attitude. I left for America with Meara and Mimm after setting up trusts for Adair's people and Alexander. I miss him and regret the loss of his regard, but I couldn't be such a hypocrite as to pretend to feel what I didn't."

Why didn't he mind pretending theirs was the marriage he wanted and not one to Helena? She immediately felt contrite. Who was she to judge? She was being just as dishonest by pretending she didn't love him.

Jamie watched Amber. Instead of commenting, she stood and walked behind the desk to look out the windows. He wished he could read her mind. He never knew what she was going to think or do next. Yet she seemed to be able to read him as if he were an open book. Life with her wouldn't be dull.

He was glad he'd left out his suspicion that his dear uncle's last plot to kill him at Adair had backfired and killed Iris instead. Amber already knew there was a good possibility that Harry Conwell had died in his stead. With the death toll around him mounting, sooner or later he'd have to return home to do something about his cursed uncle.

He wasn't trying to be dishonest by holding back his suspicions from Amber. He just didn't want to scare her witless before it was necessary. What he *did* want was to know more about what had made her the person she was.

Unable to stand the strained silence any longer, Jamie stood and moved toward her. The sky behind her silhouette was painted with streaks of bright pinks and purples against a canvas of deep blue.

After drinking in her profile for a long moment, Jamie approached her from behind. "I hope you understand that I'm a different person now. And that I answered your questions as honestly as I could no matter how badly they made me look."

Now behind her, he settled his hands on her shoulders. Even though she stiffened, sultry sensations curled through his entire body as they did every time he touched her. He was always left burning for more, but her apprehension made him just as determined not to push her too fast.

There was a delicate balance between letting her know how highly he regarded her and how much he desired her without making her feel trapped and pressured by their hasty marriage.

"You were going to San Francisco to serve as a governess? Can you tell me why a beautiful, young woman would go so far from home to help raise someone else's children? Why am I so fortunate that you're here at all?"

"I told you. Helena looks like—"

"Not what are you doing on the *Young America*. Why aren't you married with children of your own?"

"My parents died of fever when I was six," she answered, her voice distant and monotone. "I remember how much they loved each other. My aunt and uncle raised me after that. They were also deeply in love until the day she died. That was the only kind of marriage I wanted." She stopped and took a deep breath. "I was to be married a bit over a year ago. Joseph was a mineworker. The week before our wedding there was a cave-in. He was killed. After that, I didn't want to love anyone. So I didn't want marriage, either. I'd lost enough already. But I adore children. I decided that as a governess I could be with children day and night. That was as close as I thought I'd ever get to being a mother."

Ironic. He'd been competing with a miner for Helena's regard, as well, but this miner was dead. Most likely a saint in her eyes. And he'd competed with his father's grief over his mother's death until death won. A spike of anger rushed through him; he tried to put it away, but he couldn't completely suppress that inner battle. "So my adventurer was really running away to hide from life."

She rounded on him, her gaze furious, her little pointed chin notched high. "That isn't—"

"It *is* true," he broke in. "You know how I know? What do you think drove me to come to America dragging along my infant and my old nurse? Here I didn't have to face my cousin. Nor worry about what my uncle would do next. Or hear one lecture after another from relatives and other peers on the importance of securing the succession to the title. None of them want to think of Oswald as head of the family. So I ran to America as fast as the wind could carry me. What a pair we are, Pixie."

She sighed and dropped her chin, bumping her forehead on his chest. "And what a pickle we are in together, Jamie. What an awful pickle."

Jamie tipped her face to his and cupped her cheeks in his palms. "Not at all. This thing between us could be wonderful. You just have to let go and enjoy." With no thought of plans to the contrary or their consequences, he leaned down and sealed his lips to hers.

She put her hand to his chest and pressed. His heart beneath her hand sank in defeat. But before he could retreat, she moaned at the back of her throat and her hand moved upward to his neck. His cheek. Jamie deepened the kiss and wrapped his arms around her, pulling her close.

He slid his tongue along the seam of her lips and she gasped, granting him the chance to taste of her sweet depths. Blood pooled low and hard in his body. He craved more than the intimacy she had granted his mouth. But he knew that couldn't happen.

Before he did something he shouldn't, Jamie gentled his hold. Softened the kiss. Traced tiny sipping kisses across her jaw to her ear then into her hair.

And finally, he managed to step back.

It was a near thing when he saw her wide, dark eyes staring at him. And for once he thought he knew what she was thinking. She didn't know why he'd stopped, but she knew it had nothing to do with where they were. He could see that she was still willing to surrender, but he didn't want her defeated.

He wanted her because she was victorious. When she'd conquered her fear for her heart. When she could admit she loved him. And only then. Maybe by then he'd find he could say the same thing. He doubted it, but a man could hope. If anyone could unfreeze his heart it would be Amber.

He could read the confusion and the question in her azure gaze.

"I stopped because you're not ready for more than stolen kisses no matter how much I wish you were. I won't rob you of the courtship I promised you. Just being alone like this is more than a proper courtship would allow. I want you to believe in us. I want you willing to risk that heart you keep hidden behind a wall of fear." He said nothing about his own fear. That wasn't her problem. It was his.

She swallowed hard and he stared, fascinated with the delicacy of the narrow column of her neck.

But her next question snapped him back to reality. "What if that risk isn't something I can handle?"

Jamie forced the future away. His need away. *Live for the little moments,* he told himself. *Lure her with the truth of how perfect you are for each other.* And in a blinding flash he saw what he had not before. He needed to court and woo her as much as she needed him to do it. He needed what he'd never had. He kissed her forehead, then her nose. "My adventurer, too afraid to reach out and take the life she deserves? Not possible."

"But you said I was running away, not going on an adventure."

He smiled. "Did I? How foolish of me! We're both on an adventure. The most dangerous and wonderful kind of all."

She still looked confused, which made him smile even more. "Because going around the Cape is dangerous?" she asked. "But I didn't know how dangerous it could be when I thought up this trip."

"It isn't the route or even the trip I'm talking about. Our journey toward each other is going to be life's greatest adventure. Now, since neither of us seems to be very hungry, suppose we go up on deck and take in the full panorama of that beautiful sunset."

He gave her his arm and led her out of the stateroom, but it was her beauty he'd been drinking in and not the multihued sky being reflected on the surface of the ocean. And that would never change.

Not even when her blond hair was white and her smooth skin wrinkled with age. In fact, after all those years together, he'd wager he'd still have eyes only for her.

Chapter Nine

June 29, 1876—Cape May, New Jersey

Meara ran across the porch, hopping up and down in excitement. "Look, Mimm, Da's come to see me!"

There was no way her Jamie could be there unless the ship had needed to turn around and that rarely happened, Miriam Trimble thought, frowning. She pushed herself out of her rocking chair and walked to the railing of the porch on the second floor off the side of the house.

Mimm's head liked to spin right off when she saw *who* had come to call. "Out of the mouths of babes," she muttered under her breath. No, it wasn't Jamie, but that snake of a cousin of his. And if the man wasn't Meara's blood father, Mimm didn't know who was.

She'd never trusted young Alexander. As far back as she remembered, he'd always had a look in his eyes that said he wasn't telling the truth—that he was guilty of something. Still, she'd felt pity for him when he'd returned from his trip to find the woman he loved had married Jamie.

Jamie had lived with that guilt every day since.

"'Tis not your da. Probably just a tinker," she lied. "And right now, my little lamb, it's time for your afternoon rest. Hop up on the chaise inside and I'll tuck you and dolly up for a nice bit o' sleep."

When Meara was born, Alexander'd shown up out of the blue to patch things up with Jamie. Miriam Trimble was no dummy. He'd wanted access to that child. Though Meara had been a little bit of a thing, Mimm hadn't believed for one minute that she was a seven-month baby. She herself had given birth at seven months to a lad who hadn't lived and he'd looked much less finished than Meara had.

Jamie had closed the subject with one hard look when Iris's personal doctor proclaimed the tiny baby early. But nine months earlier Jamie'd not been to London yet and Alexander lived there. Not once had Jamie treated Meara as anything other than his own adored child. Her Jamie was no fool, though. He knew.

Mimm looked down at the child. Though Meara looked like Jamie, the little lamb looked even more like Alexander with her wavy blond hair only a few shades lighter than his.

And now he was in America.

The question was, why?

She closed Meara's door and went to find out, planning as she went. He could take the girl if he had a mind. With Jamie so far away and out of touch, Alexander could go to the court, complain that she wasn't being properly cared for and gain custody. He was blood. Miriam Trimble was nothing to the outside world but the hired help.

She met Hadley halfway up the stairs. "Where did you put him?" she asked.

Hadley's eyebrows climbed high on his forehead. "So you saw him arrive. He's in the front parlor. He's wanting the earl."

"You didn't say where he is, did you?" she demanded.

"I have more in my brain box than that. Last I knew, his lordship wasn't on speaking terms with his cousin."

"Not since Iris's funeral," Mimm grumbled. "When that one beat my Jamie black and blue."

"And I'd repaired what I could before you saw him. If his lordship had defended himself there'd have been a different outcome. The coward should have realized it was too easy and stopped long before he did. Therefore I saw no need to share anything with Reynolds but standing room in the parlor." Hadley regarded her for a long moment. "Shall I have tea brought?"

"He won't be here that long. Wait in the hall and ride to the rescue if you're thinkin' I need it."

"You're a suspicious woman, Mrs. Trimble."

"And I'll stay that way till there're questions answered that never have been."

She walked in and found Alexander by the fireplace examining a portrait Jamie'd had done of Meara last year. "Mister Reynolds, I'm right surprised to see you so far from England and here on our doorstep, no less," she said, startling him from his study of the portrait.

He turned to face her, his expression unreadable. "Is he about? His New York neighbor gave me his direction here. I felt the need to see my cousin. It is time."

"Have you punished him enough for being a gullible fool, then wakin' up to his countess's true heart, then?"

Thunder crossed the face so like Jamie's and his jaw went hard as rock. "What are you now? The lion at the gate rather than just his nursemaid? *Is* he here?"

"I'm Meara's nanny now as I was his. Until *someone* arranged to have me given the boot and have Jamie packed off to boarding school, then on to Edinburgh. The boy never learned a thing about how to run Adair or about the sufferin' of its people."

"But he did strengthen up there with all that icy-cold Scottish weather."

She gave a sharp nod. "That he did, though I'm sure the plan was quite the opposite. He fooled the lot of you."

Alexander smirked. "I dare say being so far from home kept him out of quite a lot of trouble."

"And you would know about that as you was probably the instigator of his every scrape at Adair."

Alexander covered his heart. "Or I was merely there to rescue him. My father was always equally angry at us both so I see no need to dwell on who was the follower. I understand Jamie has become quite the leader these days."

"And he went off this morn to do more of it. Back to New York. Your train must've passed his," she lied happily. "He plans to be gone a week or more. Perhaps you could find him at home in New York." She thought for a minute on how to put him off the scent of Jamie's true travel plans. "Or he may stay at one of the hotels there. He said he might so as not to need the whole house opened just for him."

Alexander raked a hand through his hair, but she noticed his other hand was in a fist at his side. "Are you sure? I really must see him."

"As sure as I can be. Busy as a beaver that one is. Restorin' Adair's coffers of what was stole," she added pointedly and noted that Alexander Reynolds looked quite uncomfortable at the mention of all the funds that went missing during the years his father had control before Jamie came of age and gave the man the boot.

Alexander tried to hide his discomfort with a smile, but she'd seen through him for some time now. He knew his father was a thief and he'd probably benefited as much as Oswald Reynolds.

"I knew Jamie would make a wonderful father," he said. "Meara will have quite a dowry someday." He turned to look up at the portrait. "She looks exactly like our grandmother. I must see her while I'm here. Fetch her, will you?"

Not while Miriam Trimble had any say in it! "She's restin' just now. Was quite ill with scarlet fever in May, poor lamb."

He spun to face her, looking a mite pale. "What? Is she left with any lasting ill effects?"

"Not so we've noticed. 'Tis why we came down here to New Jersey. So she could regain her strength in the sea air."

"I'll see her later, then? You do have room for me, I assume. I'm sure my cousin would like me to stay here since she's been so ill and he left her with only the help."

Mimm stiffened. She was more than the help to Jamie and Alexander knew it. "You best seek him out in New York City. I can't be extendin' his hospitality without his express say so. When last you left Adair, my Jamie was bloodied and bruised."

Guilt flooded Alexander's eyes as he looked away. "Can you at least tell me what hotel he would recommend here on the island?"

"When we came here last year, we stayed at

Columbia House between Ocean and Decatur Streets. 'Tis a very *aristocratic* hotel. You wouldn't feel at home anywhere else."

Alexander stared at her for a long moment, then growled, "I'll be by in the morning to see Meara."

"She sleeps in these days, 'til at least eleven, still gainin' her strength as she is," she told him. Just late enough that he'd miss the last train leaving town.

His lips pressed into a straight line. "Expect me then. You won't keep me from seeing my…my niece." He turned to stalk off.

Good riddance, she thought, as he charged out the door, stalking past Hadley still standing guard in the hall.

"And we'll be on the seven-thirty train out o' here," she told Jamie's right-hand man. "We have preparations to make. Have someone watch that snake of a cousin and you get over to the rail yard and order the railcar readied. Mr. Palmer writes that the house in San Francisco is all ready. We'll head to California in the morning. I don't want to be facing that snake again without his lordship available.

"Make sure to arrange for the lamb's pony to come along, as well. And wire Mr. Palmer to keep quiet on our destination. Make sure he doesn't let on where any of us have headed."

Hadley snapped a smart salute. "I hear and obey, little general."

Mimm smiled. "See that you do. We swore to protect her and I mean to see we do."

Even against her real father. It hadn't slipped Mimm's notice that if it had been Jamie killed instead of Iris that day six years ago, Alexander would have had his lady love, their daughter and eventually Jamie's title. His uncle was a demon and his son was more than likely his true spawn.

Chapter Ten

Jamie looked across the table at Amber. Tongue caught between her teeth, she shuffled a thick deck of cards with avid concentration, then looked up and smiled broadly.

At him.

Just him.

It felt as if the sun had burst through the clouds after a long week of rainy days. His heart lightened and brightened each and every time she smiled at him like that. He didn't think he'd ever tire of seeing her look at him with such unadulterated love shining in her eyes. As if he'd found the secret way to bring happiness into her life.

He grinned while picking up his cards. She was unaware of how transparent she was at moments like this when she was so good at hiding what she was thinking most of the time. "I still think all this bluffing is dishonest."

"I thought you liked all things American."

"I do, but there is nearly as much corruption here as in Britain."

Her eyes flashed. "At least here if someone has millions, kills someone and is caught dead to rights, he's put on trial. In your country if someone has a title nothing is beyond him. And, by the by, there *is* a penalty for bluffing."

"What penalty?"

"If you try bluffing, I'll remember your expression and be ready to defeat you next time."

Jamie wondered if he was ready to try it. He looked at his pitiful hand, grinned a bit and tossed in three buttons. They played for buttons from her trunk so he wasn't betting money, just information. The loser of each pot had to tell a fact about their life.

"I'll hold with the cards I have, thank you," he told her, trying to look pleased with his cards while pretending to be trying to hide his elation. This game might be good practice for business—this bluffing.

She nodded and took two cards, with a little smile, quickly hidden.

In the two weeks since dinner in the captain's cabin he'd learned a lot about her. And about himself. He had more patience than he'd ever have thought. Patience with the slow progress of their marriage. With kisses that were only kisses and not the prelude he wanted them to be. Patience with finding little privacy on the confines of the ship.

Amber still thought they were ill suited. But they were becoming friends. Which, he had to admit, was a novel idea. A wife who was a friend was nearly unheard of in his circles.

Oddly here he was, in the middle of the ocean, in a second marriage he hadn't wanted, but this time he was having the time of his life. His thoughts only half on the game, he raised the bet, trying to keep his expression neutral. She called and raised and he followed suit.

He'd come to think of the days during the voyage as a gift of time. Time the outside world couldn't intrude upon. Without warning, a crash of thunder called him back from his thoughts and vibrated the deck below their feet. The ship seemed to drop a hundred feet. Amber's eyes widened in fear and she paled. They'd been lucky so far with smooth seas, but their luck had run out. "Perhaps we should get aft before this gets much worse," he suggested.

Amber stood and started scooping the buttons into the tin, as she beat back her fear of storms. He dropped his cards on top of the ones she'd held, then added those to the rest of the deck. She held out the tin so he could drop them in. She gave in to temptation and pulled his off the top to check them. Surprised, she looked up at him. "You had nothing." But then neither had she.

He grinned. "I was bluffing. And doing quite a good job of it."

She managed a smirk, hiding her near terror. "Mine were worse."

Jamie laughed, clearly not realizing she was still bluffing.

Maybe he was right and they were made for each other.

Just then the ship dropped out from under them and she felt her feet come off the deck. She landed back in her chair as Jamie made a grab for the tin to keep it from tumbling to the floor.

His expression went suddenly tense. If the storm worried Jamie, maybe she wasn't being such a child after all. "Jamie, I'm scared."

"It's going to be fine," he said calmly. "These men sail these waters all the time. We're in good hands."

A cabin boy ran in, bringing wind and rain along. He stopped short and gaped at them. "Cap'n wants everyone tucked in their cabins," he said, rushing about stowing loose objects in the cupboards. "Looks like a right nasty squall snuck up on us."

She nodded and accepted Jamie's support to stand. But for the first time in weeks, his arms didn't feel as safe as she'd like. He had no control over the ship or the weather, after all. He could drown as easily as she could.

And *she* could drown as easily as *he*.

Or be killed in a carriage accident.

Or by a runaway team.

Like the sun coming out from behind a thick bank of clouds, her mind cleared and showed her the truth. Love was uncertain, but so was life. Did she really want to stop living to avoid hurt in the future? She didn't think so. He was taking a chance with this marriage, too. His first wife had hurt him, yet he was willing to let her be a mother to his daughter and to any other children they might have. She had to think on that.

Jamie steered her out on deck, holding her against him, sheltering her. She looked past him to the sky. It had gone nearly black; no moon and no stars shone in the dark heavens.

Jamie grabbed on to one of the ropes strung from the forward deckhouse back to the poop deck where their staterooms were housed. He tightened his hold on her and they made their way along the deck. The ship rocked to the side and seemed to leap off the crests of the waves or ride them into what the men called a trough. It looked like a deep valley with mountains of water all around.

Waves washed over the *Young America*'s bow, then sluiced back toward the stern on the uphill climb out of the trough. The water rushing under Amber nearly knocked her off her feet, but Jamie pulled her deeper into his strong hold, keeping her upright. Her skirts were heavy with water by the time they reached the mizzenmast, weighing her down and making each step difficult. The wind stung her eyes, lashed her hair into them, making a miserable situation much worse. She might as well be blind while trying to negotiate the trip across the deck.

At last they reached the door to the saloon and stumbled inside. Both of them were soaked through. Warm as it had been all day, now she shivered uncontrollably. Amber wanted to cling to Jamie and beg him to stay with her, but she needed to think, not yet ready for that step. She turned at her door and looked back at him as he entered his stateroom. Longing to run to him and cling, instead she entered her own stateroom.

She stood for a moment, as the floor vibrated under her feet and thunder cracked overhead. The lightning that flashed revealed seawater lashing the porthole. A chill rushed through her, releasing her from her frozen state. She peeled the soaked dress down her arms and over her hips, letting it drop to the floor.

She started toward the clothes press, but stopped. Tonight she wanted the comfort of her own things. On unsteady legs she walked to her trunk and opened it. Still wrapped in tissue was the light green muslin she'd made just before Joseph's death. The look on his face when he'd seen her dressed for the big Saint Patrick's

Day social had made all her work worthwhile. That night it had never occurred to her that he would see her in it only that once.

Pursing her lips, Amber pulled it out and her own plain cotton underthings, as well. She'd finished dressing and was about to toss a shawl around her shoulders when it dawned on her that she wasn't shivering from the cold, but quaking in fear of the storm. The big ship felt small and vulnerable against the furies of nature.

They could die.

Tonight.

"Pixie," Jamie called through the door, knocking softly. "Are you all right? Why don't you…?"

She wrenched open the door and ran into the safety of his arms. She wrapped her arms around his middle with no intention of letting go. Rubbing her cheek against the finely milled cotton of his snowy shirt, she closed her eyes and breathed in his lime-and-bay-rum scent. He wore no collar or cravat and he'd left his shirt open at the throat, his sleeves rolled back to nearly his elbows.

She closed her eyes and remembered the night he'd come to her pallet. She'd run her hands over that muscular chest. Absorbed the deep rumble of his groan into her body as she'd absorbed him.

It was then Amber realized it was Jamie's arms she'd run to just now. She hadn't thought of Joseph. She looked up at Jamie, tears all but blinding her. He'd replaced Joseph a little more each and every day. Amber hadn't even noticed.

She waited for pain, but felt none. It wasn't that it was time for her to forget her gentle miner, but that each day she saw more and more traits in Jamie that had drawn her to Joseph, though on the surface they appeared complete opposites.

Jamie was always impeccably groomed. Poor Joseph had needed to bathe after work before he could even approach her or the coal dust clinging to him would have ruined her clothes. He hadn't owned even one suit and Jamie seemed to have an endless supply. After their marriage, she and Joseph would have lived in the little house supplied for her as the town's teacher. He'd never have earned enough to provide a house. It hadn't mattered. Jamie had three houses in this country alone. He was apparently as rich as Croesus, but that didn't matter, either.

What mattered was that Joseph had been a man of strong character with a kind heart and a gentle spirit. Strength and gentleness hadn't been at war inside Joseph and they weren't in Jamie, either. He would protect her with his life if the need arose, but also comfort her in her fear. She could trust him with her life. And her body.

Maybe someday she would be able to trust him with her heart, as well.

The ship rocked to the side violently. She gave a little squeal, but he managed to steady them both.

"Come. We'll sit out here," he said and stepped back, leading her into the saloon. He closed her door and they made their way to the comfy velvet sofa where passengers often sat at leisure.

"I'm sorry to be such a baby," she said, perching nervously next to him. "This isn't at all like being in a row boat on a river where we could row ashore at the first sign of bad weather."

He put his arms around her just under her breasts and

pulled her against his side. She felt her nipples harden at just that slight contact.

Seemingly unaware of her reaction to his touch, Jamie settled his cheek atop her damp hair. "Try to settle your heart and mind, Pixie. I've got you. Let's have a nice little coze here, just the two of us. Try to forget the storm. Did you ever get the chance to ride on the Mauch Chunk Switchback Railway?"

"I don't have a death wish."

"Glad to hear it, but thirty-five thousand people rode it last year," he countered.

She laughed. "You mean there are that many crazy people in my home state?"

"What happened to my adventurer?"

"She's found out she doesn't like some of the consequences of her scheme to help Helena Conwell."

"And I've grown quite fond of all of those consequences."

"I cannot imagine why. Everyone else is in their rooms tucked up in bed and here you are stuck in the saloon with Miss Nervous Nellie."

He cleared his throat. "Countess Nervous Nellie, if you please."

He'd said it so soberly he drew another laugh from her. He could do that. Make her laugh at the oddest times with an understated little quip.

"You look very pretty tonight, I don't remember seeing that dress on you before this," he whispered against her ear, raising delicious goose flesh on her arms.

"I haven't worn it. It's mine, you see. Um...not Helena's. I know it's simple compared to her things and I didn't want to embarrass you by wearing an inferior garment. But if I'm going to die, I want to die as myself."

"We aren't going to sink. Have a little confidence in Captain Baker."

She crossed her arms over the one he had around her middle and found herself momentarily distracted by the crisp texture of the hair on his well-muscled arms. "It isn't him I don't trust," she explained, trying to get her mind off the memory of his body under her hand— his whole body. "It's the storm. The sea. Perhaps even the ship itself. My life has been utter chaos since I boarded the *Young America*. Which is why I wanted to wear something familiar even if it is out of fashion."

"You look very pretty in green and I don't see why you say this is out of fashion. And it certainly isn't inferior in any way." He fingered the material and she could hear the smile in his voice when he said, "It's actually quite lovely, but to put your mind at rest, you should know you couldn't embarrass me wearing rags." He chuckled then added. "Or nothing at all. Though you did put the poor cabin boy to the blush, I didn't mind in the least."

She smacked the arm anchoring her to his side. "I was wearing my shift and a blanket. You were the one who wasn't wearing a stitch. And the only reason you weren't mortified by my cavorting about in the saloon in my state of undress is because you were probably in shock over the way I'd already embarrassed us both with my wretched temper."

He chuckled again and it vibrated through her, awakening all the sensual feelings she'd fought for too long.

"I shall be forever grateful there wasn't a chamber pot handy, or I think you'd have beaned me and undone all your hard work," he said, levity abounding in his tone.

"When we get to San Francisco," he continued, "we'll go shopping and you'll have your own clothes. You'll pick them yourself and you needn't order anything just because it is in the latest fashion—unless it appeals to you." He fingered her skirt. "Except I'd like there to be at least one for every time of day in some wonderful shade of green. Though I don't think any will be as fine as this one."

"Thank you. It was my best dress. The one I wore to church and socials."

"I'm very glad you wore it tonight. Did it come this way? I know nothing of women's fashion. To hear my valet tell it, I dress like a banker or a doctor and not as my station demands." He sighed. "I do so like it in America where a station is a train depot."

She laughed. "It isn't just fashion you don't understand, *my lord.* You don't seem to comprehend the difference between being wealthy and poor. I made the dress."

"All these tiny stitches," he said, closely examining a seam. "What about these?" he asked, pointing to the darker sprigs.

"I embroidered the sprigs, as well."

"I'm now convinced I'm quite brilliant. I've not only wed a woman who is good and kind and beautiful, but one of great accomplishments, as well. And perhaps you can teach Meara how to do fine stitching like this."

He hugged her a little tighter. "And I do understand the difference. My mother was a commoner. My uncle obsesses over that blood flowing through my veins. According to him, it was the reason for my every childhood infraction. For some reason he thought he could beat it out of me. I don't know what his own son's failing was because he treated him as badly.

"It was my mother who gave me what some think of as a child's name, by the by. It was to be James after my father. I should be cross with her, but she only held me the once and called me Jamie as she did. She died later that day. My father thought to honor her by giving me the only name for me that had ever left her lips. Meara is named for her."

"That is a sad yet lovely story at once. Your father must have loved her greatly."

He tensed. "Unfortunately. Apparently he loved her more than he did me. He killed himself and left me at the mercy of his brother. A note he left said he couldn't go on without her any longer."

Amber was incensed for the boy he'd been. For the man who still bore emotional scars inflicted by uncaring adults. "What utter nonsense. You said you were seven years old? He'd borne it that long and should have been over much of his grief by then. We all have to learn to carry on after losing our loved ones."

"I thought he had. Even looking back on it with an adult's eyes, he'd seemed just fine. Busy with the estate and often preoccupied, but not in the doldrums. He was always able to tell me about her and smile. It was a great shock to everyone."

Most particularly a child suddenly thrust into an unfriendly judgmental atmosphere. Beating the sweet sensitive child he must have been! Oh, but she wanted to meet this uncle of his and give him a piece of her mind, but was just as horrified at the idea of looking upon such evil.

Just then a particularly violent motion nearly

knocked them off the sofa. The truth of their situation once again surfaced in her mind. They could die. And all she would have experienced as his wife was small talk, card games and long, lonely nights in separate beds for both of them. Except, of course, making love one glorious time only to have him call out to Helena, his lost love.

Was that truly all it had been? He'd said she was punishing them both for his confusion and anger when they woke. *Was* she punishing them? She still didn't know.

But she did know she wanted more than this. They were married. And, though there had been no baby as a consequence from their first and only night, there was the bond he'd spoken of all those days ago.

There was most definitely that bond.

Chapter Eleven

Before Amber could say anything about her change of heart, the ship rolled sharply to starboard and Amber felt them nearly slip off the saloon's long curved sofa again.

"This won't do," Jamie grumbled as he scooted them deep into the cushions again. "One more wave like that and we could wind up on the floor."

Amber twisted in his hold so she could face him but still stay in his embrace. Their gazes locked. The look in his eyes, strained and aroused, showed her without a doubt what holding her actually cost him. And she'd never loved him more.

She laid her hand on his cheek and with a quick nod of his head he kissed her palm.

"You're right. This won't do at all," she told him. "I won't go to my grave—watery or otherwise—and not feel what I did in your arms at least one more time."

His eyes blazed, but he shook his head and gave her a little grin. "We aren't going to our grave tonight or any other night aboard this ship. There's plenty of time for us."

Amber had seen that grin before—just before the

storm broke and ended their poker game. He'd been bluffing at the time. Amber fought a smile. She'd warned him that if he bluffed, he might give himself away and never be able to fool her again.

"I'd never pegged you for a liar, Lord Adair. You'd like nothing more than to whisk me into the privacy of one of our staterooms so we could be together again."

"We are together," Jamie protested.

"Why won't you just admit it?"

He sighed. "Caught out, am I?" Jamie slid an arm under her knees and lifted her on to his lap. "I've tried not to push. Tried to give you all the time you need."

She traced his jaw with her fingertip. "I appreciate your restraint, but I've had all the time I need. I'm ready."

"Because of the storm." He took a deep breath and his chest expanded, pressing against her breasts. His gaze dropped to the point of contact. He sighed again, she hoped in defeat, and dropped his head to the high back of the sofa. Then, after a few moments, he picked his head up and looked her in the eyes again. "I hadn't wanted you to have a reason other than wanting me as much as I want you. But I'm not strong enough to resist the invitation even if it means using a chance storm to get us what we both want and need."

He stood with her in his arms. She hadn't been carried this way since her father's death, but this didn't feel the least little bit childish. What she did feel was very much a woman in his arms.

"My bed or yours?" he asked, his voice deeper than normal.

"Yours is so much bigger," she whispered against his ear.

Jamie took no time getting to his door. "Twist the knob, Pixie. I'm a little busy keeping us upright." She twisted it, and the ship rocked toward that side at the same moment. The door flew open so hard it crashed against the wall. Jamie fell into the room as the two of them laughed like fools. He kicked it shut behind them as the boat righted itself, then he pivoted and bent so she could turn the key in the lock.

Then he half stumbled, half ran to the bed and stood her next to it. After sitting, Jamie reached out and pulled her into the V of his legs. Her heart pounded as she stared at his smiling lips, wanting to feel them on hers again. His mouth pulled into a broad, sexy grin and her stomach dropped, but the ship didn't have a thing to do with it this time.

"Want something, Pixie?" he asked. His voice, low and throaty, danced along her spine. Her gaze flew to his. He knew she'd been fixated on his clever mouth.

Amber swallowed. "I guess a kiss would be nice," she answered, unsure what he expected her to say. If he made her ask for specifics, she'd melt into a lump of embarrassed flesh.

He took her face in his broad, capable hands and angled her head before drawing her to him and sealing his lips to hers. How could just the pressing of their lips set off so many…well…they felt like small explosions going off inside her? She didn't understand how his nearness, his touch, could affect her this way.

He nipped at her bottom lip, then his tongue traced the seam of hers. She conceded that he surely did affect her. She shivered and gasped, giving him the chance to deepen the kiss and twine his tongue with hers. She felt that intimacy all the way to her toes, which seemed to curl in her slippers all on their own.

She was thankful he'd left the lantern lit so she could see his expression when he lifted his head. But of course, she had no idea if the look on his face was only about passion and lust or if there was caring and some small amount of love written there, as well. Oh, how she hoped and prayed that, if there weren't, there soon would be. When poets wrote about unrequited love, they vastly overstated its appeal.

"I've dreamed constantly of a moment like this," he whispered against her lips before pressing them to hers again. Then he trailed his fingertips over her cheeks.

Weeks ago he'd said, *"Our lovemaking formed a bond between us. We didn't mean it to happen, but the bond is there."*

Did that mean there would be an even greater bond now that they'd made a conscious decision to make love again? More important, did he want there to be? Did she? Knowing she wasn't brave enough to ask or answer that particular set of questions, Amber turned her head and kissed the hand he used to caress her cheek.

He looked at her with fire in his eyes, his gaze flicking over her face again and again. It was as if he was trying to memorize her features.

"I'm rather glad you got yourself all wet out on deck and had to change. This dress is intriguing with the buttons all down the front," he said at last. Then he trailed fingers down her neck and began slowly, torturously unbuttoning the front closure of her dress while continuing his intent examination of her face. His rapt gaze made her feel more exposed than his inexorable advance downward as one little button after another gave way to his nimble fingers.

Then he leaned forward and his lips covered hers again. His tongue once again begged entry and she eagerly opened for him. This time he lazily thrust his tongue forward and back in a distinct parody of the end they were rushing toward.

But Jamie seemed determined not to rush at all. His hands slid inside the open bodice of her dress and covered her breasts, kneading them through the thin material of her shift. His mouth stayed busy with hers. Then his hands moved and started on the tinier buttons of her shift.

She decided that even if imitation wasn't the sincerest form of flattery, she wanted to follow his lead. Not to flatter, but to touch and be an equal partner in this adventure.

"Speaking of clothing, I'm rather glad I don't have to divest you of a coat or waistcoat." She wanted the feel of Jamie's skin under her hands again. Fingers trembling, she worked at the remaining buttons of his shirt and tucked her hands inside, needing to touch the heat of him—skin to skin. Impatiently, she skimmed her hands upward across his chest and over his muscular shoulders.

But she lost all her ability to think sensibly when his clever fingers plucked at her nipples. She felt the tug deep and low in her belly and sucked in a sharp breath. Her knees went watery and she moaned.

Jamie's husky chuckle told her of his satisfaction. As if he knew she was about to become a puddle at his feet, he guided her bottom on to his thigh.

His mouth left hers and she uttered a tiny cry of disappointment. The regret lasted only seconds because his hungry lips were on her again, kissing a trail downward over her neck to the valley between her breasts. His mouth replaced one set of fingers that had been strumming her nipple. Cupping her breast, he all but devoured her as the other hand continued to knead her other breast.

Amber feared for her sanity when he rolled her nipple between his thumb and index finger while using his teeth and tongue on the other. She arched her back, calling his name and tunneling her hands through his thick hair, holding him to her even as he moved on to the other breast and repeated the luscious torture.

Then he kissed his way back to her lips and feasted on them again as his busy hands moved their sensual massage to her thighs. She felt as if he'd brought her to his room for a feast and she was the meal. He was her sustenance too and she'd take all he offered.

He sighed suddenly, disappointment keen in the sound.

Her brain scrambled in confusion. "Is something wrong?" she asked, shocked by the husky, breathless quality of her own voice.

He tugged her skirt up until he found the hem, then his hand caressed her thigh, skimming his fingertips over her skin. "I want to get you out of your clothes. I refuse to rush this by making love with our clothes in the way. I want to feel you under me again, but with nothing between us this time."

"Oh. I was afraid I'd spoiled it somehow."

He took her face in his hands and touched his forehead to her. They were nose to nose when he said, "Nothing could spoil this night. You're my dream woman." His face was strained as he steadied her and reached for her hem, skimming his hands up her legs to her hips, then her waist.

She shivered again, but not from fear even though the ship took a sharp dip. Nerves and anticipation warred in her. "Sinking could spoil it," she teased, however unsteadily, having nearly forgotten the storm entirely. That fear all but gone, she was, however, unsure about being naked before him.

He laughed at her joke as he slid her to her feet and pulled both her dress and shift over her head, standing as he did. The look of appreciation and wonder in his eyes as he looked down at her chased away any shyness.

"The only place I'm sinking, my dearest countess," he whispered as he pulled her against him, "is into you. And you will be sinking into my wonderful feather mattress right now." He scooped her up, then laid her down, and she sank into the decadent luxury of his bed.

Then he tore his shirt and pants off. His manhood standing proud was a new sight for her even after bathing him for days on end. This was even different from seeing him well and gloriously naked that awful morning they'd fought.

Amber was suddenly very glad for the night he'd stolen on to her pallet, because otherwise she would be beyond nervous all the way to terrified at the thought of him trying to join with her. But it had worked out spectacularly the last time.

Jamie lay next to her on the bed. Arm bent, he propped his head on his hand and traced her jawline with the knuckles of the other.

Then he bent to kiss her and the glory and delicious torture began again. This time, though, he moved more quickly from one kind of kiss to the other, from soft fondling to bold caresses. Soon she was writhing on the bed, pulling him closer, pulling him atop her, then into her.

She cried out in ecstasy at the fullness of him entering her and wrapped her legs around his lean waist, wanting him closer still.

He gasped, his entire body quaking. "I thought it couldn't have been this good."

"Why?"

"I'd thought we weren't meant to find perfection on earth."

She couldn't help smiling at the hint of the Irish accent he seemed to work so hard at hiding. "Hmm. I think you were wrong," she said, happily breathing deeply of him.

"So wrong. This is better. This is everything. Are you sure you aren't magic, my pixie? Because you've surely brought me a piece of heaven on earth."

Then he began to move in her and suddenly a storm rose. It raged within her. All around her. The waves created were waves of pleasure. They dragged her under, but she was unafraid. Her mind spun and her lungs burned as if they would burst, as if the pressure building in her would make her explode. Then she did, arching under him, shouting his name as pleasure sent her flying up to the surface and beyond—one of the million stars twinkling in the sky.

Jamie called out, too. Her name this time. She sucked in a deep, relieved and exhausted breath, floating home still in his arms. Knowing it was she who was in his mind.

He stared down at her, something new in his gaze, and then he kissed her and smiled gently.

And so did she. Yes, there was a great and wonderful bond between them. And it had just grown much, much stronger.

Jamie rolled away from the light streaming in through the porthole and spooned against Amber's back.

Amber. In his bed. In his arms. And not just in his dreams.

He found her breast and the nipple tightened under his hand. She still seemed to be asleep until she purred and stretched in catlike pleasure. He smiled. "Good morning, Pixie," he whispered in her ear.

She gasped and rolled a little away. He found he liked that she was unused to finding a man next to her when she awakened. Lying on her stomach, she pushed up on her elbows and turned her head toward him. "Um, good morning."

Her big, brown eyes peeked at him through a riot of very mussed hair. He'd taken it down and unbraided it at one point. He saw now why she'd told him it was a mistake. Apparently, it tended to tangle.

He reached out and touched the golden tresses that she usually wore swept up or braided, then wrapped around her head. Thick, fine and reaching her waist, it truly was her crowning glory, though he was sure she'd think he was lying if he told her so just then.

Jamie leaned forward and kissed her nose where it peeked out from under the messy strands of hair. How he'd loved that curtain of hair falling over him when he'd shown her how to ride him. He grinned. She showed more than great promise as a rider.

He wondered how she managed that mass of hair on her own without a lady's maid. Once they got to San

Francisco, he'd see she had that as well as a new wardrobe. She deserved that and more. He'd see she had everything a woman could want.

Now she looked around and frowned as if it took a great deal of concentration to get her bearings. "The storm must finally be over."

Jamie laughed. "It's long since moved on. I don't think I'll ever hear thunder or see lightning again without remembering last night." They'd made love through most of the night and the storm had already quieted when they'd drifted off to sleep. It seemed he'd distracted her so well she hadn't paid the storm much notice. He fought a grin. The rough passage around the horn showed great promise suddenly.

Amber rolled over, shoved her hair back and flopped down on the pillow. Smiling that bright, happy smile of hers, she said, "I'm sure I won't think of thunder and lightning in the same way, either." She looked well-rested and well-loved. The combination made her look even more beautiful and he felt even better knowing he was the reason for it.

He couldn't look away. Amber was as loving, giving and courageous in bed as she had been while saving his life. When trying to overcome Jamie's objection to Iris and the way she'd acted in the garden, his uncle had said the perfect wife was a lady in public and a wanton behind the bedchamber door. His uncle had been right, but he'd left off one important trait. Amber was honorable. And integrity could not be overrated.

This time Jamie had found the perfect wife.

And he planned to take advantage of that happy fact for the rest of the voyage. And the rest of his life. Everything would be fine now. Nothing could go wrong.

Chapter Twelve

Jamie stood behind Amber as the ship moved through the Golden Gate into San Francisco Bay. It was day one hundred and twenty-five of the most anxious, rewarding and purely splendid days he'd ever spent. On the voyage they had lived a year's worth of seasons in four months. There was a damp chill in the air as was common in this city.

The closer to the end of the voyage they got, the more subdued Amber had become. She'd also become a bit fretful about her role as his hostess and mother to Meara. She even worried that Mimm wouldn't approve of her.

He couldn't wait to get Amber to his San Francisco home where he was sure all her worries would melt away. Just before Meara took sick he'd had a letter from Fernando Nelson, his builder, reporting that the house was nearly finished. Before he took Amber there, though, he had to secure a full staff and check the house to make sure all was ready. Until then he and Amber would have to stay at a hotel.

He'd heard the Palace Hotel was now up and running. He'd take her there first. It was reputed to be elegant, with every amenity. There she'd get the rest she seemed to need. Why a delicate young woman would have undertaken such a difficult voyage to help a near stranger he would never understand. Curiosity about her home state didn't seem to be incentive enough for such an undertaking. He was selfishly glad she had, however.

"Tell me what I'm seeing," Amber begged.

Jamie squeezed her shoulders, then pointed to the right as they sailed through the Golden Gate. "That over there on the headland is Fort Point."

"That would explain the cannons," she said in an ironic tone.

He laughed at her quick wit. "Off to the left is Alameda," he went on. "It only has three small towns. It has a lot of grazing land for cattle. Still it's where they decided to move the Transcontinental Railroad terminus. When Mimm and Meara come west in my train car, that's where they'll arrive."

"I still cannot believe you have your very own train car."

"It really isn't all that costly for me because I have interests in the New York Central and Central Pacific Railroads. It certainly isn't as extravagant as it sounds when weighed against the discomfort Meara and Mimm would feel in a regular car for weeks at a time."

She pressed her hand to his where it still rested on her shoulder. He didn't seem to be able to be near her and not touch her.

Amber turned her head toward the bay again. "Oh, what is that?" she asked, pointing up ahead and off to the right a while later.

"That?" He took her shoulders in his hands and turned her slightly toward the island. "That's Alcatraz Island. Military Point and the Citadel are there."

"And more cannons. It doesn't give a welcome feel to visitors. What goes on there?"

"It's actually a military prison now. The tall thin building is the lookout tower. I'm told the lighthouse off to its right is the same type they have New England."

She nodded. "I've seen a painting of the one at Cape Cod. It's much the same."

"There are also extensive docks at the other side of the island."

"Alcatraz is from a Spanish root, right? What does it mean? Do you know?"

She had to be the brightest woman he'd ever spoken to. And she was all his. "I understand *La Isla de los Alcatraces* means Isle of the Pelican."

"Are there pelicans here? I saw a rendering of a pelican in a book on ornithology once. A very strange-looking bird. Do you think we'll get to see one?"

"I'll make sure of it. There are other rather exotic kinds of wildlife here, too." On the starboard side where they stood, he saw several streaks of gray break the surface. Their dorsal fins arched high before disappearing beneath the surface. "In fact, look." He pointed downward. "There in the water."

She sucked in an excited breath and gripped the gunwale, standing on her toes for a better view of the cavorting sea mammals. "Finally, porpoises."

"See the calves among the pod," Jamie said and pointed. "There are also sea lions in the bay. They sun themselves on the rocks."

She turned in his arms, her eyes lit from within. With

her excitement all the shadows of the last days of the voyage seem to have fled. She wrapped her arms around his middle and hugged him. "I'm so glad I became an adventurer!"

"Not half as glad as I am," he told her, wrapping her in his arms, too, and just holding his precious wife next to his heart. He was relieved to see her so animated.

As they sailed past Alcatraz Island she asked the question he imagined everyone arriving either by ship, rail or Conestoga wagon asked sooner or later. "Why is it so misty?"

"I've seen it pour in through the Golden Gate. I was told it has something to do with the difference between the temperature of the ocean and the bay."

"Whatever the reason, and cannons notwithstanding, it looks like a fairyland," she said. "I hadn't expected a terrain like this at the shore. It's as if we are in the foothills of a mountain range. It's not like what I saw in Atlantic City, New Jersey or New York City."

"It's actually a lot like Maine. And the water is every bit as cold as it is there."

She yawned and seemed to wilt in a moment. "Jamie, would you mind very much if I rested up until it is time to disembark?" she asked suddenly.

"Of course not, Pixie. Go rest. You probably have nearly an hour," he said, trying to hide his disappointment. What had gone wrong? He watched her move toward the door to the saloon and as the door shut behind her a little of the sunshine went out of the day.

"The Palace Hotel, please," Jamie told the driver as he climbed into the carriage he'd hired there at the docks.

"Are we not going to your home?" Amber asked.

"I thought we'd stay at the Palace until I can hire staff and make sure the house is ready."

"Oh," she said, sounding disappointed.

"The Palace will be a wonderful experience, I can promise you. William Ralston, the man who had the hotel built, was an acquaintance. He had a vision for San Francisco and he hoped having a hotel of its quality would steer the city in that direction. He ran the Bank of California until his death last year. It was only two months before the hotel opened.

"Sadly the bank failed. He'd overextended and Ralston's business partner, Senator Sharon, put the final stress on it with a financial maneuver and William lost it all. Sharon got the bank, the hotel and even Ralston's home. He's a U.S. senator. Too bad they couldn't pin William's death on the good senator," Jamie said pointedly.

She gave him one of her beatific smiles. "I'm glad having a great amount of money hasn't corrupted you."

He was pleased she thought so highly of him, but then her smile faded and she sighed. Jamie took her hand in his. "What is it, Pixie?"

"It's just that you've met such fascinating people."

There it was—that fretful tone in her voice again. "You mustn't worry about anyone outside our little family and getting to know Meara when she arrives."

"Do you think she and Mimm will get here soon?"

He put his arm around her and pulled her close, keeping hold of her hand. "Please don't think Mimm will not love you at first sight. You are everything she could want for me."

She nodded, but seemed to have wilted again after

her rest. Dropping her head to his shoulder, Amber fell asleep in moments. It was as if just disembarking at the docks and getting to the carriage had been too much for her. He was going to contact his old friend Malcolm. Malcolm was as fine a doctor as he'd ever seen. They'd met at Edinburgh, but Malcolm had moved to San Francisco almost immediately.

When they arrived, the motion of the halting carriage roused her. Her face lit up as she beheld the hotel's circular courtyard. He looked up and drew her attention to the seven stories of columned balconies overlooking it. The gleaming white of the marble columns stretched upward to a full skylight, turning the large courtyard into an elegant conservatory.

He jumped to the ground and lifted Amber down. "So, what do you think?"

She put a hand at the back of her head to hold her bonnet in place and looked up at the majestic glass skylight high above. "This is incredible. I'd say your banker friend outdid himself."

Jamie smiled and took her arm, leading her into the magnificent lobby. It consisted of another series of marble arches and ornate coffered ceilings and had elaborate thronelike seating and plush carpets throughout.

This time her reaction was a delighted gasp. Then she blushed. "I sound like a country bumpkin, don't I?"

"I'm no less in awe, Pixie. This is on a level with Windsor Palace. Let's get you settled in a comfy chair while I check us in." He walked her to one of the ornately carved chairs and kissed her cheek. "I'll be right back."

* * *

Through a sheen of tears, Amber watched Jamie walk to the marble registration desk just left of the fancy iron-and-glass-arched doorway they'd entered through. Why did he have to be so sweet? He made her love him more and more each day—and he still loved Helena.

Blinking the telltale moisture from her eyes, she let her gaze drift to the elaborate carpet with a pattern of golden-feathered wreaths woven against a jewel-toned background. He'd brought her to this fine place—a palace—and all she wanted to do was sleep or cry. *What is wrong with me?*

Amber knew she had to get a hold of herself and try harder to pull out of this melancholy she'd fallen into. Now she had Jamie thinking she was afraid to meet Mimm when she was actually keen to meet the woman. She desperately hoped to be able to talk to Mimm. She'd lost her aunt when she was sixteen and other than Joseph's mother, she hadn't had an older woman in her life since.

She supposed she could have talked to one of the passengers about her worries, but Amber hadn't been comfortable asking near strangers intimate female questions. There had been Dr. Bennet, of course, but there'd been no way she'd have asked questions about her very personal matters. The man gave both her and Jamie the creeps.

If Mimm was everything Jamie said, Amber was confident she'd feel comfortable discussing her very worrisome problem with her. Last month her courses had come, though late and not as heavily as usual, so she knew she wasn't expecting. Now she was tired, terribly tired, and felt the urge to cry all the time. She hadn't the slightest idea what ailed her, but she was sure

Mimm must have more experience in life than she herself did.

Her relationship with Jamie had begun to torture her heart. He'd never said he loved her, just that he cared for her. That she and their marriage was important to him. He desired her, but he was a man and men were able to bed women they desired, but didn't love. Amber very much feared she was still only the woman he'd gotten stuck with because fear for his daughter had surfaced while he'd been ill.

She should have refused when he'd begged her to marry him. She knew she should have. She'd known it then, but she didn't think she'd do anything different if she had it to do all over again. He'd been so filled with fear for his child, how could anyone have refused? Even knowing where it would lead, she'd do it again. She loved him that much.

A pair of polished boots stepped into her view. She looked up into Jamie's troubled gaze and tried to brighten her tone when she said, "Oh, you're back."

Jamie smiled uncertainly. "You look a bit wilted again. Come. We'll get you settled. I've taken a suite. That way you can rest in your own room and not be bothered by my comings and goings."

She hadn't slept alone since the stormy night they'd made love for the second time. Was he being considerate or had he tired of her already?

She stood and a wave of dizziness assailed her. "Goodness," she gasped and grabbed for his arm.

"We need to get your land legs under you again."

"I think you're right," she lied. Her legs were fine. It was the rest of her that didn't seem right.

At Jamie's side she walked across the spectacular

lobby to an elevator. It was one of five hydraulic elevators in the Palace Hotel, according to the bellboy who had been charged with escorting them and their trunks to their room.

They exited onto the upper floor where the spectacular glass roof was just overhead. The heat of the sun warmed the courtyard and seemed to have created a warm and cozy climate much different from the damp, chilly world outside.

Lining the balconies and halls were graceful statues and exquisite urns and vases that were filled with strange and wonderful plants and flowers that scented the air with heavenly aromas. It looked and smelled like a fairyland.

The bellboy opened the door and handed Jamie the key before stepping back and bowing slightly and gesturing them inside. They entered a gracious suite with a wide, deep bay window on the far side of the room that let bright sunshine pour in.

"You have a private toilet, a fire grate and ample closets if you wish your maid to unpack the entirety of your trunks," the bellboy who introduced himself as Caleb explained.

Amber tried to think of something to say that befitted the wife of a man of Jamie's station. A countess. She didn't wish to gawk like a bumpkin, but she also didn't wish to appear toplofty as if the young man was beneath her notice. She decided on, "The furniture is very unique. And it looks well made. A friend in Pennsylvania where I'm from is building a furniture factory there."

The bellboy smiled. "The hotel was furnished by a local furniture maker. Spanish styling heavily influences the design. If you tell me where you'd like your trunks placed I'll get to it."

"I'll handle this, Amber," Jamie said. "Why don't you rest for a moment on the sofa."

Amber sank into the downy cushions, wondering how to ask Jamie if he meant for them to sleep separately. She was completely taken off guard by what to her was an uncharacteristic move on his part. Why did he suddenly want them to have separate rooms?

"Is there anything else I can do for you before I leave?" she heard the bellboy ask.

"If you could have some light refreshments brought for my lady, I would appreciate it," Jamie said and handed the man some money. "Other than that, we should be fine."

After the man left, Jamie turned to her. "I thought you could use the extra room as a dressing area. Once I find you a maid, we won't be able to dress in the same place."

Relieved, Amber sighed dramatically. "And just when I'd gotten you so well trained in the profession. Very well, if I must break in a new lady's maid, I might as well get started."

Jamie tossed his head back and laughed. "Minx. You should rest. And while you do that, I have a bit of business to handle. I need to secure staff for the house and contact the builder. I want to inspect the place and make sure it's ready for us before I take you there. They tell me there's a salon here called The Office. There are supposed to be attachés waiting there to handle business and run errands and such for guests. I may as well avail myself of their expertise. Come to think of it, we'll need a carriage and driver. Perhaps one of them can deal with that, as well."

She hadn't realized there was so much for him to accomplish. "Very well. I suppose I could use a rest. Disembarking was very exciting. You aren't interested in waiting for the refreshment you've sent for?"

"That is for you. I'll find something at the Men's Grill. We'll dine in one of the restaurants this evening." He bent, cupped her cheek and kissed her. "Promise to rest?"

She nodded and he dropped his hand, worry in his gaze. Darn it all! She didn't want to burden him with even a minor inconvenience. Being married to a woman he didn't love was inconvenient enough.

"Dream of me," he ordered with a gentle smile. Then he left before she could find a way to reassure him.

Dream of him? She dreamed of little else. Thought of little else.

Amber came awake with the vague feeling that she wasn't alone. She opened her eyes in the darkened room and found Jamie sitting in a chair, watching her. She sat up and swung her bare feet to the floor. "What time is it?"

He took out his watch. "Seven. We have reservations for eight."

"You should have awakened me. I'll have to hurry to be dressed on time."

"I meant to. I lost track of time. I was thinking and watching you sleep."

What had he been thinking about with such concentration that he'd lose track of time? "Thinking about what? Is there something wrong?"

"I have news. Our house is ready and waiting. We still have to hire a few more staff, though. But the most important news is that Meara and Mimm have already arrived."

"That's wonderful! You've seen them? Were they happy or upset that you married a woman neither has met? Will we be leaving now or in the morning?"

Jamie laughed. "Slow down, Pixie. Unfortunately, no, I didn't see them. They were away from home when I got there. Hadley said they'd gone to visit with a playmate of Meara's."

"You didn't wait? Why ever not?"

"Because he said they often stay at the playmate's house for dinner. I'd left you here and you wouldn't have known where I was if I'd waited. I didn't want to worry you by disappearing for hours. I left Mimm a note telling her about our marriage, but I asked her to allow me to tell Meara. Now let us get you ready for our dinner."

He stood and opened the draperies. Rays of the setting sun poured in, backlighting him as he returned to sit at the bottom of the bed. "I thought we'd devote a day or two to a bit of sightseeing and shopping."

Amber stared at him. What was he thinking? She'd thought from the way he'd talked about Meara that he missed his child. "Sightseeing? But you should see Meara and I'd hoped to meet both her and Mimm as soon as possible."

"And you will. I've made arrangements for Mimm to bring Meara here in the morning. I ordered the suite expanded to five bedrooms to accommodate our little family and Mimm and Hadley, my valet. And your maid when one's been hired. I thought we'd go to Woodward's Gardens tomorrow. You seemed to have enjoyed the Exhibition in Philadelphia. I know Meara did. I thought you'd both enjoy this, as well. There is a zoological garden there. They have camel rides, if you can believe it. My daredevil daughter will be over the moon about that idea."

Amber frowned. What was he talking about? "Over the moon?"

"You must have heard of the nursery rhyme, 'high, diddle, diddle, the cat and the fiddle,'" he began.

"Oh. 'The cow jumped over the moon,'" she finished, glad of the education Uncle Charles had insisted upon. She'd learned the rhyme and many other facts about the land of Jamie's birth from an English literature professor, this one from one of the sillier moments in his class. Without her boarding-school experience and her Vassar education, Amber wouldn't have had a prayer of fitting in with Jamie's circle of friends and business acquaintances. Actually all she really lacked was a fine pedigree. Unfortunately, birth was often the most important element of all.

"The idiom means very excited," he went on to explain. "I've ordered a picnic lunch from the kitchens for us to take along. Woodward's Gardens are a must on any visit to San Francisco.

"The first thing in the morning, though, an agency is sending several maids for you to interview."

"Me?"

He smiled. "I wouldn't know a laundress from an upstairs maid."

As if she did? Well, now that she thought about it after the summers on the Hudson she did know what their duties were, but she'd never hired anyone. She was certainly capable of talking to the women and deciding who was pleasant, trustworthy and sufficiently industrious. The real problem was she didn't want Mimm to feel displaced as if their marriage suddenly made her a servant in Jamie's home. Clearly she was much more to him.

Jamie leaned forward and tapped on her forehead as he said, "What is going on in there, Pixie?"

"I wondered who made decisions like this before?"

"Before?"

"Before me. Who would have hired staff for your house had we not arrived married?"

"Mimm."

"That's what I thought. I'd rather include her in on decisions like this, in that case."

He smiled. "I appreciate how considerate you are and how blind to life's different stations. We'll delay the interviews until after they've arrived. Meara and I will breakfast together while you and Mimm conduct the interviews."

Which meant she'd get a few minutes' privacy with Mimm. She looked up and caught Jamie staring at her, his gaze hot with desire. "You know, I would much rather eat at nine," she told him.

"Hmm. A much more civilized hour," he agreed, his tone hopeful and a bit strangled at once.

"But whatever will we do with all the time?" she asked, but she didn't expect a spoken answer. Nor did she get one. Instead Jamie pulled off his shoes. She had come to know him as a man of action. Another of his better traits, she decided a minute later when he'd joined her on the bed and covered her lips with his. Perhaps it was his best trait of all.

She laughed and flopped back on the pillows and he followed her down.

It would be fine. He did still want her. They could build on that.

Chapter Thirteen

Jamie waited anxiously in the courtyard and finally his new open carriage rounded the end of the building. "Da! It's Da," he heard Meara shout. He couldn't wait to hug the squirming little minx whom Mimm was trying to rein in.

With Amber in their lives, the circle would be complete and they would finally be a true family. Now, his child would have a mother. A very good mother.

One who happened to be the perfect wife for him.

The now bouncing carriage pulled to a stop and Jamie reached for the door. He pulled it open and Meara launched herself out the door into his arms in the next instant. He hugged her to him and inhaled the little-girl scent that was so uniquely his Meara's.

Then she squirmed, arched her back and propped her hands on his shoulders, staring at him with her wide blue eyes. "It's me, Da. Haven't I grown? I'm a whole year older! Thank you for my birthday pony! I called him Spots. He has them on his rump, you know. We brought him along, though he was very sad all alone in the car for horses. Hadley found a stable for him near our house and we go to see him three times a week. There's a little girl there named Isabella. Only I call her Bella. She's nearly my age." She paused, took a deep breath and was off again. "And I'm learning to ride from her da. Only she calls him Papa. They have a huge horse who looks like Spots. I want to get him for you for your birthday in November. When you come meet Spots you'll meet Bella. Mimm says we are quite opposite, but only because she has the blackest hair and the very darkest eyes. I love her brown eyes. But we aren't really much different. She doesn't mind getting dirty in the least and—"

"Hush now, child," Mimm called from the coach. "Let your da get a look at you, then he can help this old woman down." She leaned forward and looked up at the building. "My goodness, your lordship, this is certainly quite the thing, now isn't it?"

Jamie set Meara on her feet and went down on one knee to get a good look at her. Curly blond hair, peeking out of her pale blue bonnet, framed her cherubic face and her bright blue eyes flashed with excitement.

"And now, Lady Meara, have you been a good girl?" he demanded, trying to look severe.

She nodded vigorously and gave him a cheeky curtsey accompanied with a wide, happy smile, then closed her eyes with exaggerated vigor and put out her hands. It was a ritual with them. He was now supposed to present her with a trinket from his trip.

He reached in his pocket and pulled out the jewelry box, clasping a tiny pearl bracelet about her wrist. Then he took out the matching necklace and looped it about her neck, fumbling with the catch.

This was the first jewelry he'd ever given Meara. Tonight at dinner he'd give Amber a matching set of pearls—a first from him to her, as well. He and Meara were going to get Amber's wedding ring after breakfast. He also wanted her to have her own betrothal ring. There was so much sadness attached to the Adair betrothal ring. His mother had worn it, then it had been Iris's. He didn't want it for Amber. This was their new life and he wanted nothing of the past to haunt them.

"Right-o, little one," he said, having mastered the clasp. "You can look now!"

Meara looked at her wrist, then ducked her chin to her chest so she could see the pearls around her neck. Then she looked up, happily, a question in her gaze. "Oh, Da. 'Cause I'm a big girl now?"

Meara was again the picture of health, thank the good Lord. She had roses in her cheeks. Her eyes, the exact color of his father's, sparkled in the bright morning light. When last he'd seen her, she'd been pale and thin after the ravages of the fever that had almost taken them both.

He remembered lying in bed on the ship, burning up with fever and asking God why, but now he knew. His suffering had not been in vain because through it God had given him a sprite of a woman to make his life and his daughter's complete.

That perfect mate waited nervously in their suite to meet her new daughter. And Mimm! Remembering that his substitute mother was still waiting, he turned from Meara and lifted Mimm to the ground. She was a bit taller than Amber, her silver-gray hair covered by a cotton sunbonnet. Her eyes were the palest of blue and her stout, compact body encased one of the largest hearts in creation. She habitually wore navy skirts, snowy-white blouses with lace collars and sensible half-boots. She called it her uniform, but he made sure only the best materials were used in everything she ordered.

"So, it's to a palace you brought the girl," Mimm said as they entered the lobby. "I suppose she'll be the type to expect such."

"Of course we're to stay in a palace," Meara said. "I'm my da's princess." She waved her pearl-decorated wrist about then giggled, clearly not understanding the meaning of Mimm's comment.

Holding Meara's hand, he dropped his free arm around Mimm's shoulders, relishing the surprise Amber was going to be for both of them. "You are in for such a treat and that's all I'm going to tell you," he whispered to her.

He led them to the elevator and ushered them inside. Meara, putting on a comical face, looked up at him and pointed to Mimm.

He glanced at the older woman. Her face looked set in stone. "This is the newest and perhaps the smooth-est elevator in the world," he told her. "You'll hardly know we're moving. I promise."

"Don't you try to reassure me," Mimm snapped. "You know I don't like these contraptions. There's noth-ing wrong with stairs and more wrong than I can say with riding in a cage hundreds of feet from the ground. Folks these days are just plain lazy."

"Seven stories of stairs would be tiring, even for you. And we have quite a day ahead so we don't want to wear you out so early."

They stepped off the elevator a few moments later and he steered them toward their door. But he stopped at the doorway, squatting down to Meara's level again, and said, "I have another surprise for you inside. There is a young lady in there I want you to meet. I met her on the voyage here. And I married her."

Meara gasped. "You mean I have a mum now! A real live mum who'll hug me and read to me and...and..."

"Oh, child, don't go thinking—" Mimm began.

"Actually," Jamie interrupted, knowing Mimm expected someone completely unlike Amber, "she'll probably do all that and more. She loves children. In fact, she went through school all the way to college. She's a very well-qualified teacher. I expect her to make quite a bluestocking of you, my dear. Now come, both of you. And keep an open mind," he whispered into Mimm's ear.

Oh, this was going to be quite a good time. He had to stop himself from rubbing his hands together in anticipation. Amber was going to shock Mimm down to her toes.

Thank God she was as completely different from Iris as could be. But then he opened the door and watched Amber pop to her feet, wringing her hands. He was drawn to her, wanting to comfort her and alleviate her worry. He glanced down at Meara, who nearly vibrated with excitement while Amber looked as if she was about to faint.

Decision made, Jamie rushed ahead and put his arm around his sweet young wife, then turned back toward the doorway. "This is my new wife, Amber. Amber, these lovely ladies are my daughter, Meara, and—"

"And you must be Mimm," Amber jumped in, then hurried out of his arms and toward them. She held one hand to Meara and one to Mimm. Jamie followed.

Meara, friendly as a puppy, giggled and, while holding Amber's hand with both of hers, said, "We *call* her

Mimm, but she isn't *really* Mimm. She is really Mrs. Miriam Trimble. You are quite silly, aren't you?"

"Meara!" both he and Mimm gasped.

Amber, her creamy complexion flushed rosy, shook her head and said, "No. No. She's quite right. I am so sorry, ma'am. I shouldn't have interrupted Jamie and been so familiar as to call you by their pet name for you. I've just been so excited to meet you both and sometimes when I get excited I speak before I think."

"I do, too," Meara said, still a bit deflated.

And Mimm smiled warmly. Clearly she saw a new, uncertain chick in the nest and swept Amber under the safety of her wing in less than a second. "Me name actually *is* Miriam Trimble. Learnin' to talk as he was when I came to the Earl's home, me lamb couldn't say that mouthful. Mrs. Trimble come out Mimm. And fine by me it were. And 'tis fine for you, as well. I scarcely remember the other name now that Mr. Trimble is passed on and I am full-time again with his lordship and o' course Lady Meara."

Mimm held out her hand to the new Countess Adair. She couldn't believe this was the woman Jamie had picked as his wife. She wasn't a thing like that greedy temperamental Iris, the former countess. And certainly nothing like that Helena Conwell who'd had Jamie's head all mucked up and his heart all a-twitter. She'd come to the New York house with her father a few days before the poor man was murdered. Mimm had noticed the cool way she'd treated Jamie. She hadn't even been able to look at little Meara without taking a step backward. Jamie said it was terrible nerves and youth that was wrong with her, though, having never before been out in society. But she'd dressed the same as Iris had. Expensive.

Wearing a simple day dress of green sprigged muslin, Amber's hair was wrapped in a shining coronet of braids, her face as fresh as spring. If Miriam Trimble hadn't lost her touch at sizing people up, this one was everything the previous countess hadn't been.

Amber sat in a chair and called Meara over to her. "Tell me what you do with your time, Lady Meara," she said, her voice as sweet as her smile.

"I ride my pony," Meara said, beaming at the special attention. "And Mimm found me a painting teacher. She says I'm very good. Mimm tried to teach me to do stitching like this." She pointed to the sprigs on Lady Amber's muslin dress. "But I'm not so good. I pricked my finger and I cried."

"Oh, I'm so sorry. You'll get better at it as you grow. My aunt taught me."

"Didn't your mother teach you?"

"No, she died when I was six of a fever and I was rather clumsy with small things like a needle back then. My da died at the same time. My brothers, too."

Little Meara's eyes opened wide. "Oh! So you was all orphaned and everything?"

"Yes, but my aunt and uncle took me in and raised me. They were wonderful to me. I was ten when my aunt taught me stitching. This material was plain muslin when I bought it, but I wanted it to be fancier so I embroidered it. Though I think Mrs. Trimble is more likely better at needlework than I am, I can help you learn anytime you want. Would you like that?"

Meara nodded vigorously.

"Princess, would you like to have breakfast with

me?" Jamie put in. "There's quite the fancy dining room down near the lobby. We can let Mimm and Amber get to know each other. Amber, perhaps you could tell Mimm how we met and I will tell you, Meara, all about how Amber took such good care of me when I was sick with your fever."

Mimm could only stare. He'd gotten that awful fever? Then Meara asked, "Was you sick as me was?"

"As *I* was, princess," Jamie corrected.

"You just said you was sick," Meara said, clearly puzzled. Then her thoughts must have turned where they often were—on food. "I want flapjacks. Do they have 'em?" she asked.

"They'd better," Jamie answered and smiled at her. "That is all I've thought of since waking this morning. I believe my stomach will revolt if I have to settle for anything less. And afterward you can help me with an important errand. How does that sound?"

"Is it a secret important errand?" Meara asked with great anticipation in her winsome voice.

Jamie, ever the attentive da, stooped to her level again. "A great secret. And you must keep it for me until I say you're allowed to say where we've been."

"Yes! Oh, I love secrets," Meara said, her little body vibrating with excitement. "And I can keep them, too, can't I, Mimm?"

"Oh, yes, indeed," Mimm agreed, hoping Meara wouldn't need to keep this secret for long. She was better, but not completely discreet yet. That was why she'd misdirected her attention back in Cape May when she'd thought her father had come to visit. And it was why she hadn't explained but to say bad weather approached as the reason they'd suddenly left for San

Francisco. She couldn't have told Meara the truth and not had her mention it to Jamie. Mimm hoped and prayed Alexander wouldn't track them here because Jamie didn't see his cousin for what Mimm feared he was—a wolf in sheep's clothing. If he did show up Mimm was in for a tongue lashing from Jamie. He'd told her he forgave Alexander for the fight they'd had and wouldn't hear of her poisoning Meara's mind against the man. But he'd never said she had to give him free access to the child or to Jamie for that matter.

"Then with your oath of silence given," Jamie was saying, "I think we should be off. We'll see you ladies later. And I'll check on the picnic basket before we return. Your breakfast should be here at any moment. I ordered it just before our carriage arrived. We will see you both about noon."

"I'm so sorry," Amber said the moment the door closed behind Jamie and Meara.

"What are you apologizing for, lovie?"

"For the shock of…of all this. There was no way to inform you about our marriage before we arrived in the city and Jamie shouldn't have just written a note and left it for you. He should have waited at the house for you to return, but he was concerned I'd worry if he was gone too long." Amber shrugged her delicate shoulders. "I confess I probably would have."

"He said you cared for my lamb when he took sick. Is that how you met? And just how sick was he?"

Amber nearly laughed at the thought of her big strong husband owning a pet name like *my lamb*. With Mimm obviously so emotionally tied to Jamie, Amber hesitated to go into how sick he'd been. But Jamie *had* said to tell Mimm so Amber gave the older woman the highlights of his illness and the reason why they'd married. It went without saying that she left out the part about how they'd consummated their marriage and who Jamie had thought she was when he'd married her. Some things were just too personal or humiliating to repeat. Ever. This was both of those things.

Which was why Miriam Trimble smiled broadly and said, "How romantic and how good you are for him. I can see it already. I told him I thought he were sickening and should stay home. He wouldn't be put off, though. A man on a mission, he was. It seems to have all worked out for the best.

"You would never have met had he listened. My heart aches that he was so frightened for Meara, though. And considering that his snake of a cousin showed up in the East lookin' for him, 'tis glad I am he weren't sick at home. I perish to think what might have happened if Alexander Reynolds had got it into his head to take advantage of Jamie when he was in a weakened condition."

"His cousin Alex? But Jamie is so distressed over their rift. He blames himself for it."

"Amber, luv, let me speak my mind. I don't trust Alexander Reynolds. Never have. And I'm askin' that you don't tell Jamie he's in America. There was always something sneaky about that one. As if he was sayin' one thing and thinkin' and doin' another. I'm not tellin' you what to think of him if he shows himself. For your sake and Jamie's and Meara's, though, you be careful of that one."

Amber nodded. "I will. But I also know we cannot judge a man by the actions and character of his father.

My best friend married the son of a mine owner. He is as different from his father as night is from day."

"Jamie don't agree with me, either, but you mark my words," Mimm said, "and be careful if you ever do meet up with him."

"You must tell Jamie his cousin came looking for him. He will be so relieved."

"I can't. I sent him off on a bit of a wild-goose chase to New York City when I knew Jamie was on the clipper. Jamie will be so angry, but I didn't dare let Alexander know Meara was all alone with just servants."

"But you are more to Jamie than that."

"I know that, but Mister Snooty Reynolds might not. I didn't think it a wise chance to take. Now, what is it you wanted to talk about, lovie? I can see all is not well. What has you so troubled?"

This time a bit more haltingly, Amber tried to explain how she'd been feeling. The tiredness. Her tendency to end up in tears at the slightest provocation. Then she asked Mimm what to do other than see a doctor.

"Well, I think you *are* needing a doctor, but don't worry so. 'Tisn't anything time won't cure on its own eventually—say in eight or nine months," she added, her eyes sparkling with mirth.

Amber didn't think she could stand feeling like this for… "Eight or nine months? You think I could be expecting? But I had my courses."

"Don't always matter."

Excitement surged through her. A child? A child of her own? No, a child of hers and Jamie's. Amber's heart swelled and she blinked back tears.

"I'd say 'tis nearly certain."

"I have to find out." Amber sniffled. "How do I find

out for sure? I don't know what doctor to trust here. You have no idea how awful the doctor was on that ship. I wouldn't have asked him about a hangnail."

Mimm chuckled. "Not to fear, lovie. I know exactly who you should see. Met him when last we were in San Francisco. About two years ago it was. Dr. Malcolm Campbell. I would imagine he would be glad to come here for the wife of a fellow classmate from Edinburgh. I will send for him at once and then you will have wonderful news for our Jamie."

He'd said he wanted more children. Would this make her more important than Helena? Help her supplant the other woman in his mind? "Don't tell him," she said in a rush of anticipation. "It should come from me. He'll be pleased, don't you think? Oh, I do so hope he will."

"Amber, take a breath. Did you see him with his Meara? The love in his eyes and she isn't even—" Mimm took a breath "—the child of a woman he loved."

As if I am? The woman Jamie loves is married to Brendan Kane and I can't even tell him so. Keeping Helena's secret had become harder and harder.

"I'll be back in a few moments," Mimm was saying in her no-nonsense way as she bustled toward the door. "I'll send a message and ask Dr. Campbell to come about eleven. We should be done with your interviews by then and Jamie isn't due back until twelve. That ought to give us time to get this bit of business taken care of."

Amber walked out of the bedroom, vastly relieved yet frankly terrified by the prospect of giving birth. Children had always been her dream, but the reality of actually producing them hadn't been quite so real until now.

It was suddenly paramount in her mind. That and the other piece of information the doctor had given her. Jamie had already asked him to come look at Amber. She had troubled him as she feared.

"There now, that wasn't so terrible, was it?" Mimm asked. She met Amber halfway across the parlor, having shown Jamie's friend, Dr. Campbell, to the door. She held out both hands and Amber grabbed on like Miriam Trimble was a lifeline that could keep her from sinking into a dark pit of fear and uncertainty.

"Your hands are like ice, lovie. It's going to be fine. Women have been doing this since Eve. And Jamie? Oh, but isn't he goin' to be so happy. But you'll need to tell him soon, himself having asked Dr. Campbell to come have a look at you already."

Amber nodded. She was reasonably sure Jamie *would* be thrilled. Just seeing him with Meara, the way he made sure he spoke on her level and had turned a simple breakfast into an adventure, made Amber love him all the more. Seeing him with Meara had reminded her of her own father. He'd had that same ability to make Amber feel loved and cared for more through his actions than his words.

But Amber was an adult woman now and she needed those words from her husband. Jamie had never said he loved her. Unfortunately, she wasn't sure she would believe him if he did. Helena Conwell's name on his lips loomed like a specter in her mind.

Maybe giving him another child to love would bring him to love her the way she did him. Maybe if he held a child that was the product of her love for him, he would love her back just as powerfully.

Chapter Fourteen

Jamie handed Amber into the elevator, then surreptitiously checked his coat pocket for the velvet pouch holding the rings and his breast pocket for the box containing the pearls that matched the ones he'd given Meara. He checked even though it was perhaps the tenth time he'd done so since he'd finished dressing.

He glanced at Amber. She seemed miles away, but a slight smile tipped her lips, giving him hope that having met and spent the day with Meara and Mimm, she'd relaxed about her new role in all their lives.

"Meara is quite taken with you. So is Mimm," he said, watchful of her reaction.

Her smile grew. "She's a lovely child. Kind and generous. You and Mimm have done a wonderful job raising her."

"She does have a tendency to be a chatterbox, I'm afraid."

"A chatterbox I can handle. I was afraid she would be spoiled and demanding. I should have known any child of yours would be adorable and sweet as she can be, but you seem to have plans to spoil me so…"

"You couldn't ever be spoiled enough. You deserve everything I can give you for all you've done for me already. You stepped in and promised to protect her."

"A promise I told you at the time I wouldn't have to fulfill." Amber looked up at him and her smile turned to a teasing grin as the elevator doors opened onto the lobby. "If she is such a chatterbox, why did you trust her with this morning's secret mission? Where *did* you go, my lord? I couldn't get her to tattle. Each time I tried to trick a location out of her, she caught on in a blink. She wanted very much to please me, yet her loyalty is firmly in your camp."

Jamie gaped at her, a bit of fear tightening his gut. "Are we to separate into camps, then? My intent was that we were to be a unified happy family. At least that was my hope," he said, a bit alarmed by the meaning of her last statement.

"As is it my hope," she said, her smile gladdening his heart. She saw family life as he did then. And he also realized she no longer spoke of ending their association, thank the good Lord.

Placing his hand at the small of her back, Jamie directed her through the lobby toward the American Dining Room. With a suppressed smile, he noted that her breath caught a bit at his touch. All he need do was continue drawing on that attraction until she couldn't do without his nearness.

"I'm very much afraid you have had no experience with families, my lord. It is a foregone conclusion that we ladies must align ourselves against the males."

"I thought it was just you and your parents until their deaths. Then you went to live with your aunt and uncle who'd been childless."

The headwaiter met them then as they stepped through the doorway of the elegant white-and-gold room. Decorative marble columns and arches reached upward to a coffered ceiling. Opulent gold brocade fabric covered the wall within the series of ornamental arches marching around the perimeter of the room. The elegance of the architecture formed the perfect background for tables covered in snowy-white cloths, fine bone china and gleaming silver flatware.

"Your lordship, your table is ready. This way, please."

Jamie was pleased the man remembered him and hoped it meant he'd remembered his other instructions for the evening. The room easily seated well above five hundred, but Jamie had wanted privacy so he'd bought the surrounding tables. It wasn't the sort of extravagance he usually indulged in, but the private dining rooms had previously been reserved and he wanted Amber all to himself on this special night. And he didn't want their conversation overheard by anyone.

The man led them to a back corner and a table for two. He pulled out a chair, smiling at Amber. She returned his smile then looked around distractedly, clearly enjoying the loveliness of the room. But in Jamie's mind and heart, the beauty of the surroundings paled in comparison to Amber's.

He cared for her deeply and knew his life was better for having her in it. He could scarcely look at her and not want to drag her to the nearest horizontal surface, though he'd thus far restrained himself quite a bit lest he shock her. His heart had ached when he'd seen how taken she was with Meara and how much Meara responded to the lavish attention Amber had given her so far. He wondered if that wasn't love. He wished he could just carelessly say the words, but he was loath to pin a label of something he didn't fully understand on what he felt.

No, he couldn't bring himself to say those words to her. Each time they made love his heart cried out to say it, knowing she needed to hear that, but his mind always overruled him and refused to let him give his feelings that name. He silently cursed his father, and Iris and his uncle, whose words and deeds always found a way to darken even his happiest moments. He fisted his hand under the table while he schooled his expression to one of utter contentment, determined not to allow those faithless people from his past to ruin the evening.

As soon as Jamie took his seat a waiter approached with a silver bucket and the bottle of champagne he'd ordered. When he'd popped the cork and poured it into the glistening crystal glasses, he retreated with a formal bow.

Amber looked a bit suspicious. "Are we to have a celebration?"

"A special night, I hope. Now tell me, what it is I don't know about families and how you learned this when you lived a solitary childhood."

"I had brothers until I was six. They died of fever when my parents did. My friend Abby in Pennsylvania had brothers. The Kanes welcomed me into their family circle often. Later, when my uncle sent me away to school, my friend Patience often invited me to her home. Her brothers were terrors and her mother gentle and sweet. In both families females presented a united front against the males. An infraction against one was an infraction against all. It was quite a lot of fun."

He grinned. "Which means you are conspiring to win my daughter. I am to be the poor, lone, put-upon male of the household."

Seeing her pearly-white teeth flash in her mischievous grin, he decided to give her the pearls first. "I purchased a gift for you," he said and drew out the black velvet pouch. He laid it on her plate.

"Is this what your secret trip with Meara was about?" she asked as she opened the box. She gasped as she drew out the necklace, bracelet and earrings. "Oh, Jamie, they are beautiful."

"Not half as beautiful as the ladies they were chosen for. They are twins to Meara's except for the earrings. I suppose they go along with your theory of homes being a camp divided. Now your group has matching pearls to wear as a standard."

"No. You don't understand. Not divided. The two camps are united unless someone gets up to mischief." She tilted her head, then her gaze narrowed. "Is there a traitor in the female camp already? Or a spy, perhaps. You are sure you had no other reason to purchase these than so Meara and I would match? Mimm hasn't said anything, has she? Or anyone else?"

Once again she'd confused him. Perhaps she thought Mimm had noticed Amber had no jewelry of quality. "What would make you think she said anything about your need of such things?"

She smiled, a beaming grin that rivaled the cheery light from the gas sconces lining the walls. "I thought she or someone else might have let you know I have a gift for you, as well. Though I am afraid you will have to wait a rather long while to receive it."

He raised an eyebrow. "A gift for me? How could you

have purchased a gift for me? I haven't yet arranged for your allowance. I will tomorrow, of course. Though I suppose you wouldn't have undertaken a trip as long as the one we just finished with no funds of your own along."

"No, I wouldn't," she said. "But this is something I am…creating."

Now he was truly confused. "As you did your green dress? You've decided to sew something for me?"

She laughed—really an adorably **unla**dylike snort. "No, silly man. I am increasing."

A shaft of elation shot through Jamie. "Increasing?" He grabbed her hands. If this heart full of joy wasn't love, then what was it? "A baby, Pixie? We are to have a child? Truly?"

Amber nodded. "Mimm says it is why I have been so tired and weepy. I do apologize for my strange moods of late. I feared there was something much more serious and tragic wrong with me. Perhaps I will present you with a member for your camp to ease Meara's inevitable defection." Her eyes seemed to sparkle and her brows arched. "I will win her over, you know."

"I will gladly remain the solitary male in our household as long as you are fine and the child is delivered safely. We must get you to a doctor. That is important, is it not? Iris had a doctor in residence with us."

"I have already seen your friend, Malcolm Campbell."

"Ah, the spy you worried about since I asked that he see you. When is it to be?"

"He promised not to tell you, but I wasn't sure he would keep silent. He says toward the late part of March. Tell me, if he studied to be a doctor at Edinburgh, what was it you studied there?"

"Engineering."

"Perhaps our son will be an engineer or architect like you," she said dreamily. "He will be a handsome earl like his father, as well, I suppose."

Jamie frankly hoped all their children were girls. Let the damned title pass to Alex. "Perhaps she will be a teacher like her mother. A shaper of minds."

"Why did you choose engineering?"

"I had to take up something and I like to build. To go from a concept, to drawing, to a tangible structure."

"My friend Abby's husband is a mining engineer. He wanted to make mining safe, but I'm afraid that will never happen. I'd like to send them and my uncle a wire to let them know of our marriage and that I am not with the family where I'd planned to be."

He knew of the man she'd spoken of. He'd tangled with Joshua Wheaton. If Jamie hadn't read the man wrong, he'd protected Helena with a pretend engagement until she'd reached her majority, then promptly smuggled her out of town with Amber's help. Then he'd married the mother of his son the very same night. Jamie owed the man his thanks for doing what he'd been unable to do because of Helena's distrust of him. And for sending Jamie on the voyage that had put Amber in his life.

"Do you want to tell those back home of the baby?"

She blushed a bit. "I'd like to keep it to ourselves just for a bit. I *will* send letters later and tell them, but right now I just want to do as I promised—let them know I've arrived safely."

"We'll go to the telegraph office in the morning. I'm sure your uncle and friends are anxious for word of you." Her mention of Wheatonburg, Pennsylvania, reminded him that he'd made contact with detectives that day in the hope of locating Helena. He needed to make sure she was safe and settled wherever it was she'd gone after leaving the small coal town. He owed her father that much.

Amber cut into the flaky crust of her apple dumpling after thoroughly enjoying a delicious dinner. The dessert fairly melted in her mouth. The atmosphere in the restaurant was regal, the waiters attentive. As was Jamie. She could have been the only other person in the room considering how undivided his attention was as he watched her. He'd not touched his cheesecake.

"Are you no longer hungry?" she asked, fidgeting under his intense scrutiny.

The left side of his mouth kicked up in a sensual smile. "Very."

Her fork clattered noisily to her plate.

He chuckled. As often happened, that deep rumbling sound made her hungry for something more personal than the delicious apple dumpling she'd been enjoying so much.

"I have something else for you," he said, his gaze blazing with aroused fire, but then uncertainty crept in. "I hope you like them. I can take them back if you'd like something grander."

"I learned early in my life to cherish any gift."

He nodded, took a small pouch from his inside coat pocket and dumped it into his cupped hand, then reached for her left hand and took off the onyx ring she'd worn since he'd placed it there and slid it back on his finger. She had an idea that she would now have a real wedding band. He slid a silver-colored ring on her finger and she could only stare.

It wasn't a plain band as she'd expected from his talk of his purchase not being grand. Instead it was filigreed with daisy-shaped flowers, tiny sapphires and amethysts as their centers. Then he added another ring, also filigreed in the same way, but with three larger flowers, diamonds at their centers, the middle one larger than the other two. The same smaller daisy shapes as those on the band filled in around the larger ones, again with tiny amethysts or sapphires at their centers. It was like a delicate bouquet rimming her finger—the first flowers she'd ever been given.

She continued to stare down at them through sudden tears, then she looked up at him. "They're the most beautiful rings I've ever seen."

He smiled and sighed, clearly in relief, then he caught a tear as it slipped out of the corner of her eye. "Going with me to the jeweler was Meara's secret. In all honesty it was she who chose them," he admitted quietly.

"Is that why you seemed so unsure?"

He shrugged, but she knew from his intense expression that he didn't feel in the least casual. This was of utmost importance to him. If so, then why wouldn't he say he loved her?

She couldn't say it first. She just couldn't. After all, she'd entered this marriage clearheadedly. He'd been the one delirious and at the edge of death, desperate to leave his child into the care of someone he trusted. His continued silence left her with no choice but to conclude that his silence was still about Helena and that the rings—the marriage itself—was about making the best of a bad situation. Yet he'd said they came from his heart. Why did he have to send such mixed signals?

"I thought Meara would tell me how excellent my taste was and we'd be on our way," he admitted, drawing her back to the topic at hand. "What I had in mind was something larger and well…ahem. Actually, the little tyrant overruled me. She called the ones I'd chosen ostentatious. I thought the jeweler would swallow his tongue. Where on earth did she get that word anyway?"

Amber bit her lip to help hold back her laughter. Leave it to Jamie to lighten a heavy moment. "I imagine she learned it from Mimm." She rolled her eyes and made him laugh. "She seems a bit scornful of the upper crust."

"I can almost imagine the context." Jamie looked so put out Amber couldn't hold in her laughter any longer. And, if she wasn't mistaken in the low light, she thought he actually blushed. She laughed harder. "Did she use it correctly?" she managed at last.

And then he smiled. "I'm afraid she did. I'm glad I could amuse you. I've missed the sound of your laughter these last few weeks."

Unwilling to touch that statement, Amber stuck to Meara as a safe subject. "Your child is quite intelligent. So tell me about the rings you'd chosen."

"Something to rival the family set that sits in a vault back at Adair. I wanted you to have my rings now—besides that, I didn't want you to wear the family rings. Iris wore those. I want the only reminder of that part of my life to be Meara. It is only because of her that I cannot regret my marriage."

"That is as it should be." She stroked the rings. "These are lovely, Jamie."

He smiled, staring at her. "You are lovely, Pixie. As for

the rings, the only part I had in choosing these is that I asked to see only those rings made of platinum. I thought that suited you. Then Meara decreed that you wouldn't like a ring that was all about show but rather that you'd want one about sentiment. Out of the mouth of babes, correct? As soon as she said it, I knew she had the right of it. I don't understand how she knew you so quickly."

"You have a wise daughter."

He cleared his throat again. "The...uh...the amethysts and sapphires—"

"Are the color of your eyes and hers?" she guessed. Jamie nodded. "She is very wise indeed. As are you for having listened to her. I love them."

Still holding her hand, he traced the ring with his index finger. She'd have sworn the cool feel of the platinum warmed under his touch. "If the baby has your brown eyes, I'll have some replaced with brown diamonds. I saw some today. They're quite unusual."

"Perhaps. Will we still be here when the baby is born? I like Dr. Campbell and would be happy in his care."

Jamie frowned in thought. "I hadn't thought that far, but I don't see why we cannot remain if that is what you wish."

"Or should we return to New York or even to Adair? You will eventually need to, won't you?"

"Again, I hadn't decided." He squeezed her hand a bit. "I thought we would make that determination together. I hate to take you away from your country. I know how patriotic Americans are. Besides which, I don't particularly want to go back to Ireland. There are so few good memories waiting for me at Adair. I would never return if I didn't have a duty to Adair's people."

"Who looks after the estate now?"

"After firing the steward Oswald had employed, I hired a man I could trust. My man of business oversees him. I trust both men completely. The local vicar also reports that things are much better for the people now that the land is thriving again. I had thought to ask Alex to stand in my stead there, but I fear he'd rather shoot me than do me any service."

Amber hated that Mimm had involved her in keeping the secret of Alexander's presence in New York from Jamie. He was so dispirited about his estrangement from his cousin that she almost told him. But Mimm seemed so canny. Could she be wrong about Alexander? Or was she right? After all, she had apparently known the man since childhood. Could Jamie be mistaken about his cousin?

"Perhaps he's forgiven you and you should write him. He could be waiting to hear from you," she said, hoping to encourage him.

"I wouldn't think so. He hasn't touched the trust fund I set up for him."

Amber drew hope from that fact. Mimm could very well be wrong about his cousin Alexander. But then again, if he were in league with his father it would break Jamie's heart. It was all so confusing and so delicate a subject. Wouldn't Alexander have used the money Jamie set aside for him if he were as mercenary and dishonest as his father? There was no way to know, she supposed. "Let's not talk of such depressing subjects," she suggested. "Tonight is for celebration."

Jamie's smile was only a bit sad. "Yes. Let's not. We have much happier subjects to discuss. Have you given a thought to names for our addition? I warn you, I'd want our son to have his own name and be his own person. I don't want to name a son after me."

"What a thing to say! That isn't at all like you. Your mother gave her life giving you yours. And as she named you, I rather like your name."

"Oh, it isn't the name at all. I rather like it myself. I gladly kept it to honor my mother and my father's love of her."

"Is this to do with something else your poisonous uncle drummed into your head?"

He winced. "He tried to force me to change my name legally to James, but I stood up to him and refused because I was determined to honor the woman my father spoke so highly of. I paid the price daily for that defiance." He smiled sadly for a second, then his eyes trained on her and his lips turned up in a genuinely happy grin. "As my new wife seems so happy with the name, I'm more than glad to have been so pigheaded."

"Someday I'd like to smack that man!"

Jamie burst out laughing, then sobered as he reached out and stroked her cheek. "So fierce. And so very lovely."

She took his hand in hers. "I'm afraid I slip out of the ladylike persona I learned while away at school a bit too often for a countess."

"I rather like it when you do." He leaned forward and whispered, "Especially in bed. Are you going to finish that dumpling? As I said, I find myself hungering for sustenance of another sort."

"I think I am, as well."

Jamie stood, and held out his hand. "Lady Adair. I believe we should retire to our room and continue this discussion in private."

She couldn't help but smile as she stood and walked to him. "Privacy is something that can never be overrated," she whispered as she passed him.

"Never," he agreed as he put a hand at the small of her back. She didn't know how he made a gesture of gentlemanly protection feel so naughtily, deliciously dangerous.

Or so good.

Honestly, she was putty in the man's hands. It was something she couldn't regret. Because even if he didn't love her, she loved him.

Chapter Fifteen

"Lord Adair, it is now we go on to California Street," Gunter called over his shoulder, as they turned onto a street with a sharp uphill rise so typical of San Francisco.

Meara bounced on the rear-facing seat of the carriage next to Mimm. Her eyes alight with mischief, she said, "This is our street so now you must close your eyes."

Jamie nodded, grinning when Amber looked at him, with a puzzled expression on her face. "It seems only fair," he said.

"Why is that?"

He leaned toward her. "You were my surprise one morning many days ago. Now I get to give you a surprise," he whispered.

The words no sooner left his mouth than Jamie wanted to call them back. He prayed she would think of the way they'd shared their bodies some time before dawn and not the argument that had separated them after the sun awakened them. In the next instant, he took note of a sweet blush spreading across Amber's face and breathed a quiet sigh of relief. Her mind must have gone where his had.

"I seem to remember that day as a surprise for me," she whispered, then added louder, "I must hide my eyes then, mustn't I?" She put her head down, hiding her face in her hands, ostensibly for the sake of Meara's game.

The brim of Amber's black straw hat hid her face from Mimm and Meara, however. But the plum satin bow with its tails forming a lovely train down her back only partially hid her blush-pink neck from his sight. The shining white ostrich feathers that decorated the brim bounced and blew in the morning breeze, distracting Meara, who seemed to watch them with fascination. They didn't distract him at all.

Her hat perfectly topped off the ready-made plum morning dress and matching jacket he had taken Amber out to find yesterday when she'd wired her uncle of her safe arrival and their marriage. She hunched her shoulders now and the jacket's black-velvet collar hid the rest of her neck from his gaze.

Not to be outdone, Jamie moved the tail of the hat's bow, and kissed the warm and luscious column of her neck. The plans he'd made to get her alone once they arrived sent a spike of need arrowing through him. He could almost see her naked in the morning light, lying among the rumpled sheets.

Mimm swatted him for his mischief and the vision disappeared. "Leave the girl be, you jackanapes. I raised you better. You know I did. Why did you have the girl hide her eyes? So you could have her at a disadvantage? Here I was thinkin' you wanted to see her face when she sees the fine house you drew up and ordered from that builder you hired."

"You didn't tell me you'd designed the house," Amber muttered behind her hands as the carriage labored up the hill.

"I hadn't wanted you to know so you'd give your honest opinion," he admitted. "I know you'll never ask for changes now, and I'll never know for sure how you truly feel."

Her head bounced up, eyes firmly closed, and she said, "That was unfair, *my lord*. Suppose I hadn't liked it? If I had said so, I would feel awful once I learned it was your design."

"Uh-oh, I'm in trouble. She's 'my lording' me again. It always means I've put a foot wrong," he told Mimm, then turned back to Amber. "I *am* sorry, Pixie. I only want to please you and to know for certain that I have."

She opened her eyes and stared straight into his. No worry of her seeing the house, even though it was only a few houses ahead. It was he she was interested in at that moment. She seemed to be silently telling him something and he was very much afraid he knew exactly what.

Tell me you love me. That's all I want of you, her gaze seemed to say. But the words wouldn't come. His throat seemed to swell, choking off the feelings overflowing his heart. Was this love? Was she telling him she loved him?

What was the matter with him? She was *not* Iris. Not even remotely like her. She was certainly not anything like his uncle. Why couldn't he find a way to define what was in his heart? Why couldn't he at least use the words even if he was unsure it was what he felt?

Jamie longed to let himself off the hook by claiming his hesitation was because she withheld the words, as well. But he couldn't hide behind that. He understood why she kept silent. He wondered when he would stop having to pay for those hurtful accusations of his that awful morning.

Then her eyes dropped closed and his opportunity was lost, but he couldn't pretend he hadn't seen the longing written in her dark gaze. He also saw guilt mixed in.

Could she still think she'd somehow ruined his life by agreeing to marry him? He didn't know how to re-assure her without saying those three impossible, elu-sive words. He hated himself and those who'd done this to them more and more each day. But how did someone who had never even witnessed love between a man and woman recognize it in himself and his mate?

"Whoa!" Gunter called to the team and brought the carriage drifting smoothly to a stop.

"Don't peek," Meara ordered. "Lift her down, Da."

"Actually I think she should see it from here," he said, sending Mimm a silent message. He wanted this moment with Amber alone.

"No. She should see it from the street!" his little one argued.

Mimm turned and said something to Gunter, who quickly hopped down, then helped her to the ground. When the driver put his hand out to Meara, she crossed her arms and stubbornly shook her head.

"Go with Mimm," Jamie told her.

"Come, *liebchen*. Leave *dein vater und dein mutter*...alone," Gunter said, still offering his hand.

Meara sighed dramatically, but stood and leaped into Gunter's arms. The older man laughed and swung her playfully to the ground. Then Meara joined Mimm, and Gunter walked to the horses and held them, looking the other way to give them the privacy he'd asked for.

"My lord," Mimm called as they mounted the front

steps, "don't you be forgettin' to carry your bride over the threshold."

The front door closed, cutting off Meara's running list of questions about how her life would change now that she had a mother and her da had a wife.

Jamie transferred to the rear-facing seat so he could see Amber's expression. He took her hands in his; even then in that moment of anticipation and preoccupation over her reaction he marveled at the delicacy of her hands. "You can open your eyes, Pixie."

She did and as her eyes widened they softened, too. "Oh, it is lovely, Jamie." She smiled. "It looks like my friend's fancy wedding cake!"

Jamie looked up at the house, seeing it in a new light, and laughed. "I suppose it does look like a wedding cake. Perfect. That is one more thing you were cheated of with our hasty marriage. Now I've managed to give you one, however accidentally. And outsized!"

He'd built the clapboard house as an investment but had designed it with Meara in mind. He'd meticulously drawn the turned Italianate columns and the fretwork on the small porch as a whimsical invitation to enter. The elaborate cornices of the two-story, stacked bay windows, and the intricately carved corbels that supported the roof overhang, were meant to enhance that feeling of whimsy. Even though he'd resisted the trend toward rather wild colors by sticking entirely to white, Jamie had apparently succeeded beyond his wildest dreams. He chuckled. Apparently, he'd built his wife a two-story wedding cake. "Would you like to go in and see the inside of your new home?"

She nodded and he helped her down.

"If you didn't know whether you'd be staying here

in San Francisco, why did you build a home here?" she asked.

"As an investment, but mostly so Meara would have a place to call her own while we're here. I may sell it when we decide to head east again. But in the meantime, she has a home to help her feel secure. Don't you think that was the worst part of being sent away to school? Not having a place to call your own?"

"I suppose it was. But I understood that my uncle was terrified to be left alone with a girl to steer into womanhood. Still, even though I understood, I did feel very much like a ship adrift with no port to call home."

"Exactly. That is a feeling I never want Meara, our baby or any who follow to feel. Wherever she goes, I want her to know she'll always have a home with us."

She smiled up at him, and he knew all he wanted out of life was to make sure she always looked at him that way. As if he was her hero. He hoped and prayed he could live up to what he saw in her eyes.

He bent and scooped her up in his arms.

"Jamie, this is silly and those steps are rather steep."

"We must ward off any evil spirits," he countered. "Besides which, you are as light as a feather. You cannot weigh more than eight stone." He carried her up the steps and through the front door with Meara, whooping and laughing, greeting them in the marble vestibule. Had his daughter not been there he'd have carried his countess straight to their room. And that second part of this bridal tradition couldn't happen fast enough to suit him.

When he'd looked around the house earlier in the week, he'd been very pleased with the house's interiors. Semi-circular columns with beautifully carved capitals stood like soldiers guarding the entrances and exits of each room. There were pocket doors hidden in each doorway, but they were barely noticeable. All the ceilings were coffered and the inset spaces were decorated with ornate papers. The walls were also either papered, stenciled or richly paneled. The floors were of inlaid hardwoods covered with thick woven rugs from all over the Orient. Remarkable iridescent tiles covered the fireplaces that sat waiting, ready to warm each room when needed.

He put Amber down in the parlor. It was a large receiving room meant to be the main entertaining space. Another public area was the dining room that lay just beyond a twelve-foot-high set of carved pocket doors that separated the rooms.

Architecture didn't seem to be on Amber's mind, however, when she sucked in an excited breath and rushed to the oil-on-canvas painting that hung over the mantel. Instead of the usual floral, it was a moody seascape he'd fallen in love with in a New York gallery.

She stared at the signature on the bottom right. "It's by Samuel Colman," Amber said. "He spoke at Vassar when I was first there." She turned around, looking at the room. It was decorated in the same varying shades of blue as were in the painting. "It's perfect in here."

"I'm not that clever, Pixie. I sent the painting to my builder, and asked that he use it as a guide for the colors of the parlor. You have an interest in art?" he asked, intrigued to learn yet another thing about her. "Do you paint?"

"At boarding school we learned both watercolor and oils," she said. "But I prefer the bolder color and contrast of oil."

"Most ladies of quality mess about in watercolors

alone," Mimm put in, standing in the doorway to the dining room.

Amber looked from Mimm to Meara, clearly not feeling free to say what she wanted. Then she turned and looked at him, raising her chin as if to say, *I never claimed to be a lady of quality.*

In case that was the message, he smiled and pulled her into an embrace, whispering, "I prefer vibrancy of color and I thank God for everything you are." He took her hand and added, "Please believe it."

She blushed a bit and nodded. He loosened his hold, took her shoulders and turned her toward Mimm, then looped his arms around her at the waist. "I told you, Mimm," Jamie said, "Amber is an original."

Mimm smiled broadly. "That she is. That she is. You should rest, my lady. I'll occupy our Meara while Jamie shows you the house and you get settled in." Her eyes sparkled as she took Meara's hand. "Come along, little lamb. It's time your da and your new mum had a bit more *privacy.*"

"They just got privacy and all Da did was carry her in. How come she couldn't walk up the steps? And how much privacy are they gonna need?" she demanded as she stomped along next to Mimm toward the back of the house.

"Just a bit now and again," Mimm said, leading the way and laughing. "Come, draw them a happy picture. We'll be all the way in the back garden," she called over her shoulder from the far side of the dining room.

"She's irrepressible, isn't she?" Amber said, watching them head toward the back of the house.

Jamie laughed. "Which one? Meara or Mimm?"

Amber laughed. "Both, I suppose," she said, turning to face him again and resting her head on his shoulder.

"I'm just glad they gave me an excuse to get you alone. Is it too early for a nap?" he asked as he wrapped her tighter in his arms. He knew the second she realized how aroused he already was.

"Jamie, it's morning."

She sounded so scandalized he laughed. "I seem to remember missing breakfast several times on the ship—"

"But the ship was different. A time out of time is what you called it."

He nipped at her ear. "It doesn't matter where we are," he whispered, the timbre of his voice already giving away the depth of his need of her. "There isn't a time of the day when I don't want you. Come play with me, my pixie. There's another threshold I need to carry you over."

Her head dropped back and when she stared into his eyes there was heat in her gaze. But her uncertainty showed in her question. "What about all the household staff you hired?"

He winked and gave her the most sensual grin he could muster. "I suppose the back stairs will be buzzing if they haven't finished upstairs yet today."

"Jamie!"

"Calm yourself." He chuckled. "I planned ahead. With the exception of the kitchen staff, all the servants have the rest of the day off. Even Lily O'Donnell, your new lady's maid. She was rather concerned that you wouldn't be able to do without her. I'm afraid I was forced to admit she'd replaced me in a job I'd trained at for months." He scooped her up again and headed for the stairs.

"It seems to me you had our morning rather carefully designed to be scandalous. I think Mimm and Meara aren't the only ones irrepressible in your household, Lord Adair."

"I'm gratified you noticed, Lady Adair," he said. Then, laughing, he vaulted up the stairs as fast as he could when carrying a pixie and an unmerciful hard-on.

"Oh, Jamie, it's lovely," Amber gasped as he carried her into the moss-green master suite with its gold-leaf stenciled boarder running near the ceiling just below the mahogany crown molding.

"That was the plan. I'm glad you like it, but the décor suddenly pales now that you're in it. It is you who are lovely," he told her as he kicked the door shut behind him.

He set her down and cupped her face, then reverently touched his lips to hers with the barest of pressure. She leaned in and pressed harder against him. Her tongue sneaking out to trace the seam of his lips nearly sent him to his knees. He broke the kiss.

"And once again," he told her, "I shall thoroughly enjoy playing lady's maid." He immediately divested her of her now slightly askew hat. After sending it flying across the room to land on the brocade chaise longue nestled in the bay-window space, he moved on to her hair, pulling pins out and dropping them willy-nilly to the floor.

She sighed. "You've become a very messy lady's maid. I fear your employment is certainly in danger. But at least as a valet, I'll have little to live up to." Grinning, she tugged on his cravat, untied it and sent it flying over her shoulder.

Jamie laughed at that and, not to be outdone, divested her of her jacket. Holding it by the collar, he extended his arm and dropped it.

She giggled, then dragged his coat off his shoulders and tossed it to join hers on the floor. Next her fingers went to work on his shirt buttons as he unbuttoned the ones that marched in a neat row down her back.

He noticed with pleasure her delicious little shiver when he reached the last button at the base of her spine and traced the indentation of her lower spine.

She'd finished with his shirt, her breathing quick and shallow, and had his trousers loosed by then. She cupped his swollen shaft in a soft hand. Jamie groaned. She was killing him.

In self-defense, Jamie stepped back and pulled her dress over her head. Then he shrugged out of his shirt and pants, knowing she'd unman him if she touched him again. But her ripe lips and delicate body called to him and he pulled her against him. After that, mouths fused, undergarments fell to the floor, hands—his and hers—touched and aroused with equal power.

Naked and needy, he stripped the covers back and lifted her in his arms before laying her on their high, canopied bed. Looking down at her enraptured expression, he felt triumphant. But he also read a look of love in her eyes and that pierced him to the quick.

He still couldn't make himself say what was in his heart. His only outlet for what he felt for her was to adore her with his body. Jamie vowed this was one interlude she wouldn't soon forget.

She held her arms out to him, inviting him to cover her with his body, but another kind of need stopped him in his tracks. "Too fast," he whispered as he climbed in bed and hovered over her.

She gave him a confused little half frown, half smile. "I thought that was the idea."

Tenderness swamped his imprisoned heart. "Change of plans," he told her and eased down next to her. Cupping her breast, he leaned in and took her nipple in his mouth, suckling it until she was panting, begging, then he moved to the other. He felt her frustrated, inflamed moan deep in his belly, but he beat back the need to feel himself slide into her. To feel her envelop him in her warmth.

Instead, he moved his mouth lower, kissing her still flat belly. "Hello in there," he whispered his lips moving over her abdomen in feather-light caresses.

Then he trailed kisses even lower. On his knees now, he pressed her restless limbs apart. Tracing kisses over her hips, he took small nips that he soothed with his tongue in the next instant. Her gasps, moans and pleas to end it only drove him on.

When he reached the soft skin of her inner thighs, she arched her back and begged him to stop, but he moved ever upward as he pressed her ankles toward her rump so her knees were bent. She called out, "What are you doing?"

He looked up into her hot and troubled gaze. Clearly she was more than confused with this new lesson. And a touch apprehensive, too. But sometimes a bit of nerves helped build anticipation. "I'm giving my lady a morning to remember. It's fine. It'll be wonderful. Trust me," he urged and realized it was now he who'd turned to begging. "Let me show you what you mean to me."

Then, without waiting for an answer he feared she wasn't ready to give, he began again on his relentless campaign to claim and worship every last inch of her. Finally when she was near insensible, he parted her nest of golden curls and laved her with his tongue, found her core with his fingers and stroked her until her hips found his rhythm and she shattered beautifully.

Then, after soothing her to near slumber, he began again. Took her there again.

And again.

Finally with a strength born of what her expression said was beyond desperation, she grabbed him and pulled him over her. Tears flowing into her hair, she hooked her legs around him and drew him home. "Jamie," she sobbed, breathlessly. And the muscles surrounding him began contracting at once. "I love you. I cannot help it. I am sorry. I love you. Please. Please."

He was no fool. He knew what she needed of him. She needed the words. But he couldn't make himself say them. He wanted to. His heart ached with the need to say them. He even opened his mouth, but the words had long ago been locked inside him. When he loved openly he lost or was crushed by those who'd muttered those dangerous words. Consumed with so many needs he couldn't sort them out, Jamie followed her into the storm and his climax took him under with her.

In that transcendent moment, he hated the people who still held the key to his inner self. He hated them with a fierceness that frightened him. She would never know that hers weren't the only tears soaking into the pillow as they fell into weary sleep.

His last thoughts before exhaustion claimed him were, *Does she understand that if I could say it, I would? Know it, Pixie. Please, know that I don't know what this is I feel. If it is love it so mixed up with pain that I've locked it inside me and lost the key.*

Chapter Sixteen

Amber woke and rolled toward the other side of the bed. She reached out a hand. Jamie's place was cold. She was alone in the room.

The musky scent of their lovemaking brought it all back to her. All the things he'd done. She remembered the words he'd wrung from her with his relentless loving.

But it wasn't *love*making. Not *lov*ing, either. He'd left love out—banished it—by his silence. She'd begged for those words, but he hadn't said them.

He'd claimed he'd been trying to show her what she meant to him. Or had it been what he *thought* of her? Well, actions had certainly spoken even louder than his silence. So what had his actions said? That he enjoyed her body. That to him what they did was about pleasure—not love.

Which made her what?

His bought-and-paid-for whore? A brood mare? Both? *Why couldn't he have lied?*

"No. I don't want a lie," she said to the empty room. "I wanted him to love me the way I love him. But I don't think that's going to happen."

After his silence earlier, she'd lost all hope that he would ever love her. After all that time on the ship together, now when the daily chores of life were about to intrude, how much chance was there that he'd even notice her enough for deep feelings to emerge? They should already be there.

Weary even after what felt like hours of sleep, Amber sat up and noticed her clothes had been picked up. They lay neatly arranged on the chaise longue. It must have been Jamie who'd done that. Lily, her new lady's maid, would have hung them up.

A mantel clock ticking in the quiet room drew Amber's attention. She squinted in the low light and started when it rang three times. "So I did sleep for hours," she muttered and swung her feet off the bed and slid to the floor.

The carpet under her feet was thick and plush. Top quality like everything else Jamie bought—everything but his wife.

Trying to shake off the melancholy, and naked as the day she'd been born, she padded to the doors on the other side of the room, peeking in the first. Jamie's clothes hung to one side of the small dressing room. A club chair and an occasional table sat near a window on the far wall and a small dresser and shaving stand occupied the other. Next to the door was a foldaway bed. Praying that wasn't for his valet, she backed out quickly to close the door, lest Hadley catch her standing there naked.

The next room was a bit larger and was another dressing room. Hers this time. As with Jamie's, her clothes hung on a pole along the one wall. No, not hers. The only ones hanging there were Helena's castoffs.

Apparently, Lily O'Donnell didn't approve of home-made dresses for the wife of an earl and wealthy businessman.

Her trunk sat just inside the room next to a dresser. There was also a dressing table and low backless chair sitting before it. A pretty beveled glass window allowed the late afternoon sun in and filled the room with rainbows.

She walked to the trunk and found her dressing gown and her other things. The robe had been part of her trousseau, made for her by Joseph's mother. She put it on and wrapped her arms around her middle. The soft fabric soothed her a little bit, though it left her hungering for the arms of someone who loved her.

She saw herself in a full-length cheval mirror, remembering the first time she'd seen the wrapper. The very next Saturday she'd been going to marry the man she'd loved. But by Wednesday he'd been clinging to life, when death would have been a mercy, just so he could put voice to his love for her one last time.

She sank onto the dressing-table bench and her tears fell like rain. She could no longer see Joseph's face in her mind. Love had a new face. A new name. Several names. Jamie Reynolds. Earl of Adair. Husband. Father of her unborn child.

She could no longer hear Joseph's voice, either, but *it* had been replaced by heartbreaking silence. Jamie was a man who couldn't love her.

Because he loved another woman.

In the dressing-table mirror, she caught the reflection of Helena's clothing hanging along the opposite wall. She wanted to scream. Defiantly she dried her tears on her hem and went back to the trunk. She pulled out her sprigged muslin and hung it up. Then she went into the next room, a modern bathroom, and ran a warm bath.

She added bath salts, determined to wash Jamie's scent away. After pinning her hair up, she soaked and scrubbed then dried off and dressed. In *her* dress. The one she'd made with Joseph in mind. Joseph, the man who'd loved her and had endured the torture of being carried, crushed from the mine, so he could tell her one more time before he'd let death take him.

Then she went to explore her new home. She had always made the best of any situation and she wouldn't stop now. Jamie didn't treat her poorly. His lack of feeling for her wouldn't hurt so much if he did. He was her baby's father and she did love him. She would have to find a way to live with the circumstances life had thrown in her way. But it wouldn't be easy.

She went out the back door of the dressing room and found a narrow hall that ran along the side wall of the house. It serviced the dressing rooms and bath. The hall connected to a branching set of back stairs.

The other branch of those stairs led to three bedrooms. Meara and Mimm occupied two of them and the third, which looked like a combination classroom and playroom. It could be used for the baby if Jamie decided to stay in San Francisco for a while. Along the other side of the building was a bedroom and bath to care for the needs of the inhabitants of the four minor bedrooms. The bedroom was decorated as a guest room.

It wasn't a large house by some standards. Certainly not if compared to the places where she'd stayed in the summers of her college years. But it was comfortable, very pretty and, because it was Jamie's, built of the finest materials.

She went down the back stairs to the kitchen.
Attached to kitchen was a cozy breakfast room. Then
she moved into an elegant dining room with thick mold-
ings, dark-paneled wainscoting, silk wall coverings
above an intricately carved chair rail. A gleaming Chippendale table and chairs sat in the center of the room
with a shining crystal chandelier hanging over it. The
table was already set for dinner with some of the same
china displayed in the Chippendale breakfront. A server
sat in a bay window with two crystal lamps on its
marble surface. The afternoon sun streaming in caught
in the crystal prisms and bounced light around the room.

She heard Jamie talking somewhere down a short
hall off the dining room. Hurt though she was, she went
toward his voice, drawn to him as always. He couldn't
help how he felt or didn't feel, after all. And she had to
make the best of her situation for their child's sake. She
hoped his smile would help cheer her.

Then his words became clear and her heart nearly
seized in her chest.

"You're reasonably sure Miss Conwell headed west,
yet you say your agent could track her only as far as the
depot in St. Louis? Then why do you believe she stayed
at the Menger Hotel in San Antonio?"

He was looking for Helena. Again. Still. She didn't
understand what he hoped to gain, but he couldn't have
hurt her more had he tried. He'd fathered her child
because he'd been so determined to make their marriage
work. Yet he didn't love her and he'd renewed his search
for the woman he did love. He must have renewed the
search while she napped on Monday.

At practically the first moment available to him.

Again his actions in their bed that morning returned

to haunt her. What had he meant? Oh, yes. She'd forgotten. She was his brood mare to get an heir on and only a bit better than a whore he used to slake his lust.

"We had looked for her for another client, but he canceled our contract. We'd been using a picture of her in our files," the man with Jamie said. "Using it, we definitely tracked her to St. Louis, and several people place her arriving in San Antonio."

"But you've lost her there."

Almost like a moth drawn to the flame that would destroy it, Amber moved into the open doorway. Jamie sat behind a desk facing the door, and the man, his back to her, sat facing Jamie.

"Our agent is once again on the trail of a young woman he thinks—"

Jamie's gaze collided with hers and he put his hand up, stopping the man midsentence. Guilt swamped Jamie's expression as he stood. The man looked over his shoulder, then stood, as well.

Amber forced her posture straight and as regal as she could make it while her patched-together heart was busy breaking into a million pieces. She walked forward. "Have a seat, gentlemen," she said, her voice not as steady as she'd have liked it.

They both sat rather uneasily.

"Please, go ahead," she told the short balding man. "Helena is a particular friend of mine. We are so alike we are practically interchangeable. Isn't that right, my lord? Oh, pardon my poor manners. I am the earl's wife." The man's surprise showed this was new information for him. "Didn't you know he had one? I might be inconvenient, but he's apparently stuck with me. When was it you thought you would know more of dear Helena?"

The man cut a glance at Jamie, who closed his eyes and nodded. The man went on. "We can find no record of her actually staying at the Menger, but our agent in San Antonio feels sure she stayed there because someone recognized the woman as a person she directed there. Our agent in San Antonio is one of Pinkerton's best. He'll run her to ground."

Amber forced herself to smile. She'd reached California so her promise to act as a decoy was actually finished. And he had implied that Franklin Gowery had cut off his search. Abby had wired her first thing that morning with her congratulations and with the news that Brendan and Helena were safe.

"Perhaps a little more information might help your search," she said. "I assume you're still looking for Helena Conwell. Perhaps if you looked for her under another name."

The man gave her a slightly nervous glance, but his condescension showed through. "Yes, we do think she's using aliases, ma'am. But that makes it harder, you see, because she'd change it often."

"No, it is you who doesn't see," she said, anger entering her voice. And she let it. She let it wash over her. "Neither does my husband. You should be trying to find Helena *Kane.* Or Mr. and Mrs. *Brendan* Kane. They were married the night they left Wheatonburg."

She turned to Jamie then and took in his startled expression. "You see, *darling,* Helena's been married to the man she loves since February. I got a wire from Abby Wheaton this morning. Abby's husband, Joshua, has managed to clear Brendan's name in spite of her guardian's lies. So you see, there's nothing you or Franklin Gowery can do about any of it. She's beyond your reach. Unfortunately, I am not. If you gentlemen will excuse me, I find I need some air."

She turned and fled through the house, heading to the back garden. Tears blinding her, she stumbled on the steps, but Jamie had followed and caught her. He helped right her balance. She grabbed onto the railing and yanked her arm from his grasp. She turned at the foot of the steps and backed away as she looked up at him. He stood as if frozen on the steps.

"Leave. Me. Alone," she screamed. "Haven't you hurt me enough for one day?" He looked as if she'd stabbed him, but he'd already cut her heart out so why should she care?

Still she found she couldn't look at that hurt in his eyes so she turned away. She saw a gazebo far off at the back of the yard and ran there.

So angry. So hurt. She found she couldn't cry. Not noisily. Not with the rage she felt. Silent tears fell as she collapsed onto the seat in a daze.

There she sat with what she'd once have thought was the perfect life. A little girl to mother and help raise and she already seemed to love her just for being. Her own child was on the way. She had a handsome, wealthy husband whom she adored. Yet she was miserable— miserable because he loved some other woman.

"Pixie," Jamie called softly, stepping into the gazebo. He slid on to the bench beside her. "Please calm yourself. You're hysterical. This can't be good for you or the baby. Suppose you'd fallen?"

"Then maybe you'd be rid of your inconvenient wife. I warn you, though, even if you were free of marriage to me, I know Brendan Kane well enough to know he won't easily give up what's his. If at all."

"I don't want to be free. And I am *not* in love with Helena. I don't want her. Only you."

"Then why are you so *obsessed* with her?" she shouted.

Jamie winced, then pursed his lips. "I'm not obsessed," he swore. His jaw flexed as if he were gritting his teeth. "When I met Helena I thought she was lovely, I won't deny it. And I was interested in her, but she had the wrong idea about why. She thought I was interested only in her money. But I didn't know that until after both of you had left Wheatonburg.

"I told you I was with her father when he was killed. And I told you I came to fear the bullet that killed him was meant for me. I promised him I'd make sure she was safe. I owed it to him, don't you think?

"When next I saw Helena it was nearly a year later. She'd already met Kane. Gowery contacted me to see if I was still interested in her. He treated her as if she were on an auction block. I was trying to save her, but she didn't understand that. To get rid of me, she told me she was damaged goods. That she'd slept with Kane and that he'd rejected her. I swear there was no love in her voice, only bitterness. I was incensed for her sake and I told her guardian what he'd done to her. That is how he rooked me into getting involved in the Pinkerton investigation. He said he was convinced Kane had killed Harry Conwell. But Kane wasn't the man I saw that day. I needed the truth for my own peace of mind. And Helena was in Wheatonburg, so I thought I could check to see if she was all right.

"Everything awful that happened to her was because of me. If she is with Brendan Kane and you think he can be trusted, I'll call off the search. That is it. That is all there is to it. I swear."

It was a warm day, but she was chilled to the bone. Numb, too. She felt as if her insides had been hollowed out. She wanted to go back to their room and pull the covers over her head. If only she'd stayed there nursing her hurt and hadn't gone looking for him. She had hoped seeing him could help her make the best of it. Except he'd wound up making it hurt so much more.

Looking at him was painful, so she sat with her hands limp in her lap and stared straight ahead. "I wish I could believe you. I want so desperately to believe you. But all I am to you is a bought-and-paid-for whore and a brood mare for your heir."

He was on his knees, taking her hands in his in the next instant. "My God, you cannot think that! I adore you. I have been trying to show you how very much I *do* love you." His eyes widened and he shook his head. "I couldn't say it. I wasn't even sure I knew what it meant. So how could I say it? It was as if my heart was held prisoner."

He raised his hand as if to touch her hair, but he must have seen her flinch because he dropped his hand back to cover hers. She wanted him to let go, but perversely took some small comfort in his touch.

"You don't know what love has been for me," he went on. "You cannot know how it was to wake one day and suddenly learn I was alone in the world. My last words to my father the night before were how much I loved him. He said he loved me, too. Then he sent me to bed and sat down behind his desk and blew his brains out.

"Iris pretended great love for me. But then she told me all she'd loved was the title that came with marriage to me."

She pulled her hands from his and slid to the side.

How did he think she felt after screaming her love with only silence in answer? If he touched her again, she'd fall apart more completely than she already had.

"Then why were you so suddenly able to say it now?" she asked, her voice sounding as hollow as her chest felt.

He reached for her again and she gave a small cry of distress and he pulled back, his hand motionless, extended toward her, anguish on his face. She turned her head and stared at the distant spire of a church.

He sat next to her again. "I don't know why I could finally say it now. Perhaps because I cannot let you think so little of yourself, Pixie."

Amber stood, feeling at the edge of sanity. "Don't call me that! I wish I were magical. I'd cast a spell. I'd make you love me. Or make myself believe what you say now. But I'm not and I cannot! I might have been able to fool myself into believing you if only you'd told me this morning. I really think I could have."

"Believe it. Believe in me," he pleaded.

She shook her head. "How can I believe you when nearly the first thing you did after we arrived in the city was to institute a search for Helena?"

"I explained. I'd have told you, but it didn't seem that important."

She stepped back a step. "It was important enough that you hired that awful Pinkerton Agency to look for her. If only you hadn't called her name that first time we made love. Did you know that you had? You thought you'd married *her*. By the time you knew whom it was you really had married, it was too late. And you weren't happy about it, were you? You were furious.

"When you talked to me about trying to make our

marriage work, you as much as admitted the truth. You're stuck with me. You needed me to produce an heir. I was only going to be a governess. Why not be a countess and have fine things and children of my own? Except every day I wear her clothes and I know you wish I was her."

She turned and fled. Half-blinded by the tears that wouldn't stop, Amber lifted her skirts, careful not to trip again. Angry and hurt though she was, she'd never risk her child. Jamie's child. She ran past Mimm and some others in the kitchen, and took the back stairs to their room.

Perhaps it was childish, but she locked each of the doors leading into their room. She didn't want any more explanations, denials or lies. All she wanted was to close her eyes and forget.

The locks weren't necessary, though. This time Jamie didn't follow.

Chapter Seventeen

Jamie sat in the gazebo hunched forward, forearms braced on his thighs, hands hanging uselessly between his knees. His mind spun. They didn't fight often. Only twice so far. But their battles were certainly epic.

And both times the fault had been his, the explosion hers.

Last time it had been bad enough when the argument was about anger and temper and injured pride with only a small amount of hurt on her side. And lots of temper.

For him it had been about leftover confusion from having been ill for so long. Unaware, he'd let Iris and Oswald's poison slip into his mind. And he'd let it overflow onto her. He'd known that.

But it was worse than he'd thought. Now he knew why that argument had cast such an indestructible shadow upon everything.

He'd called her Helena.

When compounded with his stupid, blind suspicions that morning, he'd managed to pump the poison of his past into their entire relationship.

If cutting out his tongue would help heal her, he might consider it, but he knew why she'd refused to look at him for most of their discourse. She loved him, and seeing him hurting hurt her.

She'd said her piece and now all he could do was tell her how important she was at every possible moment and show her in every possible way.

Because this last argument had been about heartbreak and betrayal. And it was all his fault for not conquering his demons before now—for not letting Amber's love heal him. For once again letting his father's desertion, Oswald's cruelty and Iris's venom poison his life.

He'd come to this country to leave all three behind, but apparently he'd packed the demons and brought them along as surely as he'd packed his clothes and personal possessions.

Why hadn't he tried harder to understand what he felt? To say what he felt? When he'd seen her need for the words, why had he kept his heart locked away?

They hadn't held the key.

He had.

And all he'd had to do was trust Amber and give her what she needed. All he'd had to do was hand her the key. She already had his heart. What could he possibly have lost?

Now it might be too late.

"Talk to me," Mimm demanded, suddenly standing over him.

He hadn't heard her approach, but he shouldn't be surprised. She'd always been there to cushion his fall. He didn't move. Didn't look up. He didn't deserve her comfort. "I don't think I've ever said this to you, Mimm, but…get the hell away."

"Oh, no, me boyo. I'll do no such thing. I'm not standin' here for you this time, but for that poor mite whose heart you've apparently tromped on. What did you do? When finally you have a whole lovely life ahead of you, what did you do?"

He looked up. Swallowed. "Nothing. It's very easy to do nothing, you know. You merely pretend it's all right to take without giving back. You let the dead influence you more than the living. And you let them and your childhood monsters prey on your mind so they can surface in the stupidest of ways.

"And somehow when you've fooled yourself into thinking everything is fine, you find you've destroyed the very thing you cherish most in the world."

"No, I don't see, at all. But you're seein' it pretty clearly from how it sounds. So go fix it. Before you lose her completely, find a way to fix it. She still loves you or she wouldn't have been cryin' her heart out when she ran past me. Now would she?"

Then the quiet pad of her footsteps took her away. And he was all alone with his ghosts and demons. He had to find a way to banish them. He stood and walked toward the house, but skirted it and left by the front-garden gate. Looking up at the house that had held such promise only that morning hurt. He looked away.

And started walking. He walked up hill and down and did so for what seemed like miles, occasionally turning, not paying much attention to his surroundings. Thinking and trying to untangle his heart from his mind.

His love from his anger.

Angry though he still was with his father for taking the coward's way out of his grief, he'd loved the man. As far as Jamie could remember, his da had never had an unkind word for him. They'd breakfasted together each day no matter how many pressing matters were lined up for his father to tend to that day. And each night he'd taken time to read to him before sending him back to the nursery and Mimm.

Jamie supposed he'd loved his Aunt Deirdre, Alex's mother. She'd died in a fall about a year after they'd come to live at Adair. She'd been kind and had insisted Mimm stay on because she'd been a constant in Jamie's life. Her only fault was that she'd been cowed by her husband's rages. Oswald had been her misfortune, too. And Jamie had grieved her loss along with Alex.

Alex. How he missed his cousin. Though five years Jamie's senior, he'd made time for his younger cousin and had taken the brunt of more than one scrape for him. He'd visited him at school so often it seemed he spent more time on the road than in London at the town house. Sunny and charming, Alex had been his light for many years. Until Iris.

Iris. Jamie couldn't even say he hated her. That would allow her too much continued significance in his life. Besides, she had given him sweet Meara. So why had he given her vitriolic words so much power over him?

Stupidity again.

Which left Oswald. He'd banished the bastard from his home almost the moment he'd reached his majority. He'd not laid eyes on him in over seven years. So why should he have allowed that spawn of Satan to hold sway over him? Why had he not worked to banish him from his heart and mind?

Stupidity…*again!*

Well, it was done. It was over. *I will not destroy myself and those I love to please him.*

Or because of the rest of them.

Jamie looked up then from putting one foot before the other. The day had all but gone. The sun was but a glow behind the surrounding buildings. San Francisco was a wonder. Not one building next to another had the same architecture. It looked like any and all the ancient cities of Europe with as many styles of buildings as it had languages. Someone not knowing it was a city not yet thirty years old would have thought it had been around centuries.

To his left a small older man struggled to drag a sign inside his shop. With the winds that often swept the streets any independent A-frame signs had to be quite sturdy or spend its day blowing over. "Here, let me help you with that," Jamie said and grasped the sign at the top. "It's quite heavy as I suspected," he said, though it was really just unwieldy.

"Oh, thank you, kind sir," the shopkeeper said with a heavy Italian accent in his voice. As they wrestled the sign inside the little shop, he went on. "Son, go home. Noon. A grandson born today." Gesturing with his hands and smiling broadly he went on, "*Buon*…a good thing, no? Four generation make…good tradition." He did a good deal of talking with those active hands. "Papa teach me. I teach son. Now grandson." He happily smacked his busy hands together in celebration. "Good day, no? *Buon.*" He gave Jamie a nodding grin.

Jamie smiled for the first time since looking up and seeing Amber standing in his office, anguish in her eyes. "Congratulations. My wife told me a few days ago that we're to have a child. Much as I understand your wish for another partner, I confess to hoping for a little girl with my wife's golden curls and brown eyes. Succession be damned."

The old man's brows shot toward his nonexistent hairline. "So good to see young love." He gave a rusty chuckle and swept his arm gesturing around the shop. "Good for business. Eh?"

Jamie looked around. It was a jewelry shop he'd wandered into and the man had a right to be proud of his work. The pieces displayed were clever and thoughtful. Well made and quite lovely with intricate and often puzzling designs.

Before he considered the absurdity of buying Amber a memento of his meandering, brooding walk, his eyes fell on a clever piece. It was a silver heart, daintily filigreed, sharing a velvet cord with a key. The tiny key was also filigreed. The jeweler explained, the key actually unlocked the heart, which revealed the piece as a locket that unfolded to hold several picture frames meant for tiny miniatures.

Jamie didn't think twice. It was as if it had been designed as a gift for the woman who had indeed unlocked his heart. And would always hold the key.

He hoped she would believe the sentiment and accept it as a token toward making up for his monumental stupidity.

He hoped and prayed she would.

Darkness fell while the jeweler gave the special piece one last polish. Jamie stepped out into the night and had just tucked the box in his pocket when a flash in the growing darkness caught his attention. Instinctively, he flinched away. Something whizzed by his ear and crashed down hard on his shoulder. His arm went instantly numb as he dove away, hitting the ground hard, scraping his jaw on the side of the building. A man came out of the darkness, a long object in his hand, and jumped after Jamie. Jamie managed to roll away from the wall he'd hit and avoided being hit again. In the next thud of his heart, a near-deafening boom rent the air. A belaying pin dropped next to him with a mild clatter. The man, who'd apparently planned to bash his head in with the thing, shrieked, grabbed his arm and staggered backward into the alley next to the shop. In the next instant he had turned and fled.

The stooped little jeweler had paid him back for his help with the sign and his purchase and then some. He'd saved Jamie's life.

"You all right, sir? *Il bastardo!*" he shouted after the attacker whose footsteps receded in the alley. "Thank God. My son load the gun—worried for me here alone."

Jamie struggled to his feet as several sets of pounding footsteps came toward them. The police. Too little. Too late. The thug had gotten away.

He let the older man talk while he thought about how odd it was that the man had attacked him. The police speculated that he'd looked like a wealthy plum, ripe for the picking. That theory seemed to Jamie to be problematical. To assume this had been a random attack over money made little sense. There was, after all, a shop full of gold and silver just on the other side of the window. And it had been clear the old man was closing. A few more minutes, one broken window later and he'd have been able to scavenge the cases of a small fortune.

No. It had felt more personal. So why him?

Jamie was truly afraid to speculate.

* * *

Amber heard a knock on her bedroom door. She'd been reclining on the chaise longue since before it had gone dark and still had no inclination to move. Or to talk to anyone.

"My lady, it's sorry I am to disturb you. I'm in a real pickle," Mimm called softly through the door. "I don't know what to do. I'm needin' your help. This is serious or I'd never disturb you."

Mimm sounded quite worried. Goodness, was something wrong with Meara? This was a day that would go down as one of her more difficult to get through. Amber stood and carefully made her way through the darkness to the door and opened it.

"What is it?"

"Jamie went walkin' hours ago and hasn't returned. And now his devil of a cousin has caught up with us, he has. He's pacin' the front parlor. I've put Meara in her room with strict orders to stay put, but 'tis only a matter of time before she revolts. She's missin' Jamie and wantin' you, as well."

Mimm stepped into the room, holding a lamp. She held it up and shook her head. "Oh, lovie, you can't meet this one with tears in evidence. Help me handle him. No matter how angry and…and…whatever it is you're feelin' toward Jamie, this is serious. Lily's here to help you get ready. Will you come down?"

Seeing Mimm all at sixes and sevens, Amber didn't have the heart to refuse. She nodded and walked into the dressing room behind Mimm. Mimm set the lamp down, unlocked the back hall door, and then bustled around, lighting all the lamps and gas sconces.

"Come, lay yourself down on the bed, my lady," Lily

ordered, a large glass in her hand. "I've got some nice cool milk, here. It'll fix you up quick."

"Lily, I hate milk. I honestly don't know if I could keep it down."

Lily chuckled. "It's for your eyes, my lady. Just put your head back and relax for a few minutes. Pads of nice cool milk. My ma taught me this. Works every time."

It did feel good. What felt the best were these two women huddling over her trying to soothe her. She shouldn't have locked them out. She should probably not have done most of what she'd done that day.

She'd been so angry. So hurt.

"I'll make sure your dress is all set," Lily said.

The resentment began to stir in her again. "What's wrong with this one?" she demanded. "Even Jamie claims to like it."

From somewhere in the room Mimm said, "Not a thing is wrong with it. 'Tis a lovely frock."

"Then why did Lily leave it in the trunk? I could only assume it wasn't good enough for his wife."

Lily gasped. "No, ma'am. I didn't have the time to finish the unpacking. You and Lord Adair arrived home so I left it for later so you could have your privacy while he showed you your rooms. He told us to leave for the day."

Amber felt like a fool. Because the trunks had been going ahead of them early in the morning, Lily had packed mostly everything the night before and in no particular order. Many of her things had never been unpacked at the Palace, which put them at the bottom already. Amber had pointed to the new plum ensemble as what she'd wear the next morning. "I'm so sorry for misjudging you, Lily."

"Not to worry, my lady. This is a new life you've stepped into. We're all bound to put a foot wrong once in a while," Lily assured her. "Missus Trimble and me will have you fixed up in no time.

"An' you'll show that struttin' prig in the parlor a thing or two when you walk in and take charge," Mimm put in, then lifted the cloth from Amber's face. "Right as rain. Now let's be gettin' you up and dressed. That pretty face and keen mind'll knock him flat on his skinny arse—!"

"Mimm! I don't want to embarrass Jamie again today. I'm not at all sure what you expect me to say to his cousin after you lied to him and gave him the slip in New Jersey."

"Oh, don't worry yourself about that. I already told him we got word the house was ready and decided to travel before the weather got too warm for Meara. It don't sound too kind, considerin' he expected to visit with Meara the next morning, but he knows deep in his heart why I wasn't wantin' that to happen. Said he understood and I saw the double meaning there."

"Mimm, Jamie is going to find out what you did to Alexander now."

Jamie's rock pursed her lips and nodded. "Alexander said he weren't going to say nothin'. I expect he thinks it leaves me beholdin' to him. But it don't."

Amber shook her head. "I don't want to lie to Jamie."

"It's an omission. We'll cross that bridge if it winds up in front of us."

Together, Lily and Mimm had her dressed in Helena's gold lace and white satin gown in no time. It was more indecent now than it had been on the ship. Mimm frowned and shook her head when she came around the front to survey their work. She gave Amber's mostly exposed breasts a pointed look. Amber blushed, pulling at the neckline as Lily scrambled to the dresser and produced a fichu to tuck inside the bodice. It did a passable job concealing Amber's swelling breasts.

She was uncomfortable in the constricting dress, but ready. And Jamie was still not home.

Mimm said he often walked when he needed to think. If he was trying to think of a way out of the conundrum he'd made of their lives by consummating their marriage when it should have been annulled, he might not be back until after she was delivered.

Either way, as she'd loved him already, she'd have been hurt, but at least an annulment would have been quick.

At the top of the stairs, Amber took Meara by the hand and led her down the main staircase to meet her uncle. With Meara chattering like a magpie, Amber remembered what Jamie had said about not being able to regret his marriage to Iris. It had given him Meara. Just as this marriage to Jamie had given her a child growing under her heart—a child she loved already. And the one she held by her hand also had a piece of her heart.

Amber couldn't truly regret their marriage, only the state of things between them.

She opened the doors to the parlor and got her third nasty surprise of the day. Alexander Reynolds turned from studying the Samuel Colman painting over the mantel. He wore a nervous smile and the face of the man she loved. About the same height and same breadth to his shoulders as Jamie, he had only a few fine lines around his bright blue eyes and a head of wavy, blond hair to differentiate him as other than a twin to Jamie. He was a man Meara resembled even more closely than she did Jamie.

That thought set her mind whirling and Amber stood dazed. Thinking. Calculating. Jamie's twenty-eighth birthday was to be on Thanksgiving that year. On his twenty-first birthday he'd tossed his uncle out of his life. That was one month after his wedding to Iris. Meara had told her all about the pony Jamie had arranged to have waiting for her on her seventh birthday. Her *late May* birthday. Which meant she'd been born seven months after their marriage.

Meara's father must be Alexander! Why didn't I put it all together before? Because I hadn't seen Alexander Reynolds. Meara's father. Dear God, Jamie could have warned me. Mimm could have warned me! No wonder Mimm had worried about telling Alexander that Jamie was on the clipper and out of touch.

"Expecting my cousin?" Alexander asked, calling her back to the problem at hand. His arrival. Jamie's absence.

"Yes… No… He isn't at home just now. I'm told you are the earl's cousin, Alexander Reynolds."

Alexander arched one of his eyebrows and gave her a charming smile, then advanced toward them. She felt Meara peeking around behind her.

Would he figure it out?

Or did he already know?

She forced a smile and turned, putting her hands on the shoulders of a very silent Meara and bringing her to stand in front of her. "My name is Amber. And this is Meara." Past a knot of nerves in her throat she managed to add, *to lie,* "Meara, this is your cousin Alexander."

Alexander stared at Meara with what looked to Amber to be love and longing. And she knew. He did know this was his child. Which brought up another question. What would he do with that knowledge?

More important—did he hate Jamie for being Meara's legal father?

As she'd seen Jamie do so often, Alexander squatted down to eye level with Meara. "Good evening, Meara. That is a very pretty name for a very pretty girl."

Meara curtseyed nicely as Amber had shown her to do before they came downstairs. "Thank you, cousin. I didn't ever think I'd get to meet you. Da misses you, but he says you live far, far away. You should stay till he gets home. He'd be sad to not see you."

Alexander stiffened and gave Meara a slightly tight smile. "Perhaps I'll wait then. Do you know who you look like, Lady Meara?"

Amber stiffened involuntarily.

Meara looked up at her with puzzlement, perhaps feeling her tension. Amber smiled, then Meara's gaze drifted back to Jamie's cousin. "Mimm says I look like my da."

His jaw went rigid. "I'll bet she does," he muttered, then he forced a smile. Amber was nearly sure Meara was taken in by the charming grin, but Amber saw anger and some other emotion that only the man himself could explain. "Actually you look very like our grandmother and therefore like us both since we favor her. She was a great beauty, much to my cousin's and my good fortune." His grin turned teasing, then he mugged a silly face and said, "Grandfather looked rather like a tall troll."

Meara giggled just as, "Dinner, Meara," floated up the hall from the back of the house.

"Oops. That's it for your visit for a little while," Amber broke in and Alexander stood to his full height.

"Please make yourself comfortable and excuse us a moment. I promised to deliver Meara on time," she said, then took Meara's hand, knowing she'd made no such promise. She wanted a word with Mimm—the traitor. "Come, sweetheart, time for your dinner."

"I thought I could eat with you and Da tonight."

"He had to go out unexpectedly, remember. We'll do something special tomorrow evening. All right?"

That seemed to appease the confused child and she skipped at Amber's side to the breakfast room. "Here is Lady Meara for her very special dinner, Mimm," Amber called out as she entered the breakfast room.

Mimm bustled in from the kitchen, carrying a wide soup bowl. "And here is your favorite chicken stew. Cook just finished thickening the gravy."

Meara scrambled into a chair and Amber pushed her in. Then she took Mimm by the wrist and pulled her out into the hall. "You could have warned me," she told the older woman in a whisper.

"I told you he's not to be trusted."

"I mean the resemblance. *And* the dates."

Mimm's face went beet-red. "I didn't say because Jamie refuses to discuss it. It was his place, not mine. She was a little bit of a babe. The doctor said she was early, but—"

"I saw the look on Alexander's face the moment his eyes fell on her," Amber whispered.

Mimm nodded and in as quiet a tone she said, "As did I when he came after she was born. Oh, he knows the truth of it. And I've never figured out why he didn't throw it up at Jamie when they fought. I expect he's biding his time. I tell you, waitin' for the other shoe to drop now that he's here is gonna' be the death of me."

"Perhaps you misjudge him. Perhaps not."

"I know what I've seen often enough. That one was

around and trouble always found Jamie," Mimm said with a stubborn set to her chin.

Amber sighed. "We can only wait, as you say. But his estrangement from that man has hurt Jamie."

Mimm pinned her with a penetrating look. "My lamb has someone else in his life now, lovie." Amber guessed disbelief showed in her eye because Mimm squeezed her hand and said, "Believe it. He don't need that one anymore. Now you had better get back before he's rootin' through the drawers."

Amber sighed. "We just moved here. There's nothing in the drawers. He's more than behaved himself thus far," she quietly assured Mimm, then returned to the parlor.

Alexander stood as she entered and smiled, seeming to ooze charm and friendliness. "And you, pretty lady?" he said. "You have not told me exactly who you would be in Lord Adair's household. The governess, perhaps, if I am lucky?"

Amber stiffened, uncomfortable with his flirting. "I would be your cousin's wife, sir," she said a bit too sharply.

Alexander frowned—his charming facade slipping a bit—before he managed another smile. "Jamie is wed? When did this happen?"

"We met on the ship. Actually, we were married on the ship. There was a minister on board. Jamie didn't want to wait."

"Swept you off your feet, did he?" Alex asked, his grin almost gentle, but his eyes were uncomfortably penetrating.

"It was more the other way around," Jamie said from the doorway. Tension, thick and heavy, flooded the room as Jamie advanced and dropped an arm possessively around her shoulders.

Amber whirled to face him, shocked at his sudden entrance. Then she gasped, for a whole different Jamie than she was used to faced her. Dirt smudged his face and his jaw was scraped, as well. She stepped back and saw that his normal impeccable grooming was gone. Blood stained his white shirt and the knee of his charcoal-gray trousers was torn, as was the shoulder of his frock coat. And he held himself stiffly as if he were in physical pain and not just affected by the tension in the room. Then a frightening thought added guilt to her worry. Had Mimm keeping Alexander's presence in the country a secret put Jamie in harm's way?

In spite of all that had gone before—all the hurt and disappointment—she was suddenly terrified for him. He'd been in danger.

Love, it seemed, wasn't nearly as fragile as she'd thought.

Chapter Eighteen

"Perhaps this is a bad time," Alex said, his voice tight and controlled.

Jamie shook his head, and noted that while his neck hurt his head didn't. He drank in the sight of Alex. His cousin had not changed much in the years since he'd seen him. After so long, though, Jamie was nearly unable to comprehend that Alex actually stood before him—nearly half a world away from his London apartment. "You should know that any time you might show up at my home wouldn't a bad time, Alex. The fault between us lies squarely on my shoulders."

Alex stared for a long minute, then he raked a hand through his hair. "It takes two to quarrel. As Mrs. Trimble pointed out, you were the worse for wear when I last cast my eyes on you. It was nearly a year before I realized you'd barely defended yourself. Ever since, I've felt the coward where you're concerned. How then could I be sure of my reception?" He narrowed his eyes. "Actually, you don't look at all the thing tonight." He put a teasing spin on his words, but Jamie was sure he saw concern in his cousin's gaze. "Been brawling again, cuz?"

Jamie gestured toward Amber with a message to watch what he said. He didn't want to worry her. "I should change. Is Hadley above stairs, Pix…ahem… Amber?"

Her lashes swept down, hiding the sadness he knew he'd written there. Had he even destroyed something as simple between them as his pet name for her? Or perhaps the look of sadness was about his hesitation to use it. Was she regretting the afternoon's argument even half as much as he was?

"I believe Hadley is having his meal in the breakfast room with the staff," she said and turned to his cousin. "You will stay for dinner, Cousin Alexander?"

Jamie almost let his sigh of relief become audible. Apparently, Amber was at the very least willing to act as his hostess in front of Alex. "Yes, please. We need to talk," Jamie put in. He looked at both of them in turn. He needed to talk to each.

An idea occurred to him. If Alex were to stay there, Amber might rein in her temper enough so that Jamie could apologize before she shouted him down. And if Alex were in residence, Jamie might find a way to put back the ease between them that had always been there. An ease Iris's entrance into their lives had destroyed. "Perhaps you would be our guest during your stay here in San Francisco?"

"I'll see to having the guest room made ready, in that case," Amber said with a forced smile.

Jamie heard the strain in her voice and centered his attention on at her. "How can I reassure you that all is fine? Just a tussle with a cutpurse," he said, couching his question so that she could respond to whatever was the cause of her upset.

Her worried gaze went first to Alex, then back to his own. "Are you sure it was just a robbery attempt? Are you sure it wasn't a serious attack on your life?"

So it was both his worse-for-wear condition and Alex's presence. Mimm must be casting doubts about Alex to Amber. He would talk with her again. And not for the world would he tell Amber that the attack had felt like an attempt on his life. "I'm fine. Just a little dust-up outside a jeweler. The cutpurse didn't get a dime." He forced a smile. "Or your gift."

She blinked. "Losing an object would have been preferable to your putting yourself in harm's way. You have Meara to worry about."

He took a chance, cupped her cheek. "I have two others to worry about, as well. I assure you the thug was more than likely after what he could easily steal. He ran readily enough from the jeweler, who was not much taller than you." Jamie left off the sound of the shotgun, as well.

Having given Alex time to think of a response to the invitation to stay with them, Jamie looked over at his cousin, who seemed a bit far away and more than a bit disturbed. "So are we to be graced by your presence for a while?"

"We can easily get reacquainted if I stay on at the Occidental Hotel where I've registered."

"I won't hear of you staying elsewhere. You are family. Your place is here. I'll send my driver to retrieve your things. Do you have your valet with you?"

Alex's lips curved in the mischievous grin that used to drive Oswald into a fury. "We mere misters learn to travel light. I've managed to tie my own neckcloths for years, cuz. Laundries do a passable job of starching my collars, as well."

"Amber, would you ask Gunter and Hadley to ride over to the Occidental after their meal to pack and retrieve Alex's belongings?"

Alexander sighed. "You've learned to play lord of the manor quite well in the intervening years." Shaking his head, he took out his room key and his calling card, then placed them on the console table near the doorway. "I paid in advance. If they could leave the key with the front desk—"

"Of course," Amber said, still more than a touch tense. He foolishly basked in the sound of concern in her voice when she went on to ask, "Jamie, are you sure you're all right?"

He nodded.

"Then I suggest you go clean up. If Mimm or Meara see you...well...go clean up," she said and turned away to play his hostess.

As he watched her go, a shaft of longing struck deeply. She had to listen. Had to forgive him. Not for his sake, but hers. She deserved so much more than he'd given her thus far.

"I must say, your lady is a surprise. Wherever did you find a woman who values your skin over something from a jeweler's case?"

Jamie's lips curved in a helpless smile. "Some things are just meant to be, I suppose. I'll tell you all about our great romance if you care to come along while I clean up. You can help with my damned neckcloth. Unlike you, I am lost without Hadley. And especially as I am not sure I can lift my right arm."

"Glad to play valet. It won't be the first time, will it?

Nor the first time I helped repair damage so Mimm won't find out you've been in a scrape." He chuckled. "Another scrape, I should say."

"No, it won't." But it would be the first time in over seven years they'd shared a moment like this. He felt a bit lighter going up those stairs than he had climbing the steps to the front door minutes earlier. He could only credit Amber's concern and Alex's arrival for the change.

"The house is quite nice," Alex said, following him into the master bedroom. "I see your fine hand in it everywhere I look."

"That would be because I designed it. I had much of the furniture sent from New York, as well. I wanted a comfortable place for Meara when we're here. Little did I know I was building my bride's wedding cake. At least that is what she said it reminds her of."

Alex smiled. "I will have to see it in the daylight to see that effect, I suppose."

"So, how did I meet Lady Adair?"

Jamie started off warning Alex to go light on references to his and therefore Amber's title even though Mimm refused to. Then he took off his ruined clothing with Alex's help, and told him about how they'd met and married. He left off the more personal details, only saying that they'd decided to make a go of the marriage after he'd recovered. He added that he was deliriously in love with his wife. It felt even better saying it to Alex than it had to the jeweler.

Alex understood better than anyone Jamie's fear for Meara and once again, as he'd been doing for years and years, apologized for the father he loathed. Then he asked. "Are you ever coming back to England? Or at least to Ireland? I kept waiting, then I decided I had to seek you out."

"I was in no hurry to return before meeting Amber and now I have an American wife."

"She was quite a surprise." Alex grinned, his easy charm much in evidence. "I'd hoped she was the governess."

"Actually she was headed here to become a governess to one of the original families of the area," he said, but then he groaned as he tried to get a shirt back on.

Alex stepped in and helped him. "That's some bruise raising. The blighter obviously meant business. It's a rather odd place to strike his victim. You did say you had the box in your pocket already so he wasn't trying to get you to drop it."

"I caught his shadow and flinched away. Had I not he'd have rattled my brain box for sure."

Alex paled a bit and looked away. "You should be careful. Perhaps a bodyguard is in order. Now tell me more about your lovely wife."

"She's quite the bluestocking. Educated at a degree-bestowing college in New York called Vassar."

"As it happens I've heard of it. Quite serious about their studies, I hear."

"She is very intelligent. And don't let the diminutive size fool you. She tends to speak her mind. If she ever runs into your father, she's liable to box his ears."

Alex looked surprised. "I can hardly get my mind around that. I saw her with Meara. She seemed so gentle and kind. And I do believe she'd need a ladder to reach The Bastard's ears."

Jamie grinned. Between each other they'd been referring to Alex's father as The Bastard for years. "Well, eventually in the next year or so she may get her shot." He turned away so he wouldn't give his inner feelings away before saying, "There are a few…problems…that need tending back there. So are you and dear Uncle Oswald still not speaking?"

"I still give him the cut-direct if I am ever unlucky enough to attend the same function he does. On the subject of problems," Alex said, "those between us were his doing. But I fell into his trap. I was a fool to let him drive a wedge between us. He's been trying to accomplish that since we moved to live at Adair."

"And I was a weak fool to buckle under to his demand to marry the woman you loved. I am sorry I couldn't make her happy." Not for anything would he hurt Alex by telling him his own father had been behind the accident that had killed her. After trying and failing to get his hand up long enough to do up the top buttons of his shirt, he turned back to ask for help and encountered fury in Alex's gaze. He quickly masked it, but Jamie knew Alex. He knew what he'd seen. "I'm sorry she died that way. I truly am," he added. Perhaps even a little honesty wasn't the way to go. Perhaps there was really no hope for them to patch up things between them.

Alex shook his head and stepped forward, making short work of the top two buttons. But the anger began to simmer again in his blank gaze. "I know the truth about the accident, Jamie," he said finally, reaching for the neckcloth sitting on the dresser. While looping it around Jamie's neck Alex proceeded to tie it and said, "The stable boy who found her decided to try his luck in Bath. He recognized me and made it his business to tell me about that day. I have my theory, cuz. What is yours?"

Jamie closed his eyes and when he looked back the

anger he'd seen was banked, but still there. "That I've come to hate my title. I swear I would find a way to surrender it to you if there was a way to bypass him."

"Do me no favors."

"If it's any small consolation, had the accident been mine you'd have got Iris back. Perhaps that was the plan all along when he pushed me to marry her."

"A very small comfort. Sometimes I actually understand why Mrs. Trimble used to call me the spawn of Satan."

Jamie groaned. "Another outspoken woman in my life."

"One who will no doubt find a way to blame your problem earlier on me."

"It was random," Jamie said quickly, but he was sure it hadn't been. And Alex had shown up just after. Jamie prayed it was a coincidence, hating his suspicions.

Amber paced the parlor, wishing Jamie would return from changing. Angry though she still was with him, that didn't mean she wanted anything awful to happen to him. She glanced into the hall at the stairs. She supposed she could easily go up and see if he was all right, but she didn't want to intrude. Jamie needed to heal from his turbulent life and perhaps a reunion with his cousin was the first key to that.

At least she hoped he was a key and not a danger. It was uncomfortably coincidental that Alexander had arrived the same day Jamie was attacked. Her mind whirled with unpleasant possibilities. Especially that Meara was his cousin's child and not Jamie's.

Had Jamie invited a viper into their midst?

Voices on the stairs drew her back into the hall. "I'm

told dinner is ready," she informed the men when they reached the front hall. "Shall we go in?"

She turned back into the parlor and moved through it and into the dining room. The room was set on the informal side with the three places at the far end of the table. Jamie at the head, she and Alex flanking him. Jamie rushed to help move her chair in, and then he leaned over her shoulder to put a box on her plate. She sucked in a breath at his nearness, drawing in his lime-and-bay-rum scent.

She was at first relieved when he moved away. Then he took his seat beside her at the head of the table and she was bereft of his closeness. She looked down at the box and let her anger grow again. Staying angry seemed her only defense against her feelings for him. Did he think a gift could make up for what had happened that day?

That day?

Had it really only been hours since they'd arrived at the California Street address? How had so much changed so quickly? The velvet-covered box filled her vision. She flicked her gaze to Jamie. With so much changed, how could so much remain the same?

She still loved him.

She nearly touched the box, but pulled her hand back. Her emotions raw as an open wound, she had to blink back tears. She couldn't let on there were problems, not without knowing if Alex was in league with his father. Not for anything would she give that monster the joy of knowing Jamie wasn't happy.

"I saw it and thought of all that having you in my life has done for me, Pixie," Jamie said, his voice pitched low, but not so low that his cousin couldn't hear. It had an intimate sound. She closed her eyes when they started to sting more. "I think Divine Providence took me to that shop."

"Considering you were attacked outside it, I doubt that," she said and frowned. "You should have handed it over." She reached out to pick it up, then looked up at him again and her heart tripped over itself. She wanted him safe. And she wanted what was best for him. To deny that would be stupid.

Amber called Helena Conwell to mind even though Jamie now swore it was Amber he loved and not Helena. Though Amber had felt sorry for Helena in the situation with her guardian, the girl had been a little spoiled. Used to having the things she wanted. She wouldn't have been good for Jamie.

It was also a bit of a help to know that while Helena was safe from her guardian all was probably not going exactly as the heiress had planned. She'd wanted Brendan and she'd gotten him. But according to a letter from Abby in March, there'd been interesting doings that cold night in February before the three of them had fled town, Amber for New York dressed as Helena, Helena and Brendan for points west. Abby's brother had indeed married the heiress in the local church, but it was at the point of a gun. And Abby had been holding that gun.

Amber knew Brendan. Helena had a very annoyed tiger by the tail. Jamie's hand covering hers called Amber back to the dinner table. Her dinner table. She blinked.

"I'd worry about that smile, cuz," Alexander said with a teasing grin. "You know pixies are known to play a trick or two every once in a while."

"Not my pixie." Jamie gestured to the box in her hand. "Open it. I saw it and knew it was designed for you. It is a symbol of everything you are to me and everything you have done for me."

Hands unsteady, she reluctantly took the top off the box. But she had to beat back her anger again. He'd put her in an untenable position if she were to keep their quarrel between them. She glanced up before peeling back the swatch of velvet covering to see what lay beyond.

Then she gasped when she saw the gift. Of their own accord her eyes flicked up and her gaze flew back to Jamie's. "It is lovely."

Jamie stood and came to her side then crouched down so his eyes were even with hers. He took the key hanging next to the heart on the black velvet cord. Fitted it into a keyhole hidden within the complicated filigree work. He turned it just a bit and the heart fell open in her hand. "You have my heart. And you are the key to it. You've opened that heart as surely as I just did this one." He laid it in her palm. "Just as you hold this heart in your hands you hold mine. I love you, Pixie. You don't need to cast a spell. You cast one just by turning your sunny smile upon me on the deck of the *Young America* the day we sailed."

His words, so close to his earlier thoughts on his cousin, struck her. Even Jamie recognized that his heart had been imprisoned by his past. And he sounded so sincere. She looked at him. Their gazes locked, but her voice remained paralyzed. It was all she could do to keep her tears at bay. So she nodded.

She wasn't sure she believed him or that he believed what he had said, but that wasn't something that could be fixed with a gift or even words. Time, she thought, would have to heal them both.

"Give me time," she whispered.

"All you need," he whispered back. Then in a slightly louder voice he said, "I'll commission photographs or miniatures of each of our children. There are places for several."

"It will have to be a miniature. I can imagine Meara might be persuaded to hold still long enough for a photograph, but it will be quite a while before the baby could be trusted not to move."

"Baby?" Alexander asked, his voice ringing a bit sharply to Amber's ears. When she looked up, there was little doubt that this was no pleasant surprise to him.

"It happens," Jamie said mildly and stood, his gaze on Amber. She was sure he hadn't seen Alexander's reaction. "We were wed in May. As you were my instructor in the pertinent facts, I am sure you are aware of the mechanics."

Charming smile back in place, Alexander laughed. "Of course. For some reason I was still thinking of you as newly wedded. I was merely taken by surprise. Congratulations, Lady Adair…uh…Amber. Perhaps this will be Jamie's heir."

She merely smiled in a noncommittal way. She watched Alexander as Jamie launched into his wish for a daughter. She watched throughout the meal and afterward as they sat in polite conversation in the parlor. Finally she excused herself, claiming exhaustion. But it was a while before she was able to put that odd look in Alexander's eyes out of her mind or get past the thought that a mere reunion with Jamie was perhaps not his sole reason for coming to San Francisco.

She'd asked for time from Jamie. For some reason it felt as if time had already run out.

Chapter Nineteen

Jamie heard Mimm in the hall outside his office and wondered if Amber had awakened yet. She'd been sleeping so soundly when he'd retired that he'd crept as quietly as possible to the bed, and then slid carefully beneath the covers. And this morning he'd stolen away as she'd once again been sleeping like a top.

Last night was the first night since they'd moved Amber into his cabin aboard ship that they hadn't gone to bed at the same time even if they hadn't made love. In truth, one of the reasons he'd been so furtive, nearly slinking in next to her, was that he would have been devastated if Amber had asked him to leave.

But today was a new day.

Today he planned to take her shopping to eliminate the problem of her being forced to wear Helena Conwell's clothing. Not for anything would he allow her to continue to be wounded because her own clothing wasn't appropriate for his wife. While they were out shopping he'd have Lily take Helena's clothing to the Ladies Protection and Relief Society. Mimm had mentioned that Meara's clothing was growing too small, as well, so both his ladies would get new wardrobes.

Alex went out exploring the city, promising to return that evening or meet them for dinner. Last night after Amber had gone off to bed, he and his cousin had talked far into the night. Alex had retired, but after their conversation Jamie had been troubled. He'd sat up deliberating on ways to repair his broken relationships with two of the most important people in his life.

Meara entered his office, pulling him out of yet another brown study. Her hair, braided in front and pinned in a coronet the way Amber often wore hers with the back flowing in curling waves, caught the light like a nimbus as she skipped toward him. Amber followed and her hair was done exactly like Meara's. "My girls!" he called out as Meara rounded the desk. "How lovely you both look."

"Lily fixed my hair to look like Mum's," Meara said, fairly bursting with pride. She hopped onto his knee where she cuddled up close. As he kissed the top of his daughter's head he noticed that Amber looked a bit unsure of herself.

Then he learned the reason when Amber said, "Mimm just told me we're to go shopping this morning."

Jamie smiled, hoping to set her at ease, but he wouldn't put off that day's mission unless she was feeling unwell. After all, he noted that she wore the same dress she had on yesterday—the plum one he'd bought her while they'd been staying at the Palace. He didn't think a woman wore the same dress two days in a row when she had a half-dozen others available unless she saw those others in a less-than-flattering light.

"Mimm would be right. Unless you aren't feeling up to it, that is."

"No. I'm fine, but—"

"It's about time you had your own clothing. Don't you think?"

"I didn't mention Helena's clothes so you would—"

"Of course you didn't," he interrupted. "You should have a trousseau, though. I insist."

"But my shape is changing and—"

"All the more reason," he said, purposely stepping on her words again. Yesterday even her pretty green dress looked far too restrictive across her chest. Now that he knew about the child, he understood why her breasts seemed to show more in the dresses she wore than they had at the start of the voyage. While he enjoyed the view, he'd noticed the fichu she'd added last evening to hide the new wealth of creamy breasts from being on display. "I can see you've grown a bit in the—" he stopped quickly, couching his words because Meara was in his lap avidly listening to their exchange "—a bit uncomfortable," he finished and noted a small curve to Amber's lips at his discomfort. But he didn't mind. He'd gladly play the fool if it meant hearing her clear-as-a-bell laughter ring out once again.

Instead of laughing, however, she nodded, resigned and not excited as he'd hoped at the prospect of a new wardrobe. "In that case I'll have Lily put the rest of my hair up before we leave the house."

He shifted the leg where Meara had taken up residence. "You look lovely. Don't be foolish."

Her jaw set. "I try not to be foolish, but lately apparently I've been failing."

So he'd misspoken again. He held back a sigh and

tried to recover. He decided to redirect her thoughts to Meara. At least she had a soft spot for his daughter. "I can scarcely remember you being anything but intelligent and sweet. Just like my other girl." He hugged Meara. "In fact, I rather like my ladies matching. We must find you some mother-daughter day dresses. Our Meara's dresses are quite short and should be replaced as Mimm has pointed out.

"You are growing by leaps, Lady Meara. Perhaps we need you to balance a cobblestone on this head of yours," he teased, tapping on the top of her head. "That ought to keep you small and manageable a while longer. What do you think, Mum? Will that keep our princess small?"

"Perhaps," Amber said, "but it is my experience as a teacher that little serves to thwart time."

Meara frowned and crossed her arms. "I don't want to be small, now. I'm going to be a big sister, Mum says. I cannot be both small and big. That makes no sense."

"I hope you don't mind my telling her," Amber said. "But as you told her uncle, I didn't want her to hear the news accidentally said in passing."

"It is your news, too, Pixie. In fact, I've planned a celebration. I've sent word to the Maison Dorée that we will dine there early this evening. It is recommended as one of the city's finer restaurants."

"Yea!" Meara shouted.

"Is your cousin coming, as well?" Amber asked at the same time. She didn't sound a bit at ease with that possibility.

Jamie glanced at Meara, picked up a piece of paper and scribbled a note. He wanted time with Amber to undo some of the distrust of Alex he saw in her gaze. The less said in front of Meara the better. After sanding the note, he handed it to his little pitcher. "Princess, would you take this to Mimm or Hadley? Your mother and I will be along in a bit," he explained.

She hopped down. "Privacy time again," she grumbled and exited, displaying all the drama of a Shakespearian actor's death scene.

Amber didn't even smile. She just stared at him, sadness still so deeply imbedded in her gaze it hurt to see it and acknowledge himself as its cause. Perhaps he shouldn't have sat up with Alex. Had he made things worse? He couldn't put a foot right these days. But he had to keep trying.

Working to remove one shadow from her eyes at a time still seemed the best course. "Come, sit," he said, gesturing to the chair still at the side of his desk where his new banker had sat not an hour earlier.

Almost nervously she sank into the leather chair. Only then did he swivel to face her. "Yes. I invited Alex to join us. Do you object?"

"He didn't seem as if he wished to celebrate our good fortune last evening at our dinner table. In fact, I thought he looked angry. Or at very least deeply disturbed by it."

"I don't know if he'll come. He hadn't decided when he left this morning. But I hope he will. I think I know what is Alex's problem. It isn't that he begrudges us our good fortune. I believe seeing Meara and knowing we're to have a second child has brought home to him once again what he lost when he lost Iris to me. And she is dead and I have you. It seems so unfair to him."

Amber looked at him with a piercing question in her gaze. "Perhaps it isn't a kindness protecting him from the truth about her. If some part of your life was not what you thought it was, wouldn't you want someone to tell you if they knew?"

To someone who'd been loved by all the adults in her life while growing up that probably sounded like a simple question. "I'm not sure. Sometimes one can stand only just so much pain and disappointment. Alex's father is a singular bastard, Amber. He twisted my life with his cruelty and it has left its mark as you have unfortunately discovered. I fear for Alex it is worse."

He rolled his chair a bit forward and chanced to take her hand. He was heartened that she didn't seem to object. "I at least have the comfort of knowing the man isn't my father. As bad as it was having my uncle as a guardian I knew my father had been a good man even if he was weak."

"But Alexander is his son," she protested.

"Yes, and because of that, what has Alex to hold on to? He has the dream of who he thought Iris was. I don't know how he has managed to excuse me as much as he seems to have for the part I played in his loss of Iris. Though she was not the kind of person he thought she was, it was still a great loss to him. And now he has yet another burden to bear."

"Is our child an emotional burden in some way, do you think?"

"You're remembering Alex's initial silence last night." He sighed. "Quite possibly, but that isn't all I'm referring to." Half-truths had hurt her too much already. He let go of her hand and pushed his chair back a bit. "There are a couple of facts I've left out about my first marriage. When Iris trapped me into marrying her she was already increasing. Meara is Alex's child, but I'm legally her father. I didn't tell you because, as she is part of Alex, I couldn't love her more were she my own."

She didn't seem shocked, but she should be. "I already came to that conclusion," she explained. "It wasn't difficult once I saw him and put all the dates together. And I know she is your child in your heart. I just wish I'd been warned."

He grimaced. He should have told her sooner and was done with secrets. "I also hadn't wanted to tell you the whole story of Iris's death, but keeping things from you has caused you heartache. Iris's death wasn't an accident."

After he said it that way, he realized how it must sound after he'd once told her that Alex had blamed him for Iris's death. But Amber only looked expectant. He supposed it was a plus that she didn't think him capable of murder.

So he went on. "For months Iris tried at every turn to anger me, but I didn't care enough to be drawn into her arguments. Until the day I reached the end of my rope when she persisted in demanding to be allowed to return to London. I finally told her to go to London, but to leave Meara behind where Mimm would be a better mother than Iris ever would. My parting shot was that no matter what she did while there I wouldn't challenge or accept a challenge in defense of her honor as she had none. She stormed out of the house.

"My favorite horse, Poseidon, was saddled in the drive ready for me to ride out with my steward to check on a few cottages that had need of new thatching. She mounted Poseidon. When he returned without Iris or the saddle, we organized a search. The entire neighborhood searched for hours, but it was too late. She'd fallen at the border fence to a neighbor's estate and had been killed instantly. The cinch on the saddle had been cut nearly through. My saddle."

She blinked. "Your uncle made an attempt on your life? Yes, you certainly did leave that out. I'd thought it was a suspicion that he had planned to make an attempt, but that by banishing him you thwarted his scheme. You never told me he'd actually tried to take your life before Harry Conwell was killed. How awful for you. Why, after all you've told me of the man, do I continue to be so surprised by anything he would do?"

Jamie shook his head sadly. "And the worst of it is that Alex has found out. He knows it is more than likely that Iris died as a victim of his own father's failed plot to kill me. That she died instead of me."

"So you don't want to disparage Iris to him. Because you believe you are all he has in the world while you have—"

"I have you and Meara and our child on the way," he told her so there would be no doubt what was in his heart. He wanted no more misunderstandings between them. "I think I can bear up under any residual anger Alex holds toward me. It is nothing compared to what he must think of Oswald and what my marriage did to him."

"I suppose there is little to say. We will see if he joins us. And if he cares to celebrate tonight. But still, the woman he loved died in your place. What if his loyalty belongs to his father rather than you?"

"I cannot believe that of him. Please don't let Mimm color your feelings toward Alex. She holds a grudge for something that turned out to be the best thing that ever happened to me. Alex thought I would be better away at school. He talked Oswald into firing Mimm and sending me north to Scotland. It changed my life for the better. I had been sickly and I grew strong there. What she saw as a curse was the saving of me. Then there was the fight he and I had after Iris died."

He stood and held out his hand, gratified that she took it without hesitation this time. She allowed him to assist her to stand and escort her toward the door. "Shall we go make the local merchants wealthy?"

"Oh, dear," she said, sounding worried that he would spend too much blunt on her. Alex was right. She was a gem and so he laughed. He refused to be anything but cheerful today. It was a new day. And he was the luckiest of men to have so perfect a wife. And it seemed she'd surrendered and was about to allow him to try to make up for his stupidity in hurting her.

Lily waited in the front hall with Amber's hat, the jacket to match her dress and a parasol. He was nearly sure she'd never used a parasol in her life. She certainly hadn't been shy of the sun aboard ship. She'd just finished buttoning up when Meara came dancing down the stairs, wearing her bonnet.

Then they were off.

Amber stared at the shopkeeper, who stared back with her mouth thinned to a straight line. When she spoke it was with an accent not unlike Jamie's. But from this woman it grated.

"My lady," the shopkeeper intoned, looking down her nose, "it matters not if the dress is practical, as long as it is the height of fashion. And this dress is. It is the design of Mr. Worth, so it is just the thing right now. He dictates much of the latest in fashion in England. He has slenderized the silhouette in front and is putting the emphasis on the back of the dress with the elaborate train."

"What a shame," Amber retorted, annoyed, "as I'm increasing and my front will soon be anything but slender."

The woman's eyes bugged out, then she recovered herself. "It will be waiting for you after your confinement when you're presentable again."

Amber had not thought she would become unpresentable. She knew women did not go about in society in those final ungainly months, but women in her home town had no such luxury. Deciding not to take exception to what had sounded like an insult, Amber said, "Still, I see no reason to drag the weight of all this material around behind me."

"These days, ladies of *consequence* wear trained dresses and not only as a ball gown. As you have married into the aristocracy you must at least *appear* to be a lady of consequence. Shall we show the earl how you look in this one? So far he's liked every item I've selected." With that said the woman swept out of the dressing area, expecting Amber to follow.

Her temper simmering, Amber did follow, but only to take her case up with Jamie. The ensemble was lovely. She didn't dispute that. The dress was made for the most part of an exquisite rose satin. It had short, set-in sleeves and a high ruffled neckline with a full skirt that ended in a ruffle that continued all along the extensive train. Designed to complete the outfit she also had on a rose, white and pink striped tight-fitting over-jacket the woman called a paletot. It had a high, collarless neckline and was nipped in at the waist, then flared smoothly over the hips. The problem was that to her, a walking dress with a long train was ridiculously impractical. The entire train was covered with large, wide bows made of both the rose and the striped materials. The tails of the bows gently curved and dipped as if unfurling toward the hem, artistically crossing over each other.

She loved it and hated it at once. It would take two hours to iron. And she just couldn't do that to Lily.

Jamie stood when she re-entered the main shop room. He was instantly alert. Meara, who had been making faces in a mirror, turned then. "You look beautiful, Mum."

"Lady Adair feels it is too much, but it is one of Mr. Charles Worth's latest styles, your lordship. Day trains are all the rage. Of course, only the wealthy wear them, which makes them a necessity for her. I've tried to explain that she must dress to her new station."

Amber glared at the woman's back.

She could see Jamie fighting to keep from showing some emotion. She just wasn't sure which one. "Do you like it other than its impracticality?" he asked her.

"It's very pretty, but—" She lifted the weight of the train in one hand. "I understand trains on ball gowns, I do, but this is ridiculous. Can you imagine how dirty it would get just walking from the door to the carriage?"

He held up a hand. "I see your point about the impracticality. Why pay street sweepers if ladies are cleaning the roads with their hems?"

Meara giggled. Amber found herself smiling, too. Jamie still didn't seem to be taking the exchange lightly though he'd made the joke. "Suppose we do this." He turned to the shopkeeper and handed her a card. "Box up the dresses I marked so far for Lady Adair. And this one, as well. Have them sent to that address."

Amber sputtered, "But...Lily will have to press all these bows and—"

At the same time the woman also sputtered, "But Lord Adair, you said an entire wardrobe."

He turned to Amber. "Do you think the ones so far have been as lovely as I do?"

"Yes, but it will be so much work to maintain such complex gowns."

"Lily is employed to care for your clothing," Jamie said. "Without you she would be unemployed and living a much less comfortable life. This will be perfect for a tea at home or perhaps a party in the garden. You needn't wear it when we go about the city. I suggest we return to where we purchased the plum dress you're wearing today."

He turned to the shopkeeper then. "This will be all then, madam. We will need to continue our expedition elsewhere. I must say I am disappointed. I was told this was a place where my lady would find everything she needs."

Minutes later they left a much-disappointed shopkeeper behind as they made their way to the carriage. Jamie went to speak to Gunter after handing her and Meara in. He climbed in as the driver mounted and got them moving.

"I'm sorry," she said. "I should have just let you buy what you thought I needed."

"What have you to be sorry for? You looked exquisite in the gowns you'd tried on so far or I'd have cancelled the order and not just cut off our shopping there. I heard the way she spoke to you. You would be a lady of consequence in rags, Pixie. And not just because our marriage bestowed a title upon your head."

Amber was grateful for his support and was much happier at the shop they both remembered so fondly. The proprietress managed to combine fine styling, workmanship and materials with common sense. She also sold girls' dresses that matched some of Amber's gowns. There were other dresses with trains, but none so elaborate as the rose gown.

Her favorite dress was a royal blue taffeta trimmed with black lace. The lace was sewn toward the bottom of the full skirt in a herringbone pattern, making a very smart design. The woman promised to alter it so the waist sat higher than usual to hide Amber's blossoming shape.

Next he made sure they were both outfitted with shoes and hats and gloves at other shops. As with the gowns from the first shop they would mostly be delivered the next day. Jamie left her and Meara at a lingerie shop, having given instructions to supply both of them with an unnecessary number of high-quality items, turning basic needs into indulgences. Then he fled, heading, he said, for a shop just two doors down. There was a dangerous glint in his eyes.

As she and Meara giggled and selected a dizzying array of unmentionables, which the shopgirl had no problem mentioning, Amber realized she was having fun. Had been having fun since Jamie rescued her from the clutches of that first officious shop owner.

He'd made the day better than she'd thought possible. The trip that had instantly unsettled Amber when Mimm told her of Jamie's plans had shifted from an embarrassing chore to a carefree romp.

She had, in fact, dreaded the entire day from the instant she'd opened her eyes. But then Lily and Meara had swept in, opening shades, giving good-morning hugs respectively, which buoyed her heart. Jamie had finished the job by showing her that, in buying her things, he wasn't trying to buy her affections, meet an obligation or class her up. He was trying to make up for not recognizing what was in his heart and not giving voice to it sooner.

When she stepped out on to the sidewalk, she saw that not surprisingly Jamie had gone to a jewelry shop. The man was positively obsessed with hanging things about her neck and wrists and from her ears.

Next they would be on their way to the restaurant, Maison Dorée, where Jamie hoped Alexander awaited them. Amber wasn't sure whose version of Jamie's cousin was right, Jamie's or Mimm's. It was all very confusing. Had Alexander come to bury the hatchet and become friends again? Or had he come to bury the pro-verbial hatchet in Jamie's back?

Amber didn't know, but she intended to watch care-fully.

Chapter Twenty

Seeing Jamie's carriage near the end of the block where they'd begun their shopping, Amber took Meara's hand and started that way. It was toward the end of the shopping day so there weren't as many people around as when they'd gone inside although it was still a lovely, sunny afternoon. Oddly, a dilapidated-looking milk wagon with an even more disreputable-looking driver sat between their gleaming open carriage and the intimate apparel shop where they'd just been. She would have thought it the wrong time of the day for a milk wagon.

Meara was chattering about her pretty new night-gowns and how they were nearly the same as Amber's. Amber, determined to resist the temptation of glancing inside the jewelers, kept her eyes on Meara to make sure she resisted, too.

As they passed the old milk wagon, Meara screamed in terror and her hand jerked out of Amber's.

Amber pivoted in time to see Meara being tossed into the open back of the shabby wagon. Rushing forward to rescue her, Amber realized her error as the man grabbed her. They were being kidnapped!

She screamed for help as she fought the burly, foul-smelling man, knowing they'd never be seen again if she meekly let them be taken. She drove the end of her closed parasol from under her arm hard into the man's stomach. A deep, satisfying "oohff" burst into the air. Having taken the assailant by surprise, she got one arm free, but he didn't loosen his hold on her other one.

He was big and ugly with a bald head. And strong. If anything his anger made him cling tighter as he dragged her inexorably closer to that open door. Meanwhile, he began shouting, "You whore. You hadn't ought to have run off and taken me little girl with you. You're coming home with me, bitch."

To any fellow shoppers it sounded for all the world as if this was a domestic problem. Consequently no matter what she said no one there would help. So she decided to gather her breath and fight like hell. She tossed her head, trying to get enough momentum to pull away. Her hat pulled painfully on her hair, but the pain reminded her of another weapon at her disposal.

Her hatpin.

She made a grab for it with her free hand. Her hat flew off into the attacker's face. He batted it away, but that gave her the time to position her thumb on the heavily jeweled end of the pin and get ready for a chance to use it. She was sure it would be her last chance to free her new daughter.

Meara, meanwhile, had started scrambling backward on her belly, trying desperately to get out of the wagon. The thug reached out, clearly intending to grab her and push her back inside, which was all the chance Amber needed. Quick as a cat, she took advantage of his momentary distraction. Dragging the tip of the sharp pin across the back of the hand he'd reached out toward Meara, she laid the flesh open. He howled and pulled his hand off Meara, raising it to slap Amber.

Using his strength and momentum against him, she drove the pin into and through his palm as his hand swung toward her. He howled again.

Meara reached the ground and Amber shouted for her to run, but instead, with hell-to-pay in her blue eyes, the little girl turned and kicked the big ugly thug in the shin while screaming for her da to come help them.

Gunter was shouting and running toward them by then, as well as several men who'd realized the thug clearly wasn't her husband or Meara's father. Apparently knowing his mission had failed, the thug shoved her to the ground and turned to flee, shouting for his accomplice to run, as well.

Jamie, sprinting toward them from the jewelers, intercepted the attacker. He planted his fist into the man's belly, then into his face. The thug toppled backward like a fallen tree. Then Gunter and the other men took charge of the downed would-be kidnapper and Jamie ran toward her and Meara.

Shaking and still sitting where she'd been pushed to the sidewalk, Amber hugged Meara in her lap. The poor child was quaking and crying and clinging all at once. Jamie reached them and knelt down, putting his arms around them both. "It's fine. It's fine," he crooned, but he sounded terribly rattled himself.

"Mum saved me from the bad man, Da. She's the best mum in the world," Meara told him as her tears began to subside.

"I think you saved each other, princess. As I was running toward you, I saw you kick that awful man a good one."

"He was hurtin' Mum! Are you okay, Mum?"

Trembling and trying to keep her voice even but failing, Amber said, "I am fine, my little warrior. Thank you for your assistance, but you should have run. You are too precious to your father and me to risk your safety."

"I'd rather you were both safe," Jamie said, his voice as unsteady as Amber's sounded. He could have lost them. Lost everything. He closed his eyes and kissed the top of Amber's head while rubbing Meara's back to calm her.

"Thank you, Pixie," he said when his heartbeat had settled a bit more. Having them safe in his arms helped.

Then Jamie started noticing things other than the two precious treasures in his arms. People had gathered, all sharing with each other what they'd seen and all of them proclaimed Amber a heroine. One man said the accomplice had stolen a horse. Someone shouted that the police were on their way.

And his injured shoulder burned like it was on fire. Jamie had no idea how he'd managed to plant that facer on the hoodlum. He supposed he never would know. His shoulder had been smarting all day and now it hurt even more. But somehow he hadn't felt a thing except rage when he'd seen that miscreant with his hands on his wife and child.

"You were so smart and brave to find a way to delay him," he said to Amber. "I'm sure your quick thinking saved the day."

There was a new flurry of activity as the police arrived

with a wagon. The man was soon being handcuffed, loaded inside the wagon to be taken away. Perhaps he would provide a clue as to who exactly was involved in all of this. Though Jamie was sure who was behind it.

As the wagon passed, he raised his eyes and got a good look at the attacker for the first time. His was a face Jamie would never forget. The face of the man who'd killed Harry Conwell. So the bullet *had* been meant for Jamie. Last evening's attack had not been random, either. Nor had today's. But today's had been against Amber and Meara. So what had changed? His heart stuttered. As of last night, his marriage and the baby were new information only to Alex.

"Sir," a voice above said, "we need a statement. And we'll need you to swear a complaint against the man we've taken into custody."

Jamie looked up and stood. He scooped Meara up and stood her on her feet then helped Amber stand. He kept an arm around her and pulled Meara closer.

"Have you any idea what this was all about?" the officer asked.

He was terrified that he did. "I have an uncle in England who is next in line for my title. He would cheer at my demise. And now my wife carries a child who could be my heir. She is therefore possibly standing in the way of his succession. It is the only thing that makes sense.

"Also," Jamie said, pointing at the wagon as it rounded the corner at the end of the block, "that man killed a man in New York in the winter of seventy-four. I can now only imagine the bullet was meant for me."

The officer nodded gravely. "You folks will need to come to the precinct."

Jamie nodded. "Should we meet you there, officer?"

The policeman frowned and shook his head. "I'll ride along if you don't mind. Another set of eyes wouldn't hurt, eh? Just in case."

Jamie agreed wholeheartedly. It looked as if he'd have to hire bodyguards. He'd thought Gunter would be enough, but he'd obviously been wrong.

Because the attendant paperwork at the police precinct was expected to take a while, he sent Gunter to Maison Dorée to see if Alex awaited them. He didn't know what his being there would prove or not, but Jamie couldn't condemn his cousin without further proof of guilt. But neither could he dismiss out of hand the evidence mounting against him. Amber and Meara's safety depended on his being vigilant. On his protection.

They stepped out of the police precinct as the sun dropped behind the buildings, lending a chill to the day's warmth. Alex stood talking with Gunter and turned to rush their way when Meara called out his name.

"Hello, sweeting. I hear you had a terrible scare."

"It was bad scary, but Mum and me trounced him good. Da says we were brave."

Alex nodded and looked at Jamie as he guided Amber down the steps. "Everyone is all right?" his cousin asked. "Has the man you caught given any information?"

Jamie eyed Alex. Had he imagined the anxiety in his voice? Was it worry of being implicated or worry for Meara and Amber? Hating the suspicion growing in his soul, Jamie tried desperately not to let it show on his face. He turned away and handed Amber, then Meara, into the front-facing seat of the carriage.

Once they were settled, and he was more composed, he turned back to Alex. "Thus far he's said nothing," Jamie told him. "But he's facing murder charges in New York. The police think a night in a jail cell contemplating his fate if he's extradited instead of a trial here on these charges may loosen his lips. Come morning they'll offer a deal in exchange for information."

"What happened exactly?" Alex asked.

"I was in another shop when Amber and Meara were headed to the carriage. He grabbed Meara first. Tossed her into a milk wagon like so much baggage, according to a bystander. They all thought it was a family affair and didn't wish to get involved. When Amber tried to go to Meara's aid, he made a grab for her, calling her vile names and shouting that she'd stolen his child. Thanks to her determination, Amber slowed him down. Gunter and I were on our way to help them and Meara began shouting for my help. He and the one ready to drive the wagon must have realized the bystanders were about to step in. They ran in different directions, but the one who'd grabbed them ran square into me. His accomplice got away."

Alex looked deeply troubled for a moment, glancing into the carriage then back to him. "It isn't like you to make enemies. Perhaps it's all about money and they'd have asked for ransom."

"I would think that had I not been attacked last night." He sighed. "And seen this man kill a friend. I always feared the bullet was meant for me. Now I'm sure it was.

"Amber is exhausted. I need to get them home. Needless to say we won't be celebrating tonight. That's why I sent Gunter for you."

"Of course. Perhaps you should send for her doctor."

Jamie nodded. "Perhaps. Will you act as an out-rider for me?"

"Be honored, cuz. Let's get your family home."

Jamie nodded and climbed into the rear-facing seat. They turned onto California Street some minutes later and the setting sun flashed into Jamie's eyes. They had gone only a few hundred feet when Amber looked up at a roof and shouted for him to duck. All he could think was to protect them. He dove forward to cover Meara and Amber with his body. Two sharp reports in rapid succession echoed between the buildings.

The horses screamed in fright and took off at a gallop. Jamie pushed himself off Amber and Meara and turned to see why Gunter wasn't in better control. But his eyes fell on Alex, who made a saluting motion as he wheeled his horse down the side street, leaving them to their own devices. Gunter had been shot and had dropped the ribbons. He seemed to be listing forward.

Jamie made a grab for him, keeping the big man in his seat, as he climbed over the seat back and up next to Gunter. Two drivers on cross streets just managed to pull their own teams up in time to avoid a collision. With no other option, Jamie leaped onto the back of the lead horse. After a few frantic moments during which he nearly slipped off and under their hooves, both animals finally slowed.

Now that the jangle of harnesses, the clatter of the hooves and the loud rumble of the wheels on the cobbles had ceased, Jamie could hear Meara shrieking in fear for him. "I'm fine, princess," he shouted over his shoulder. "It's all fine." But that was a lie. He'd never lied to her before. Nothing was fine.

As he made a move to slip to the ground the horses

shifted nervously under him. "Whoa," he heard Alex call out over the clatter of hooves. "What are you doing up there, cuz?" he asked and jumped down, taking hold of the horse's head so Jamie could slide free.

His temper simmering, Jamie grabbed the ribbons and pulled them back toward Gunter to check him. He was holding his arm and blood seeped through his fingers, but he nodded and said, "Am fine. Am fine."

He didn't look fine and a glance at Amber and Meara's pale faces said they weren't fine, either. "What the hell did you think you were doing?" he demanded of Alex, stalking back to the front of the horses where his cousin stood holding their heads. "You rode off and left us! We're lucky we weren't all killed."

Alex looked genuinely confused. "I saw that you were fine so I went after the gunman. I was sure Gunter would gain control of the team."

"Gunter was shot, you imbecile. He dropped the ribbons."

"I didn't realize he'd been hit and certainly not that he'd dropped the ribbons. I'm sorry as I can be. And the blighter got away, besides. His horse was a good bit quicker than this city nag I hired. When I realized I couldn't catch him, I broke off the chase."

Jamie could only stare. Then Alex seemed to understand without him saying a word. "You can't—" There was a world of emotions in his eyes, but all were suddenly unreadable to Jamie. "Oh, but of course you can. Life is not always black or white, cuz." The mocking tone cut Jamie to the quick. Alex's smile in the growing darkness shone white and sarcastic, finishing the job of destroying the one constant in Jamie's life. It died a slow and painful death there on that deserted street. "I am the spawn of Satan after all," Alex said. He turned away and mounted. "I'll send someone round for my things. It's time I gave up."

He mounted then and rode back past the carriage. His back unnaturally stiff, Alex stopped and stared down at Amber and Meara for a long, tense moment. Jamie was about to rush back to send him on his way, but Alex tipped his hat then rode off at breakneck speed. The deep shadows of the side street swallowed him in moments.

Staring after him for an endless minute, Jamie heard Meara ask where her uncle had gone. He shook his head and put mystery, danger and bone-deep sadness out of his head, getting back to the matter at hand. He couldn't worry about abstracts—what was the truth, what wasn't. He had the here and now to handle.

He couldn't look back anymore. Amber, Meara and the new baby were his future.

Amber heard Jamie tiptoe back to bed. The mattress shifted under his weight. Meara lay sprawled between them, somehow managing to take up most of the space.

Meara had done well at pretending it was all a great adventure until it was time for bed. She'd frozen at her doorway and had looked up at them and asked if they were sure that man who shot at them wouldn't come to get her. Her fears weren't unreasonable childhood fears. There was someone out there who wanted to hurt them. Meara was too intelligent not to understand that. Even for Amber that fact was nearly too much to contemplate.

She and Jamie were almost too tired and heartsore to deal with Meara's frightened tears. But they were perfectly willing to cuddle with her in their bed all night if that was what it took to help her feel secure.

"Ouch," Jamie hissed after a while in the bed. "We have to fatten her up. She's all bones and angles."

Amber chuckled.

A moment later Meara's hand flopped across Amber's face with an audible slap. The bed shook. He was laughing. After the day they'd had, she couldn't even mind that it was at her expense. He was laughing.

Compared to a life-and-death struggle, their differences were unimportant. If in fact there were differences at all. Why had she allowed love to make her so distrustful? "I love you," she said simply.

She did not wait even a heartbeat to hear him say, "And I love you, Pixie. More than life. More than death. More than anger or tears. Lying in this bed is my world. I *will* keep you safe. If I have to hire an army, you and my children will be safe."

She got out of bed and walked across the room to the front windows. Then Jamie was there, behind her, holding her by the upper arms and kissing her shoulder. "I'm sorry for trusting Alex so blindly. And that marriage to me is such a disaster," he said.

"No." She turned to face him and lay her hand on his cheek. "It's I who must apologize. I am sorry about yesterday. About demanding words when I should have seen your feelings in the things you did and the way you cherish me. You never once told me I couldn't still love Joseph, but I demanded you not love Helena. They are our past. If you say you love me now, I know your heart is large enough for both of us."

"That is more than generous of you, but I *never* loved Helena. I felt only obligation for her. And today proved I do indeed owe her that. Her father *did* die in my stead. For you I feel all-encompassing love. If there is obligation it is *because* I love you. Do you see the difference?"

She nodded.

"I will keep you safe. Somehow we'll have a good life if I have to petition the crown to give up my title. Alex will eventually inherit. If he wants the title so badly, he's welcome to it. He and my uncle both are. I am so sorry for the fright you had today. Thank God Malcolm is convinced you and the baby weren't harmed."

She put her hands on his shoulders and stood on tiptoe to kiss him. His arms engulfed hers and he took the kiss deeper, transporting her to a place she could only call love. When he raised his head, she laid her head on his shoulder. "It isn't your fault that the jealousy of others has endangered all of us. Or that my jealousy endangered our marriage. I'm sorry for doubting you."

"You had a right to the words you needed. I love you. You shall have them day after day until you are sick of hearing them."

"That won't happen," she warned him.

"Good, since I'll never tire of saying them."

She stepped back and took his hand in hers. "I am so sorry about your cousin. You love him. And he's hurt you. I thought I could like him. I wanted Mimm to be wrong."

"It is all so difficult to sort out. It has to be Iris who changed him into someone I don't know. She poisoned his soul."

Sighing, Amber sat on the chaise. "I think I may retire the field, sir. This chaise longue is looking rather comfortable."

"No. I insist you and Meara share the bed. I'll pull the roll-away into the room and sleep there. Let's get you settled in. Malcolm said you were to rest."

She climbed back in bed and watched as he made up the roll-away in silence, then she closed her eyes. Even if there was still danger to her and Jamie, she knew he would protect her and not because of obligation, but because he loved her. For tonight that was enough.

Chapter Twenty-One

Jamie stared up at the bedroom ceiling for what felt like hours. He could hear both Amber's and Meara's soft breathing. It soothed him knowing they were both safe. Amber had quickly surrendered to exhaustion and the rest Malcolm Campbell had ordered. Jamie would be forever grateful neither of them had been harmed physically, but he was deeply saddened that they'd both been so badly frightened.

He'd begun to drift off when a noise roused him. Heart pounding, he sat up. Once again, he heard a sound foreign to a house in slumber. Footsteps? The rustle of paper? It could be one of the staff. But could Alex have returned for his things? Or could he be there to create trouble?

Jamie tucked his heartache away and stood. Still wearing his trousers and shirt because Meara was in the room, he crept into his dressing room and grabbed the revolver he'd bought after Harry Conwell had died. His older friend's killer was at last incarcerated only a few miles away. But there was still the person who shot Gunter and those who'd hired him.

Creeping to the door leading to the back stairs, Jamie carefully opened it. After checking on Mimm who was sleeping soundly, he checked Alex's room. It was deserted and nothing had been touched.

In his stocking feet, Jamie returned to the back stairs and descended them carefully. He'd gotten halfway down when the overpowering smell of lamp oil hit him. He kept going and had just gotten past his closed office door when he heard the distinctive click of a revolver being cocked behind him and sound of the pocket door rolling open.

"Hallo, nephew," a voice from his nightmares sneered. "A gun? How very brave of you. What a surprise you continue to be. Drop it, turn around and kick it over here."

Jamie saw little choice but to obey. Still, he wasn't dropping his weapon until he'd made sure there actually was one leveled at his back. He started a slow turn.

"Can you never learn to listen?" Oswald growled. "I said drop it. I can kill you now or later. It's up to you."

Having turned enough, Jamie was able to see Oswald and that he did indeed have a gun. Jamie was all that stood between Amber and Meara and his vile uncle so he did as ordered. Perhaps the staff below would hear the thud. Then he completed the turn to face his nemesis.

His uncle's gray hair made him look older, but he was still nearly as tall as Jamie. He looked a good deal like the father Jamie remembered, except for the perpetual sneer on his once handsome face. It was as if evil had corrupted his features and turned them into something sour and repulsive.

"You've been extremely difficult to kill," Oswald complained. "And now look what you've done. Leave it to you to spoil a surprise. You never learned to cooperate." He stepped back into Jamie's office. "Come in. We'll have a bit of a reunion. And then I'll need to come up with a new idea now that you've spoiled my original plan."

Instead of kicking the gun toward his uncle, Jamie stepped forward as casually as he could, pretending to ignore it. In the hope of distracting him, Jamie said, "I'd rather our reunion took place in hell, you bastard."

"Tisk tisk, nephew. Such bitterness. Shocking. Now get in here." Slowly, Oswald backed into the study, the gun still steady in his hand.

Jamie followed, thankful his uncle had forgotten the gun Jamie'd dropped. Which meant if the noise had awakened someone sleeping in the staff quarters below, the gun would be there to aid in a rescue.

Even without help, though, Jamie wasn't going down meekly. He had reasons to live. Reasons to fight. He looked around at the ransacked room. "Taking up burglary, Uncle?"

"I decided I was tired of bungling inferiors. If I want you dead and buried, I suppose I'll have to do the killing myself."

From the disarray of the room, Jamie must have heard Oswald searching the office. And papers all around the office were doused in the lamp oil he'd smelled.

"Been looking for something?" he asked sarcastically. As if surveying the damage, he walked behind his desk. With a piece of furniture between them, Jamie figured he might be able to dive for cover when his uncle decided to fire his weapon.

"Far enough! I've been looking for your will, dear

boy. And preparing a bit of groundwork to cover up my presence here, as well. I must say I'm disappointed that I wasn't mentioned in the document except to be excluded. I suspected as much and wondered who would stand to profit from your demise."

"What do you care? You won't see a penny, you bastard."

"I need a scapegoat. Alexander will have to do. I'm sure your driver will let the police know he was there tonight and rode off after the gunman, but that he suspiciously returned empty-handed. Oh, and you really should watch who you call a bastard," he said and chuckled.

Jamie wondered if the man was evil or insane. Or both. Then he remembered how Alex's impudent grin used to enrage Oswald. Hoping to throw him off balance a bit, Jamie did his best imitation of it and said, "The Bastard was a pet name for you, you know. It was a joke between Alex and me. Actually, for me it was a wish. It would mean I'm not related to you at all."

"Alexander," he groused, his eyes full of fury. Then he took a deep breath and visibly calmed himself. "He's been a trial, always getting in the way with ideas of his own for you."

Jamie's heart broke a little more over Alex's defection, but he had no intention of dying. "You may get the title if I die, but nothing else will ever come to you."

"No, I imagine it goes to your little wife. And, of course, if her child is a boy, I wouldn't even inherit the title at all, would I?"

So Alex had passed the information along to his father. Jamie wasn't even surprised by how much that hurt.

"Wondering how I knew about the addition to your

family?" his uncle asked. "You really should learn not to insult shopkeepers. Especially women. They have loose lips, especially when given the opportunity to complain. I heard all about the crass American pretender who had snapped up a title she couldn't possibly appreciate. As an American, your Amber would annoy any well-bred Englishwoman. I'm assuming judges here would allow her to retain custody of your possible heir, as well as your fortune." He paused significantly, his eyes glittering with malice.

Jamie felt his stomach turn over and fury burn through him. If Oswald weren't armed, he would do what he should have done years ago. He would strangle the bastard with his bare hands. Then his uncle continued speaking and Jamie nearly lost control—gun or no.

"No. No. We can't have that," his uncle went on, smiling superciliously. "She's a pretty little thing, but she'll have to die. I plan to spare little Meara, though. She'll be worth a tidy fortune come morning. And she'd be all alone in the world. Poor child. Until I step in, that is. I'll raise her just the way I did you. Using her fortune so she'll appear to live in the manner she's become accustomed to, of course.

"When you think on it, that is only fair. It's Meara's *déclassée* mother's money, after all. You were in debt up to your clavicle until I arranged for you to marry the lovely Iris—the heiress whore. But you were always ungrateful." He shook his head and gestured around the room. "Look at all I've given you. I could have made sure my son married her, but I gave her to you."

"Because you knew you'd never see a penny from Alex," Jamie said. "I've been thinking about this all night and I remembered something. I'd been Alex's beneficiary for years. If he and Iris had married and something had happened to them, you'd have had to kill me next to get at the money. A trail of bodies that long would have alerted the authorities. Even as blind to the crimes of the aristocracy as they are, you'd have gone to the gallows. So tell me, Uncle. Was Iris to die eventually after she married me?"

"Of course," he answered, sounding appallingly jovial. "She'd have been despondent and would have had to kill herself over the heartbreak of losing you."

Jamie stared at his uncle, recalling those exact words said before. His mind traveled across the years back to that awful night. His uncle and his Aunt Deirdre had been visiting Adair the night of his father's…murder…not suicide. Fury and elation warred inside Jamie.

"Putting it together at last, cuz?" Alex asked from the doorway.

Jamie's gaze flew to Alex. He wondered if he'd done this well with the sarcastic smile Alex had perfected so many years ago. Then Jamie noticed Alex held a gun. The gun Jamie'd dropped in the hall. He didn't know if his chances of survival had just gone down or up. But he was nearly sure Amber's and Meara's had improved considerably.

If there was a quarrel between him and Alex, it was because Iris had died in Jamie's stead, and because Jamie was raising Alex's daughter. He also knew his father had arranged the accident that had caught and killed the wrong person. He wouldn't let anything happen to an innocent woman and child.

Jamie remembered then that Alex had been at Adair the night Jamie's father died. But mostly he remembered him being there the next day. He'd held Jamie's hand and told him he'd be moving in with his mother and father. He'd promised to protect him as much as he could. Jamie remembered thinking his cousin was being very nice, but what did he need protecting from?

He'd soon found out.

"How long did it take you to figure it out?" Jamie asked Alex. "I'm apparently quite slow to see to the heart of these evil plots your father devises."

Alex kept his gaze pinned on his father. The sarcastic smile fell away and his face took on a bleak expression. "There was nothing to figure out. I couldn't sleep that night and Uncle James had mentioned a new book he'd gotten especially for me. It was called *Everyday Life in the Wilds of North America* by Ballantyne. I'll never forget that title though I never could bear to read it after what I saw when I went to the library.

"I arrived in time to see my father walk up behind Uncle James and blow his brains all over the draperies. Blessedly, your father never knew his life was in danger or that yours would be once he was gone. He'd fallen asleep at his desk. I didn't know what to do. My father had just killed a man. His own brother. He was my father. Was I to send him to the gallows? And then I thought, what if no one believed me? Would he then kill you and me?"

"You knew he would want me dead. That's why you promised protection that morning. You were always there when I found myself in danger."

"I was so ashamed. I finally broke down and told my mother about a year later, thinking she'd know what to do. I was never sure. Did you kill her, too?" he asked his father. "I already know you killed Iris."

"*You* killed Deirdre when you told her. But she didn't

let on you knew. I didn't give her enough credit for being that cunning. She said *she'd* seen me. She must have been suspicious before you told her because she never looked at me quite the same way after we moved to Adair. I assumed she'd known for more than a year when she confronted me. Stupid woman. Did she think I'd let her live?"

Alex bit his bottom lip, still keeping his eyes on his father. The gun was pointed that way, as well.

Feeling encouraged yet still trying to feel him out, Jamie asked Alex, "Then the rowboat with the leaks that suddenly developed overnight was his doing. Everyone knew I rowed to the island in the middle of the lake to get away from him. You didn't get a thrashing because I nearly drowned, but because you saved me. How did you manage to force him to send me to Scotland?"

"I said I'd tell anyone who would listen what he'd done if he didn't send you away to boarding school. I was finally as tall and strong as he was. I took his pistol. He wasn't very brave unarmed, I found. That is, of course, why I left Adair when you did. He'd have killed me in my sleep after that. I was nearly sure of it. I hadn't known he'd send you so far, though."

"I was sure the cold ride with no coat would kill him. God, nothing I do kills you!" Oswald said, teeth gritted, eyes glittering with something close to madness.

Unwisely perhaps, Alex laughed. "I took him warm clothes later, but I waited up the road with blankets when I saw him ushered out with no coat."

Jamie's guilt over Iris doubled. "And I took Iris from you. After you spent your youth watching over me. No wonder you came to hate me. I am sorry. He truly trapped me into it, Alex. I really hadn't compromised her. It just looked bad to her father."

"Oh, tell him the truth, for God's sake!" Oswald shouted, his face twisted with rage. "She was a whore who slept with any man she could tempt to her bed."

"Don't," Jamie shouted, praying the servants below would hear.

"I'm sick of the two of you protecting each other. Coddling each other. You'd have been dead years ago but for his interference. He's still interfering. Choosing you over me. You, the cousin keeping me from succession to the earldom. And him, too. I am his *father.* But that means nothing to him."

"Oh, it means something," Alex said, all the bitterness he felt showing in his tone and expression. "It means no matter where I go I am your son. You are universally hated in Britain, Father, and I am looked at with suspicion because of it."

"You think I care?" His eyes darted from Alex back to Jamie. "If you won't tell him what she was, I will," Oswald growled, moving toward the library table, still keeping the gun on Jamie. "She used you. Pumped you for information about him so she could make him think they were well suited. But he wouldn't have it. So she had to trap him. She was all over him on that terrace. He was so busy trying to keep her hands off him, he didn't see her father and me observing the proceedings. She wanted that title. It wasn't that Iris was afraid to wait for you, Alexander. She had me send you away. And she didn't care if she had to pass your bastard daughter off on him. She wanted to be a countess."

Alex's eyes cut to Jamie. "I'm sorry. You weren't to know."

"I've known since she told me she was increasing. I can add."

"You love Meara. I didn't want to take that away from you. Or Meara."

"She is a part of you. The champion of my childhood. The best friend I've ever had." The cousin who was once again stepping in to save him—and his family, too, this time. "How could I have doubted you?"

"Because I'm the spawn of Satan, Jamie." Fury had engulfed Alex's features. He was again looking at his father. The hand holding the gun vibrated as if he was fighting to hold himself back from pulling the trigger and was about to lose the battle. "How were you to know I wouldn't ultimately choose him over you after the bad blood he caused between us? I was angry at first tonight, but then I realized how bad my actions looked. And then it dawned on me that, if I'd defended myself, you'd have listened.

"I came looking for you in America because I've had my father watched for years. He met up with a very unsavory bloke then booked tickets for the two of them. I hopped a steamer the day after. But you weren't easy to find. Neither was he. He must have made it here to San Francisco before me because the trouble had already begun."

"This is all very touching," Oswald put in. The hand holding the gun wavered. "And I know I promised a reunion but I'm tired of standing here listening to you two. You don't have the guts to shoot your own father, Alexander. You couldn't turn me in during all these years and you still don't have the guts. And he's still going to be written up in the morning papers as the man who was attacked and killed in his study. And that little

American is going to be the wife burned to death with him after a lamp was knocked over in the struggle that killed him. I'll let you go rescue your daughter, Alexander, but that is as far as my generosity goes."

His uncle's eyes glittered, but not with madness. With joy. It was clear he saw his dream of the earldom within reach. He put his hand in his pocket, pulled out a match and struck it on the grip of the gun before dropping it into the pile of oil soaked papers he had ready on the floor. A whooshing sound erupted under the library table. He stepped back as the fire leaped up the oil soaked wallpaper.

Jamie thanked God Meara wasn't in her room. It was right over the study.

"Alex. Go," Jamie ordered. "Meara's with Amber. Mimm is in the middle room. Save them."

Alex blinked, but kept staring at his father grimly. Oswald laughed as the draperies caught. This wasn't the act of a madman, but by a cold calculated mind bent on having life as he wanted it no matter who stood in his way.

Smoke and heat engulfed the room and Oswald moved toward the desk, his full attention centered on Jamie.

"Don't do it, Father. Don't move another step," Alex warned.

Then the whole bizarre scene seemed to spin out of control in a heartbeat. Everything happened as if with deliberate plodding slowness but in the blink of an eye, as well. Oswald took aim at Jamie, now standing too close to miss. Jamie dove to the side as two shots exploded simultaneously.

"Jamie!" Alex shouted at the same moment the shots rang out.

Jamie managed to move quickly, but a bullet caught

him and spun him around. He hit the floor on his back. Hard. His head smacked on the hardwoods and swam. But there was another thud and this one shook the room. Jamie knew what Alex had done. To save him, he'd killed his own father.

Then Alex was kneeling over him, ripping off his neck cloth and tying it around the wound on Jamie's upper arm. Tears that probably had nothing to do with the thickening smoke ran down Alex's cheeks. "God, I'm so sorry," he said. "You're going to be okay. We have to get you out of here, though. Come on. You think you can stand?"

Jamie nodded and got to his feet with Alex's help. "Your father?" he asked his cousin as they stumbled from behind the desk.

Alex nodded toward the middle of the room. Oswald lay in a heap on the floor, flames raging all around. "Sent him to hell where he belongs. I'm sorry, Jamie. So sorry."

"Don't," Jamie told him as they skirted the flames. "You were a child, too."

They made it to the door of the office just before the flames would have cut them off. Flames quickly engulfed the back hall in their wake as they scrambled toward the dining room. Oswald must have spread the lamp oil throughout the first floor.

The combination of the gunshot wound, the crack on the head and the smoke had his head whirling. Only Alex's support kept him moving forward. Apparently, Alex had been propping him up since the awful day Oswald had cruelly taken Jamie's father away. It seemed to Jamie they'd both lost their fathers that day.

Mimm shook Amber awake. "Lovie, I think we've some nasty company. I heard voices in Jamie's study.

Unfriendly voices. And Jamie's down there," she said, glancing at the empty cot where Jamie had settled for the night. The older woman had lit the oil lamp on the nightstand that illuminated the room a bit.

Meara was sleeping soundly next to Amber and she wanted to keep it that way. She got out of bed and quickly pulled on her wrapper. Then she reached into her nightstand for the little derringer pistol her uncle had given her for protection on her trip. She'd never really thought she'd need it, but now she loaded it with shaking hands and turned toward Mimm. Ready to use it if she had to.

"I see we have a plan," Mimm said. "I'd thought more on the lines of hiding you and the little one somewhere."

"I can't let Jamie be hurt and I don't want to chance Meara hearing or seeing something she shouldn't. She should be fine here."

Mimm picked up a small oil lamp she'd left on a table in the hall then they made their way down the stairs. They'd just reached the first landing when two shots rang out.

"Lord in heaven," Mimm cried.

Amber froze, horrifying possibilities running through her head. She had Jamie's baby and Meara to protect. If Alex had killed him—perhaps she and Meara should hide as Mimm had thought. But this was Jamie. She started forward, fear making her heart pump so hard it seemed like thunder in her ears. Mimm followed.

The smell of Mimm's oil lamp seemed to engulf Amber, turning her stomach. But then as they made their way through the dining room and were within sight of the back hall, Alex and Jamie stumbled from the office, flames following on their heels. Blood darkened Jamie's sleeve.

"Jamie!" Amber screamed.

"Go. Get out!" he shouted at Amber and started coughing. Alex was coughing too as he clung to Jamie's side. Fire seemed to be spreading inordinately fast. Confused though she was, it was clear Alex wasn't the villain they'd all begun to think he was. He kept moving with Jamie till they reached the front vestibule.

"I'll go for Meara," Mimm said.

"No, Mrs. Trimble." Alex stopped her. "You three get clear. I'll go. My father dumped lamp oil everywhere. You'd never get her out."

"We left her in the master. Oh, do hurry," Mimm cried.

Amber glanced back at the fire as it engulfed the first step of the staircase. "Alex!" she shouted, pointing.

"Go. All of you! His socks and your hems are probably soaked in oil." Alex turned and ran, leaping over the flames, then charging up the stairs.

Mimm got the door open. "He'll never get her out!" she fretted, stepping outside.

They followed quickly, the fire following, Jamie pulled the door shut and they rushed down the step. "Alex won't let anything happen to her," Jamie assured both of them.

Together they left the front steps behind. The staff streamed out the garden gate. All of them had made it out, which left only two inside. Alex and Meara.

Jamie seemed steadier on his feet. He let go of her and walked to the staff, sending two young men running for the fire department. He sent another man back along the side of the house to shut off the gas supply to the house. The rest of the staff moved to the other side of California Street.

Jamie backed up too, but only to the middle of the street, and Amber went back to join him, leaving Mimm crying on Lily's shoulder. She and Jamie stared up at the bay windows of the master bedroom, repeating a litany of prayers.

But it was the bathroom window that suddenly tore open. Then Alexander climbed out on to the roof of the small porch over the front door. He turned and leaned back in, emerging seconds later with Meara, wrapped in a sheet.

They disappeared from view, then.

"The fire department will get a ladder up to them as soon as they get here," she assured Jamie.

But Jamie shook his head and pointed. Alexander came back into view at the edge of the porch roof with Meara clinging to his back. He'd wrapped the sheet around them both and tied it around his middle, anchoring her to him. Then he started climbing down the turned columns of the porch.

Jamie put his good arm around her shoulders. "I'm afraid your wedding cake is a bit burnt now, Pixie."

"They'll be able to save some of it." Amber hugged him as Alexander and Meara moved ever closer to the porch. Once there, Alexander didn't waste time, but ran down the steps and over to them. Jamie embraced them both.

"Come on," Alexander said. "We'd better move back. I heard a few small explosions."

A neighbor met them at the crowded sidewalk and offered Jamie shelter for his household. Jamie nodded to Alexander who carried Meara to the neighbor's porch. There they all kissed her then Mimm took her inside where it was warmer.

The fire department arrived and in minutes the firemen were working the pumps and pumping water onto the fire, subduing it quickly.

Jamie turned to Alex. "Before the police get here, give me the gun."

"I dropped it behind the desk when I got to you."

"Fine, then you were sleeping and heard a noise before the women did. You got there just as we shot each other. They know someone was trying to harm me and mine. They'll see it as self-defense. I see no reason for you to face their questions."

"I killed my father, cuz. You can't erase that."

"Not from your memory, but I can make it a little easier. You've been taking care of me for years—this time I'm taking care of you."

Alexander nodded, resigned.

"We'll be at the Palace. Perhaps you should disappear for a while. And draw on your trust, damn it! It's yours. You've more than earned it."

"Not necessary. My father gave me the money to buy a commission when I was twenty. I wasn't about to be got rid of when I knew he needed watching. I bought into a mill. I've put together a tidy portion with it and a few other enterprises over the years. I do fine, cuz. And if you think on it, I'm sure the money he gave me was embezzled from Adair. So, in effect, you already gave me a good start toward independence."

Jamie smiled sadly and nodded.

"Now, cuz, why don't you go sit over there. I'll see that someone sends for a doctor, give that nice officer approaching the story you've cooked up and then I'll make myself scarce."

"I'm sorry, Alex," Jamie said.

"Not half as sorry as I am. It's a little much to comprehend right now. See you around." He winked at Amber. "Pixie. Take care of him. He gets into a dizzying number of scrapes."

Then he turned and walked away.

"Do you think he'll be all right?" she asked.

"I wish I knew. I really wish I did."

As they watched the firemen's efforts, Jamie told her all of what he'd learned that night during their three-way confrontation with Oswald Reynolds. It was all so shocking she didn't think she would ever understand the mind that had committed and tried to commit such heinous crimes.

The fire was out completely before dawn. They'd saved much of the house from the flames, but there was a lot of smoke and water damage, Jamie said after walking through it with the police. Alexander had already disappeared. The police accepted Jamie's story without question and they left for the Palace Hotel.

Malcolm Campbell arrived there and dressed Jamie's arm and checked both her and Meara. Thankfully, Jamie's uncle's was the only life lost. She really couldn't feel he was a loss at all except for the damage ending his life had done to his son.

Amber slept till noon. Sometime before she woke, Jamie managed to have some of the clothes they'd bought the day before delivered to the Palace. She dressed with Lily's help, and then went in search of Jamie. Amber found him in the parlor writing a letter. He stood and held out his hand. She went to him and he seated her next to him on the settee. "Feeling all right?" he asked.

She nodded. "I'm fine. How about you?"

"I think I'll avoid facing down madmen in the

future, but I'll be fine. I wanted you to know the Pinkertons found Helena. She is indeed going by Mrs. Brendan Kane. And Helena Kane. I want your permission to write her to tell her that her father's death was meant for me and that the men responsible have been arrested or killed. I don't want her thinking there is even a chance Brendan Kane was involved. I know what trouble misunderstandings caused in our marriage. I don't want to be responsible for that happening in theirs. Alex has been by. I thought I'd send it with him. Give him something to do and think about for a while."

Amber nodded, shocked that his plan caused her no worry. No upset. That he wanted to contact Helena sounded reasonable.

Jamie handed her the letter he'd drafted. It said exactly what he'd said it would. "It's fine. But you didn't need to show it to me. I trust you, Jamie."

He smiled. "I know. And I thought I'd add my thanks to her for being so damned hard to track down. She inadvertently led me to the perfect woman."

Amber knew her grin was cheeky. "Actually, the masquerade was my idea, remember?"

Jamie's laughter rang through the suite. And in the next moment he was kneeling in front of her and taking her hand in his. He reached into his pocket and pulled out her wedding rings. "I found these on the nightstand when I went to survey the damage."

Then he looked up into her eyes, his love in his gaze. "With this ring I thee wed, the woman of my dreams. My true adventurer."

* * * * *

*Harlequin Intrigue top author Delores Fossen
presents a brand-new series of
breathtaking romantic suspense!*
TEXAS MATERNITY: HOSTAGES
The first installment available May 2010:
THE BABY'S GUARDIAN

Shaw cursed and hooked his arm around Sabrina.

Despite the urgency that the deadly gunfire created, he tried to be careful with her, and he took the brunt of the fall when he pulled her to the ground. His shoulder hit hard, but he held on tight to his gun so that it wouldn't be jarred from his hand.

Shaw didn't stop there. He crawled over Sabrina, sheltering her pregnant belly with his body, and he came up ready to return fire.

This was obviously a situation he'd wanted to avoid at all cost. He didn't want his baby in the middle of a fight with these armed fugitives, but when they fired that shot, they'd left him no choice. Now, the trick was to get Sabrina safely out of there.

"Get down," someone on the SWAT team yelled from the roof of the adjacent building.

Shaw did. He dropped lower, covering Sabrina as best he could.

There was another shot, but this one came from a rifleman on the SWAT team. Shaw didn't look up, but he heard the sound of glass being blown apart.

The shots continued, all coming from his men, which meant it might be time to try to get Sabrina to better cover. Shaw glanced at the front of the building.

So that Sabrina's pregnant belly wouldn't be

smashed against the ground, Shaw eased off her and moved her to a sitting position so that her back was against the brick wall. They were close. Too close. And face-to-face.

He found himself staring right into those sea-green eyes.

How will Shaw get Sabrina out?
Follow the daring rescue and the heartbreaking
aftermath in THE BABY'S GUARDIAN
by Delores Fossen,
available May 2010 from Harlequin Intrigue.

HARLEQUIN *Presents*

Bestselling Harlequin Presents® author

Lynne Graham

introduces

VIRGIN ON HER WEDDING NIGHT

Valente Lorenzatto never forgave Caroline Hales's
abandonment of him at the altar. But now he's
made millions and claimed his aristocratic Venetian
birthright—and he's poised to get his revenge.
He'll ruin Caroline's family by buying out their
company and throwing them out of their mansion...
unless she agrees to give him the wedding night
she denied him five years ago....

Available May 2010
from Harlequin Presents!

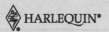

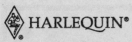

LAURA MARIE ALTOM

The Baby Twins

Stephanie Olmstead has her hands full raising
her twin baby girls on her own. When she runs
into old friend Brady Flynn, she's shocked to find
herself suddenly attracted to the handsome airline
pilot! Will this flyboy be the perfect daddy—
or will he crash and burn?

"LOVE, HOME & HAPPINESS"

www.eHarlequin.com

HAR75309

Former bad boy Sloan Hawkins is back in Redemption, Oklahoma, to help keep his aunt's cherished garden thriving and to reconnect with the girl he left behind, Annie Markham. But when he discovers his secret child—and that single mother Annie never stopped loving him—he's determined that a wedding will take place in the garden nurtured by faith and love.

REDEMPTION RIVER

Where healing flows...

Look for

The Wedding Garden

by Linda Goodnight

*Available May 2010
wherever you buy books.*

www.SteepleHill.com

Steeple
Hill®

LI87595

Introducing

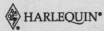

HARLEQUIN®

Showcase

Reader favorites
from the most talented voices in romance

Two titles
available monthly
beginning May 2010

HSCIBC0410

REQUEST YOUR FREE BOOKS!

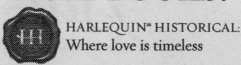

HARLEQUIN® HISTORICAL:
Where love is timeless

2 FREE NOVELS PLUS 2 FREE GIFTS!

YES! Please send me 2 FREE Harlequin® Historical novels and my 2 FREE gifts (gifts are worth about $10). After receiving them, if I don't wish to receive any more books, I can return the shipping statement marked "cancel." If I don't cancel, I will receive 6 brand-new novels every month and be billed just $4.94 per book in the U.S. or $5.49 per book in Canada. That's a saving of 20% off the cover price! It's quite a bargain! Shipping and handling is just 50¢ per book.* I understand that accepting the 2 free books and gifts places me under no obligation to buy anything. I can always return a shipment and cancel at any time. Even if I never buy another book from Harlequin, the two free books and gifts are mine to keep forever.

246/349 HDN E5L4

Name _____ (PLEASE PRINT)

Address _____ Apt. #

City _____ State/Prov. _____ Zip/Postal Code

Signature (if under 18, a parent or guardian must sign)

Mail to the **Harlequin Reader Service:**
IN U.S.A.: P.O. Box 1867, Buffalo, NY 14240-1867
IN CANADA: P.O. Box 609, Fort Erie, Ontario L2A 5X3
Not valid for current subscribers to Harlequin Historical books.

Want to try two free books from another line?
Call 1-800-873-8635 or visit www.morefreebooks.com.

* Terms and prices subject to change without notice. Prices do not include applicable taxes. N.Y. residents add applicable sales tax. Canadian residents will be charged applicable provincial taxes and GST. Offer not valid in Quebec. This offer is limited to one order per household. All orders subject to approval. Credit or debit balances in a customer's account(s) may be offset by any other outstanding balance owed by or to the customer. Please allow 4 to 6 weeks for delivery. Offer available while quantities last.

Your Privacy: Harlequin Books is committed to protecting your privacy. Our Privacy Policy is available online at www.eHarlequin.com or upon request from the Reader Service. From time to time we make our lists of customers available to reputable third parties who may have a product or service of interest to you. If you would prefer we not share your name and address, please check here. ☐

Help us get it right—We strive for accurate, respectful and relevant communications. To clarify or modify your communication preferences, visit us at www.ReaderService.com/consumerchoice.

HH10R

HARLEQUIN® *Blaze*™

is proud to present

***New York Times* bestselling author**

Vicki Lewis Thompson

**with a brand-new trilogy,
SONS OF CHANCE**
**where three sexy brothers
meet three irresistible women.**

Look for the first book

WANTED!

*Available beginning in June 2010
wherever books are sold.*

---

red-hot reads

www.eHarlequin.com